Made in Cambodia

Robert Horne

Published by
The Book Reality Experience
Western Australia

For Pip

with thanks for her faith in me.

Part One

One way of describing it was to say that he had escaped. But he wasn't that runaway type by nature. To leave loose ends and tangles in the path behind him would only create issues that would weigh on his mind, and there was enough crammed in there already. If anything, he would seize up about something he even *might* have done wrong. He'd wake up in the night and ringing in his ear there would be a word he had said out of place to someone at a party the night before. He knew, with the kind of logic that for some reason is never good enough for us, that probably no-one had even registered his mistake, let alone remembered it. But still things nagged at him.

Of course, he was not alone in the world where bouts of anxiety were concerned. But this time it would be truer to say he was running from something he *hadn't* done, or rather from what was being done to him as a result of his not having done something. If you can't imagine what that means it will become clear soon enough.

For the moment he stopped in this curious sultry street, then stepped into the shade of a three-storey apartment block to check the map on his phone. He looked up to the windows and the washing lines and the glimpses of human forms he might find there; this was all still so new. Stucco had eroded and crumbled from the building. It looked as if it hadn't seen paint since the golden days of Sihanouk, the 1960s, before the American coup and the Khmer Rouge that, with the clear vision of hindsight, had followed as inevitably as the switching of the tides on the Tonle Sap. No painters or plasterers through the Vietnamese occupation either, and now in the time of Hun Sen and the capitalists he wondered what would come first, the renovators or the bulldozers.

He liked to get about on foot. At home he had grown up walking paths on rocky cliffs that looked over the Pacific, a stiff tang of salt and seaweed on the breeze – freewheeling, solitary motion that was a pleasure and a solace. Khmer people never marched around the place like that unless they truly had to; this walking lark was a Western idea. And jogging was out of the question in a place where people's whole lives happened on the footpath: washing out to dry, motorbike parts spreadeagled, babies in pink plastic bathtubs. In the morning it was easier to walk in the middle of the street before the sun burned hard. His hat was a narrow-brimmed thing, light brown with a charcoal band. It wasn't much of a sunhat but he liked its neatness that twisted the tourist normal a little; plus, it was a perverse souvenir reminder of his trip to Turkey and Greece with Amanda. He held on to delinquent ironies like this as a little badge he could hide behind.

He tried to focus on the streets and their numbers.

'Tuk-tuk, sir.' A little caravan drew up and its driver grinned and raised his eyebrows suggesting a small commercial resolution to his transport problem. Ryan had had his first tuk-tuk experience the evening before: a wild fifty-minute ride from the airport – squeezing between motorbikes, up on footpaths, between the bowsers at petrol stations, anything to get through the traffic or around it. His driver's concentration had never wavered; he had turned and grinned at Ryan a few times as he gunned his clapped-out motorbike engine. At the end they'd had a conversation, about the clouds. That tuk-tuk man said no-one had ever asked him about the sky before.

But this was not the man he had talked to about clouds and there were only a couple of blocks to go.

'No, thanks,' he shook his head, and the driver moved off with an agreeable nod.

Map, focus, think. The numbered streets of Phnom Penh were easy, in an orderly French colonial grid. It should be only a couple of blocks to Street 51.

Amanda. Girls. Women.

Amanda was supposed to be the one, or rather, remain the one. He'd been told it was time to settle down. When we think of the word 'settle' we shouldn't jump to the idea that he was the type who was always out on the drink and chasing girls – far from it. He would more likely disappear with a book for hours and his imagination would run away with him. He would be messy and hard to pin down. He liked a drink all right but in a different way. His old school friends perplexed him when they 'played up' every week, still. Every Friday, every Saturday – even the hazy other-worldliness of Sunday sessions, their own brand of escape. He remembered a joke retold often by a certain Australian writer:

Q: What's the difference between a sensitive new age guy and a rabid hoon?

A: Two schooners.

No, when people said 'settle down' what they really meant was 'be more productive.' He got it. He should be aiming higher than to be a relief teacher who believed in little and wasted his time tinkering with poetry that wasn't going to make him famous or wealthy. Whatever his lack of faith in virtually everything to do with family and tradition and church, it had simply been accepted without words being spoken that things would roll on in the direction of Amanda and that there would be grandchildren soon and an increase in ambition and all that kind of thing.

And that there would be a wedding: Amanda, the family, the nestling friends, they all wanted it. The life-journey signpost: the notice in the paper, the costumes, the closure, the … containment of it all. It would be wrong and a little clichéd to say that he was dead inside, but he had been, how shall we say it, somewhat deadened. His older brother Dermott liked to characterise his oddball attitudes as just making trouble for the sake of attention.

But he didn't want the attention. He didn't want a wedding *because* of all the attention. Dermott had told him he was causing trouble in the family. It was as if he was the point of attraction to a centrifugal force and Dermott spoke for a maligned world that was spinning into him – for the family members and faithful friends who were shaking their heads at his intransigence and ingratitude. It was all because of what he had done.

Or hadn't done.

So, he had sought a place of inertia to escape what he hadn't done, or what was being done to him as a result of what he hadn't done. To not marry someone because you think you were two people who got together too young in life and then just grew away from each other is one thing. But to find out six months later that your ex is engaged to be married to the same older brother Dermott, who had just criticised you for not getting married, is another thing altogether. That is another matter all-to-totally-gether. And his brother knew him well enough to know that being lectured-down-to would achieve its opposite effect; that being told to marry Amanda would reduce the likelihood of that happening to zero. Now it seemed as if it had all been tactical.

He had reached Street 51. He stabbed a finger at his phone and the map disappeared. Between him and his destination building now was just the usual mess of merging tuk-tuks and motorbikes. This traffic was all so … close, almost a personal thing; you could touch it here. You merged with it when you crossed a street. You could smell the petrol and the sweat at the arms of shirts. If he'd thought of Cambodia as a place of inertia to escape to, it seemed to be encouraging him to rethink that assumption.

On this corner some boys sat lounging on their motorbikes. One straightened on his arrival.

'Sir, motorbike? Where are you going?' Where was he going? It was a question that could be answered two ways.

'Sorry,' he motioned to the building opposite, his destination.

'Ohhhh,' said the boy, grinning, 'is ok. I take you there. One dollar.'

It was his first taste of Khmer irony.

Ryan looked up at the building – three storeys of blue glass and white plastic – new, ten years old at the most, a purpose-built English language school that put the ragged shops and cafés and the sleazy bars around it in the shade. A symbol of the new Cambodia, shaped up from the rubble. It was almost too clean.

A chubby security man in blue uniform watched as he ducked across the road then raised his right hand in a gesture that was half a salute and half a shy little wave. Glass doors rolled open and Ryan stepped through to a waiting area that was spacious and plain – tiled floor and picture windows – cool and empty save a girl in big round black-framed glasses who sat behind a long counter. When he stated his business and she said 'Oh', with surprise, and went on in good English, 'You have an appointment with Mr Dith?'

She glanced toward five plastic chairs that were braced into the wall near the main door. He was fifteen minutes early. He sat his document folder on his knees and closed his jet-lagged eyes to listen to the honking, revving traffic of the perplexing city outside. It was his first day in the kind of Asia that wasn't Singapore. Soon a rumbling came on the stairs and a stampede of feet and suddenly there were young people finished Saturday morning classes – laughing, joshing, giggling, everyone headed for the rolling doors – all of them somewhere in that group that could have been aged between sixteen and twenty-eight. At the tail end of the migration a ginger-haired bloke stopped at the door and looked Ryan over for a second. Then he pointed an index finger and said a cheery 'Hey', before disappearing into the mad street.

The silence resumed and he shook out thoughts of home and rubbed his eyes. He idly thought of conversation openers that could engage the girl on the desk, but they were all too predictable for him to be happy with. Anyway, she was totally focussed on her work –

hadn't given him a glance. Another class thundered down the stairs, even more lively than the previous. Their open faces smiled at him, not because he was anything in particular, he thought, but just because he was.

'All finished for the week?' he said, about the students.

'Many of them go to their jobs now.' The girl on the desk was deeply earnest, but finished with a questioning smile.

Ah, he thought, of course. He had walked around the town the night before and seen the endless hustle – a happy enough hustle it was mostly, but a hustle nonetheless. You wouldn't go anywhere in this place if you rested on your laurels.

After five minutes the girl sent him up to the third floor. From the panoramic window outside the lift he could see down into the street. The crush of students had already dispersed a hundred different ways, but the merging of motorbikes and tuk-tuks and pedestrians was the same. He closed his tired eyes for a moment and thought of the girls in the foyer a few minutes before. Their legs had all been modestly covered with pants or knee-length skirts; even their sleeves were mostly rolled down.

He thought of Amanda at his gate. He counted backwards in his head. Was it only … eight days? Little more than a week, anyway. He heard now the whine the gate hinge had made that morning. He'd screwed his head around from his book to look up the front path, as he did in the rare event of a visitor. Amanda there – blonde bob, cream suit, tanned legs and gym-three-times-a-week calf muscles that yelled out 'look at these.' She'd turned on her court shoe heels and looked up towards his door. Her mouth had been held tight; was that from her determination, or confusion?

Mr Dith was waiting.

Ryan shook his head as if to turn the memory out, but it came straight back.

'Dermott and I are getting married,' was what she had said, as she drained the last of her glass of water. She had refused coffee, and tea – she wasn't staying that long.

Dermott. Ryan had exiled himself to a unit in the south. He hadn't kept his eye on what was going on in the old places. What Amanda did could generally be her business but, with Dermott?

'Ah, well,' he'd said, buying time, mind racing. *Do not show the shock.* He had to make a remark here and Amanda had given no hint that her news was negotiable. 'I guess you could make the perfect wife for a man like that.' It was the only barb he could think of that wouldn't be outright rude, only in a measured way, the 'like that' at the end of the sentence implying so much. Of course, whatever she did was quite immaterial to him, or so his face would tell her. 'Why didn't you just send me a text?'

'I wouldn't *do* that,' she'd said, placing her glass on the table too harshly, her own mind far away from practical, functional things. A discordant clunking noise hung in the air. Her face pleaded for understanding, for something. 'So impersonal,' she said, as if the fact that she had delivered tidings in this personal way should count as a victory in itself, but her voice had tipped upwards at the end as if asking something.

'Got an Open Inspection in the neighbourhood?' he had to follow through on the tough-guy front page. 'Not like you to drive all the way down here, just for me.' His counter sounded harsh, even to himself. But everyone has a darker side and people will push you and push you and push you until you show it. He knew that was part of the game, but still he had to bite back.

She drew breath for a moment. 'There *is* a lease inspection, a quarterly.' At least she was honest about it, he thought. That was one thing about Amanda. She might have changed sides in the war of life, but at least she didn't pretend that she hadn't – not to him, anyway.

'Some poor bastard of a tenant to torture, eh.' Words like that would once have been delivered with an ironic grin, and received an ironic answer. But not today.

'Is that all you can talk about?' Her voice now rose to *his* bait. 'Tenants, Opens? I've come here to tell you something important about … about us, and all you can do is … is … I don't know, cavil.'

And then she'd cried. Right there in his living room, surrounded by his novels and books of poetry and all the other symbols of what she'd decided two years before was his failure. He stared at his morning toast crumbs and half-drunk cup of coffee, which had already begun to evaporate, its surface congealing into a distraught milky film.

She cried and told him that she still felt for him; there had always been that connection. Life wasn't as simple and clean as he thought. Dermott would look after her. She wasn't an animal, so why did he keep treating her like she was? 'It's not about fucking!' she'd finished, too self-consciously it seemed to him.

And abruptly she had left – handbag over one arm and tissue at her nose. It had been a Thursday so, nine days ago. He'd stood in his place for a minute, stunned, then walked out to the gate and looked up and down, half expecting that she would have stopped the car down the street to think, to reconsider everything. Perhaps she would be walking back up the street to him.

On-the-edge Amanda: his first and only love, who had moved from Arts to Law, had taken to drink and judges' sons for a year, and then come back to him – who had never finished anything. Amanda, who, at the age of twenty-seven, had then drifted into business – Real Estate.

Cavil, he thought. How would she ever get on in Real Estate with her vocabulary? They will look sideways at her with clouded eyes.

And he'd spent the weekend wondering what it all meant, this visit. He left his phone turned on, and in his shirt pocket, but there was no call from her. His head said that she was never the right girl for him, but his heart didn't talk to his head every day of the week.

Then on the Monday he received a card in the post. It had been addressed in her handwriting – so neat and small that it looked studied, like everything she did. But he felt something like tension rise in his throat as he walked the card inside. He stopped inside the door and looked at it for a moment. This might be so important that it could not be just opened like a gas bill. He boiled some water and made a cup of tea, then sat down in his comfortable reading chair and opened the envelope.

It was a wedding invitation.

Without a thought he crunched it up in his hand and made to throw it at the wall. Then on second thoughts he opened the crumpled card and flattened it out and checked the detail. There was the address of the same Anglican Church that he and his brother had been christened in. It would be the full catastrophe: the bride would be in white, same colour as the horses and the carriage. Dermott would wear a top hat – a short one, nothing too pretentious.

He looked down into the Phnom Penh street again: the same honking and constant negotiation of position – no traffic lights, no road markings, no rules.

Figures were indistinct from that far up but he could make out two Western types, tourists – on the same spot he had been no more than twelve minutes before. He thought that, in a strange way, a great deal had happened in those twelve minutes. The tourists were hesitating at the edge of the street. Go on, plunge in, he thought. The boy on the corner raised his hand to the couple from the seat of his motorbike. 'Sir, I can help you. Where are you going?'

Ryan could hear the words in his head, and he smiled. I am actually here, he thought, and he could barely believe it.

The door to Mr Dith's office was half open and it moved beneath his knock.

'Ah, Mr Davey, welcome to Cambodia.' Dith rose from his chair to greet him. 'We are very pleased to have you here in our fine school.' He grinned and nodded, dipping his shoulders in a half-bow of welcome.

'Well, I am very happy to be here.' In his airplane-tired state Ryan did his best to match Mr Dith's welcome and held his hand out. Dith was no stranger to the Western greeting; his shake was firm and quick.

'Please,' he motioned to a couple of chairs, white plastic body frames and tubular steel legs. They brought back memories of the Ikea store and the Broad Australian Suburb. Mr Dith sank into a large swivelling imitation-leather chair with arms, the kind of executive chair some people use to play body language games with – to turn away to the window, to lean back in. But while Mr Dith wore his chair with comfortable pride, he did not use it to assert any of that desultory air of authority, no game of power. Rather, he quickly sat forward, picked up a pen and tapped it on the desk twice as if to call a meeting to order. He was somewhere above fifty years old, hair receding to the point where he could almost be called bald, a cheerful but watchful face – wary.

'How are you feeling after your long plane journey, Mr Davey?' He pronounced the name with a long soft aaahhh. Ryan learnt later there was a Khmer girl's name, Davy, said that way, and that he would forever be referred to in that tone. He liked it that he could have a different name.

'Well, it always takes a couple of days to recover,' he admitted.

A big window showed the tenement across the street; an old woman was moving slowly about in an apartment – above that a huge sky with streaks of cloud.

'I am pleased you could come and see me today. We all work in the morning on Saturdays and it is of course the last working day before you begin on Monday,' said Mr Dith, with an uncertain smile. There was little Ryan could say in reply, so he made the most acquiescent face he could manage.

'We have Phnom Penh's finest English language school here, Mr Davey. And we make what you call a "tight ship," yes?'

The metaphor seemed to please Mr Dith, so Ryan smiled appreciatively. He knew the school was one of the best three, probably running third in that group.

'I can't wait to get started.' The remark seemed to please Mr Dith and he got into his speech straight away.

'You must wear a long-sleeved white shirt each day with a dark-coloured tie.'

Mr Dith had already listed the dress requirements in his email, so Ryan had gone fossicking at the local op shops and picked up the three brightest whites he could find.

'Long dark pants, please. Black or charcoal are preferred. Oh, I am forgetting. You may roll your sleeves up to the top of the forearm.'

He hadn't heard of that relaxation of the code.

'Very generous,' he murmured. If Mr Dith understood the mild sarcasm, he gave no indication of it; but looking at him now Ryan could see that this was in no way a dull man. Sure, he was repeating his routine checklist now, but that was not all there was to him. A glance at Dith's eyes showed that. And anyway, why would he not lay down the rules; he'd hired a teacher sight unseen and this was his only shot at him.

'We have to attract people to our school from the best families in Phnom Penh.'

Around the corner one hundred metres up Street 114 was another school. He'd seen parents in 4WD vehicles that morning, picking up children all dressed up in uniforms: close-fitting beige waist jackets and white shirts for the boys, matching dresses over white shirts again for the girls. They went to school every day trussed up as if for some nine-year-old's birthday party, in beige and white – preoccupied fathers, mothers who do lunch – Prime Minister Hun Sen's elite. Ryan had seen no Mercedes vehicles with tinted windows outside this school when he'd walked up that morning.

'Do you take primary school kids?'

Mr Dith looked blankly back at him.

'Young ones, like around ten years of age.'

'Oh no. Most of our students are young adults, making their way in the working world. English is very important for them to get ahead. Many wish to enter university, or to work with tourists.'

'I see,' he said. He had already seen the keen young kids in the foyer, sticking their heads up to get a part of whatever was left in the new Cambodia after the elites had licked off the cream.

'Many of our students are young women. In fact, seventy per cent,' Dith said with some rising note in his voice, as if he still couldn't quite believe that women were taking whatever chance they could, while their brothers were stuck to their motorbikes on street corners.

'Our students want value from every lesson. What you teach them they will try on their customers in cafés, or at the university – some have office jobs. It is very important.'

Ryan was impressed by the urgency of Mr Dith's delivery. This was turning into a top order opening pep talk.

'I am looking forward to the opportunity to help them,' he replied.

Mr Dith eased his elbows off the desk, and when he sat back in the light, lines of care became visible in his face. Running any business in Hun Sen's Cambodia would be perilous: corruption was rife; he had read in the *Post* that even teachers took extra money from their students in some places. The owners of the school could be quite close to real power. It occurred to him that anyone of Mr Dith's age must have been a Khmer Rouge survivor. Even the tuk-tuk driver who had brought him from the airport the day before must have lived in the time of Pol Pot – the reign of terror. Everyone of that age must have been a survivor.

Or a perpetrator.

Mr Dith motioned to the corner of his desk closest to Ryan, to a large white folder, three centimetres thick with quarto-sized paper. Tabs in primary colours indicated chapters.

'This is the text book for your advanced class. They are a very good class. I have marked the place for you to begin.' Ryan noticed that Dith used 'is' and 'are' in every sentence – the first person he had encountered in Cambodia who did so. His English was good. 'Other teacher was up to here,' he pointed out the place. Ryan hadn't thought until that moment that he was taking over from someone, another person. He looked at the imprint page; the book was from the United States, for teaching English as a Second Language. It looked like his first lesson would be about the U.S. economy.

'Your other teacher had to leave?' he said, making conversation.

'We have many teachers here. All very good English. But it is good for our school to have native speakers. Very good, but expensive. You are paid a little more than Cambodian teachers.' He nodded twice in his enthusiasm, but Ryan noticed that he hadn't answered the question. Then Dith lowered his voice and cast his eyes down as if to announce the arrival of a difficult subject. 'But you must be teacher, always a teacher only.'

He didn't get it for a moment. Mr Dith hesitated, showing his preference to not speak directly about any matter, wishing rather to inflect and infer and that such subtleties would be understood that way, as they would by people of his culture; and that the response to his oblique words would be returned to him in similar subtleties of nods and inclines of head and that all would be understood. But no such affirmation did he receive, just open-mouthed wonder from the man sitting opposite him.

Mr Dith's smile crinkled in embarrassment over this last important thing he had to say, 'Always maintain appropriate distance with your students.'

Mr Dith pressed the two open palms of his hands together and raised them in an apologetic way to the level of his nose in the Cambodian sampeah expression.

'Of course,' Ryan said, more confused than he had been a half a minute before. 'Of course. An appropriate distance at all times.'

He had imagined the Phnom Penh riverside area differently – the 'quay.' It was the Sisowath Quay after all, and that word conjured all the romantic imagery of the neutered pomp of the kings of the colonial era. He'd imagined boats chugging in and out – puffs of black smoke trailing behind like something out of Joseph Conrad, cargo stacked on piers, nets of fish winched up, spilling from wicker baskets on to rustic wooden jetty planks.

But in the place of that there was a busy modern street with one side of the road packed with cafés and shops, bars and travel agents – footpaths jammed up with menu boards and spruikers, racks of polo shirts obtruding onto the footways. Still, this was one of those cities where quaint and rural touches remained: one coffin maker still sandwiched between bars and hotels, from the days when the Phnom Penh quay was like a village high street; an old Peugeot tray truck came by with hay stacked high above the driver's cabin, and on top of that a boy, propped up on one elbow – consciously nonchalant. A hay truck in the main street of the capital; he liked it.

On the river side of the street there was a wide paved area that caught every degree of the hazy heat and radiated it back at you; here and there sorrowful little trees made twisted fingers of shade. Then there was a low concrete wall and the Tonle Sap. The river was down now at the end of the dry season and the concrete supports of the quay stuck out like the ribs of a starving man, leading down to a scurf of mud and debris at water's edge. Away to the north a sight-seeing cruise boat chugged in and out from a dock every now and then, and six hundred metres or so to the south, past the Imperial Palace, was the murky confluence with the Mekong.

It was said that when the real rains came and the rivers flowed like they meant it, the waters of the Mekong shouldered into the smaller river with such force that they pushed the Tonle Sap all the way back to Kampong Thom two hundred kilometres upstream. The river then flowed backwards.

Looking down into its sturdy progress now, he could not believe it. He walked along the strip towards the confluence as far as the Foreign Correspondents' Club, then down a side street where there was an English language bookshop just wide enough to fit shelves on each wall and two long ones back to back in the middle. Soon a girl glided out and placed the palms of her hands together, then lifted them in front of her face. It felt natural to return the gesture and when he did she smiled shyly and bowed her head. She was a slim and tall picture of elegance; a small bare-footed child looked around from behind her close-fitting neck-to-floor dress. After a few minutes he found himself buying a pirated copy of Somerset Maugham's *The Painted Veil*, with photocopied pages bound together into what was a reasonable facsimile of the original cover. All that to make three dollars – without considering paper and copying.

He'd heard of pirated CDs and illegal downloads, but photocopied books? In an economy like this every single dollar had to be striven for.

He had the number of a family friend – Colin, a university pal of his father's who'd never quite lost touch. He pulled out his phone and looked at the name on the contact list. It was Saturday afternoon, an auspicious time to visit. But not now; he wasn't ready for an Aussie or anything to do with home.

He pressed on up the river towards the Chaktomuk Theatre, surrounded with big trees and all closed up. It was quiet here. The intensity of the city slipped away and he was suddenly alone. Across the Tonle Sap, on the point of the peninsula that is the final point of its separation from the Mekong, there was a brand new luxury tourist and high-roller hotel that stared out over the waters as if it was the proprietor of the river itself – big money and big-noting. There, suddenly before him, was Amanda at his gate again; he was too slow to stop her running out – tissue at her face. What if he had held her arm at his front door, given her an option that breathed and loved? What if, what if. Amanda and Dermott together – the luxury hotel. They would love it there.

Or would she? Some days she was the conscious and pre-meditated lady, on others she would shoot baskets with the boys and you would have to watch her elbows or end up bloody-nosed. There was no knowing.

He turned and hurried away.

Back in the middle of town, life burst around him again. In places there was new building work, and scores of shirtless lads in thongs toted barrows of cement and erected bizarre bamboo scaffolding on which they worked, five storeys up, still in thongs, no safety net. The buildings of Angkor had been made this way, nine centuries before.

On the footpath a couple of mechanics had wheeled out motorbikes and squatted, one with a screw driver dismantling a carburettor. Some of the boys hung about, smoking, slapping down cards – grease up to the middle joint of their fingers. Motorbike parts lay around like spent shrapnel.

At the next shop-front two women sat behind a plastic stand – grilled bits of scrawny chicken and fatty pork on sale. Beside them a clothes rack: four shirts, five pairs of undies, two bras and a range of children's things. He stepped to look closer, but this stuff was the women's own morning's washing out to dry, right there in the street. The women laughed in a cackling, crone-like way when they saw his realisation, and meant no offence.

Wedged up by them was a man asleep in his cyclo. Then another man squatted over wrought iron gates which were planked across the way, sparking at them with a welder. Beside him sat plastic bags of waste from bars and restaurants, coconut husks and banana peel fermenting in the tropical heat. An old woman who must have been seventy squatted by a pile of hessian sacks full of charcoaled branches, chopped into one-foot lengths, waiting for the cafés to pick them up for the evening grill. Among the smell of rotting vegetables and charcoal fires and petrol fumes came the dank and fetid smell of sewage. A saffron-covered monk hurried by him, briefcase in hand – business awaited him somewhere.

The irresistible, clamorous rabble of Cambodian life had kept him wired for two hours since the chat with Mr Dith. But now he could feel he was tiring with every minute that his senses were stretched in this extraordinary place. *The Painted Veil* was in his little backpack.

He decided to turn back towards the Kandal market and then up the quay to his room at the Indochine. But still, motorbikes made a slalom pathway around him, tuk-tuk drivers hailed him. A man marched past him with a basket of bananas on his head. A foot-powered cyclo glided through, one stick-thin loin-clothed gent trotting between its sticks. A boy of around ten pushed a wooden cart piled so high with spinach leaves that he had to peer around his cargo as he went, first one side then the other. A chicken crossed the road pursued by an even smaller boy. A motorbike ducked around him, a lad steering with his left hand, text messaging with his right, glancing up and grinning.

Then from the crowd a hand stuck out, grabbing him by the arm. Sudden. He gasped with the shock of it – he had been in the middle of it, but until that moment viewing it all as an apparition. He cried out loud, 'Ugghh!'

'Hey, you ok?' said the owner of the hand. Ryan looked up to a freckled face and gingery blonde hair. It could have been the head of a surfer. But he didn't know any surfers, and this face was familiar.

'I saw you earlier on today,' said the head. Ryan stared back with his mouth open. Today? What had he been doing today? He woke up in the hotel, had eggs in the café downstairs, went to see Mr Dith, walked along the quay.

'At the school,' the blonde head went on.

'At the school?'

'Yeah, buddy. You were waiting downstairs, in the lobby. You're the new guy.'

'Jesus. You were there.' Now he remembered, the guy who came down the stairs with his class, pointed at him and said 'Hey.'

'I'm there, six days a week. Well, five and half. And don't call me Jesus, the name is Tom.'

'I'll call you Jesus if I want,' he said.

'Huh!' Tom crunched a snort and threw his head back. 'You're an Aussie,' he said.

Ryan had to admit that it was true. 'Awesome,' Tom said, though 'ossom' was the way it came out.

'You can find your way through all this ruck?' said Ryan.

'Well, it's easy to say it's easy when you've been here for a while, but you have to learn to kind of merge into the chaos. There's a different equilibrium here. You make your own balance in this country.'

'Young bloke back there was steering through this and sending a text with the other hand.'

'Ah, you're not one of the guys if you can't do that. They're born on the back of a motorbike, almost literally. You gotta learn to sway.'

'I guess so,' said Ryan uncertainly. 'You've been here for a while then?'

'Two years, mate. From Minnesota. I came to Cambodia for three reasons: it was warm, it was cheap and someone said it was interesting.' The guy's story loped easily out of his mouth as if it had been told a hundred times. Ryan wondered what might have been left out.

'And you stayed two years.'

'So far,' Tom said, looking around him at the street, the people, all of life's pageant tottering along on a shifting canvas. 'It's kind of like that. You get used to it. Then you realise you're not used to it at all, then you start all over again and you just keep rollin' along.'

Ryan stumbled over his own reasons for coming, left out all his important bits and said that someone had told him it was interesting here too.

'Yup, interesting is the word – literal and Chinese senses in abundance. We need to go out sometime. I'll show you what I mean.'

'Can't miss.'

'You sure you're ok?' Tom said before he left.

'I'm fine. My hotel's just up the street. A nice cheap one.'

'Can't miss.' Tom repeated Ryan's phrase and pointed his finger at him for emphasis, as he had back at the school.

Tom seemed a bit rehearsed in his manner, but that was what you get when you travel; everyone has a quick story, a pitch. The great thing was that he had made a contact in Cambodia, two if you counted Mr Dith, then three if you counted Colin. He told himself to stop thinking so much, to stop looking so hard. It was only when you gave up hunting for something that you would find it.

That's what he told himself.

He slogged through his first day with the elementary classes. There were hours of repetition as eager newcomers tried to grasp the impossible sentence structure of English and its flowing pronunciation all at once. The business of learning was serious and taxing.

'You seen Dith yet?' said Tom at the end of the day.

'Saw him a couple of times coming down the corridor.'

Dith had gone past with a folder under his arm, all business-like, ears tweaking.

'If he hasn't sat in on a class yet, he must be busy.'

'He sits in on classes?'

'At first, yeah. That's the procedure. Then there's reports and feedback surveys. But you're a mid-term start-up – weird.' Tom wagged a finger to show that protocol was everything here.

Ryan just held his hands out and shrugged as if to say, what happened?

'Dith did two or three classes himself last week; we all did a couple.' He sat forward on his metal lunch-room chair. 'The last guy left in a hurry. Your email came through the day the fan and the excrement gon' boogaloo.'

'I took the hint there may have been some "inappropriate relationship" involved.' Ryan held his fingers up to make the ironic quote marks. 'I hate that term. It could mean anything from the full shag to touching someone on the finger.'

'Yeeaaah,' Tom drawled it out, 'something at the real business end of that scale, you'd have to say.' He was ready to show what he knew and to advise and help; Ryan could feel that the departure of the other teacher and his own arrival had both been good for Tom. 'But he was just basically slack about everything. You're already a grade up from that. Si, claro.'

Even though Tom was from the freezing north of the USA he liked to use the Spanish expressions, as if he was some Tex-Mex wrangler dude. He'd visited the Southwest once, Arizona. He stayed a while and worked in a gas station, talked to all the characters. Told himself he'd never go back to the lakes and the twin towns – moved on to Asia. That was the story.

'What happened to the girl?'

'She stayed. They pay Dith; Dith pays you.' He pointed his finger at Ryan once again for emphasis. 'Money doesn't talk around here, it swears. I guess it all depends on what you really want and how keen you are to stay. Women in this place? Different agendas to back home. It's a mystery game.'

'I think I get that.'

'Mind you, gorgeous chick.' Tom spoke with the air of someone who would know, or at the very least someone who would notice. For the moment Ryan asked no more questions about agendas and decided to keep quiet and make his own observations.

The second morning, Tuesday, was the advanced class, the one he had been looking forward to. The kids would have been up before seven for the early class at eight. Many would race away after the lesson to universities and technical colleges for eight hours of study before work in the evening, the boys buzzing tourists around on motorbikes, the girls putting plates on tables.

There was a little phalanx of five or six girls at the front, jeans with white shirts or coloured tees, delicate faces, some with a blush of makeup and with little caps sitting by them on the desk. Then the boys, the entertainers in the middle of the class and the slower ones at the back, following the lesson from whatever the better ones said.

'Ok, turn your books to Chapter 5, page 3.' A rustling of paper followed as they found their places – they could all get the numbers and were keen to show it.

'This next section is about the economy of the United States.'

'Yes, teacher,' many of them remarked in their eagerness.

'Are any of you doing Economics in university?'

They looked up at him in surprise. They weren't used to a lot of conversation with their teacher that went away from the book.

Three or four hands rose sheepishly.

'Have you learnt anything about the economy of the United States … or of Cambodia?'

Two of the boys whispered to each other in Khmer for a few moments and then were joined by a girl who sat behind them and seemed to admonish them mildly. It was she who spoke.

'Economics is mainly figures and stas…statis-tics,' she said. Then, concentrating very hard she said again, 'Statistics. That is a difficult one to pronounce.' The girl coloured slightly and smiled a sweet shy smile. She had spoken the best student English he'd heard in Cambodia, rivalling Mr Dith.

'Yes,' he said, 'I'll bet it is. And what is your name.'

'I am Malee,' she said, colouring more deeply.

The girl next to her raised her hand and Ryan nodded to her. 'Malee is the best student in class. Alway.' A number of students around her, both boys and girls, nodded and murmured approbation. Malee bowed her head modestly.

'Very good,' he said. Ryan was happiest when formality was broken down, but he could see by the way they looked at each other that this was not the style they expected. He glanced at Malee again as he began to read from the book. She was small and neat, her hair was tied back in a ponytail that revealed delicate ears and neck. Her features were smart and sharp – no make-up. She was beautiful in a withdrawn and book-wormish way that contrasted with the girls in the front row, who stared confidently at him, their tongues playing lazily around their lips.

'The United States is the world's largest single national economy,' he read. 'It was worth 18.8 trillion dollars in 2015. Does anyone know what a trillion is?'

The class was silent, twenty-two faces looking back at him.

'A trillion is one thousand billion.'

'Billion?' said one of the economics boys.

'A billion is a thousand million.'

The eyes of the class bored into the pages of their books. He didn't want to confuse them more so he stuck to the script for most of the lesson as they trudged through all the positive news of the American economy. With five minutes to go he'd had enough and he was curious about what they knew.

'All right, then. Can somebody tell me about Cambodia's national economy?' Suddenly eyes lit up; this was something about their own country. 'What industries are important here?'

A boy named Thuon raised his hand.

'Yes, Thuon, what do you think?'

'I think … is very difficult to become rich economy like Japan or United States.'

Two girls sat at the front, Sophy and Chi. They had spent the lesson alternately looking at their books and making eyes at him with open-mouthed expressions. Sophy spoke up now.

'In Cambodia people work very small wage. In Western place everything ok.'

Suddenly everyone in the class was giving him some advice on the Cambodian economy, everyone except Malee. He held his hands up for quiet and the class quickly toned down.

'Malee, do you have anything to add?'

Everyone looked to Malee and she hesitated, gathering her thoughts, still looking down at her desk. Where all the others had been blurting, she had been thinking.

'I think in Cambodia people work for very little money.' Heads nodded around her. 'I think everything owned by very few people. *Is* owned,' she corrected herself. 'Everything *is* owned.'

'One per cent of the people own all wealth,' said one of the economics boys, Tang. He spoke as a smart guy who was showing off a fact he had learnt in his university class. 'Factory own by Korean and Taiwan.'

There had been a trace of emotion in Malee's voice when she spoke. Ryan was interested and couldn't help digging a little.

'Do you know people who work in the factories?' he said, looking at Malee, holding one hand up to silence Tang and the other boys.

'Yes,' Malee said, looking up for the first time, 'my sister works in a factory.' Her astute chin protruded faintly as she spoke; he thought of the statues at Easter Island. 'She makes garments, she sews up shirts. They pay her eighty-five dollars every month and if she works overtime half a day she makes five dollars more. From her money she helps pay for me to come here learn English.'

It was not said with animation, or anger; but within the shell of her matter-of-fact tone there was hidden a pearly note of defiance. She had said more than she needed to; and four sentences with only one mistake.

'Garment making is the most important industry in Cambodia – more than 600,000 workers.' Malee lowered her head as if to say that her statement was concluded. In this context, within this classroom, it was quite a speech.

He remembered seeing something on TV the night before – un-happy workers. Was there a strike threatening? In this country? After only a few days in Cambodia he could see that this was not a place that would be friendly to striking workers. When the elite rolled their huge imported 4WD vehicles through the crowded streets – tinted windows, bullet-proof glass – people looked over their shoulders, moved aside. Worried looks crept over their faces. He remembered the parents he had seen outside the rival school, dropping their liv-eried children from huge Mercedes vehicles.

'Does anyone else have family in the garment industry?'

Two of the boys raised a finger, as if embarrassed, and the girl who sat next to Malee put her hand up as far as her shoulder. The rest of the class was silent, their pursed lips disassociating them from any stain of garment worker family.

At that moment a bell rang to announce the end of the class. Ryan could not pretend to be unhappy about taking a break. The mood changed instantly and they all began to pack their bags.

'Thank you, teacher!' many of them cried happily. 'Goodbye, teacher.' Every one of them gave him a farewell. He got the feeling he had been a hit.

When most of them had gone only Sophy and Chi were left and Malee, who was methodically and thoughtfully packing her bag. So-phy smiled and said thank you again for the lesson. They finally made for the door and Malee was just behind them. He wondered whether Malee would stay to say something to him, but she slipped through the door behind Sophy with her head down.

Then suddenly the room was empty. He straightened some chairs. His first lesson with the top class had been interesting – tiring, hard. He tried to remember details from the TV news about the industrial trouble brewing. The place had suddenly become more real to him; it was closer and that felt good.

As he stepped out into the corridor he saw the figure of Mr Dith, sitting on the bench outside the room, his back rigid and his hands on his knees – an almost military pose for a man to be waiting in.

Dith rose and turned towards him, his face serious. He brought his hands together in front of his nose and tapped his fingers as if to summon his thoughts.

'You are a good teacher,' he said. 'I was listening for ten minutes. I apologise that I was not able to sit in with your entire class. Students like you very much – it is easy to tell.' He took a deep breath, as if about to make a pronouncement. 'But I think you must follow the book. Very few students from the garment worker background come to this school. Malee is an exception. She is assisted by UNICEF and her sister works very hard to help her. Many students in this school come from a … higher background. In future I think you must follow the book.'

'Yes, Mr Dith,' Ryan said. 'I think you might be right. In future I will stick to the book.'

Mr Dith bowed seriously to him and without another word he walked away in the direction of his office, deep in thought.

Ryan made it back to the Hotel Indochine.

'Hello, boss. You want go somewhere?'

It was the tuk-tuk man who had brought him in from the airport, taken up residence outside the Indochine now. Ryan wondered whether his choice of spot to perch had anything to do with him, but guessed it must have been as good a place as any to work from.

'Not now, mate – too tired.'

'No worry, tomorrow good. We go Mt Oudong tomorrow – thirty dollar, cheap.' The man chuckled with the preposterous nature of his own proposition. Sure, he could take Ryan to Mt Oudong if he wanted to go, but it was big long shot.

'Nah, no go Mt Oudong tomorrow.' Ryan smiled too, tired and sorry he couldn't do more for this man – to be a proper tourist spending money.

'Killing Field, very nice.' Irony oozed from him like the sweat from his pores.

'Not for now.' Such tourist pleasures would have to be put on hold.

'Ok, boss.' One thing about the drivers here, they seemed to feel a responsibility to be entertaining while they were making a pitch, but knew when to give up.

He got a beer from the fridge in the little lobby and a sleepy-eyed boy stirred from his nap, slid his key across the bar and placed a stroke next to the word 'Beer' on Ryan's tab. The passageway outside Ryan's room gave out onto a couple of metres of balcony that looked over the river. He sat on a plastic stool for a minute and watched the water roll by towards the Mekong. The beer was cold.

The man had brought him in from the airport. When they stopped by his tuk-tuk in the carpark Ryan had looked up to his first Asian sky. It had been low and intense, dark and sulky – as if it had been contemplating rain but just couldn't collect the energy.

He had said something to the tuk-tuk man about the sky.

The man had looked at the sky.

The man looked at Ryan, then looked at the sky again.

'You know, boss,' the tuk-tuk man had said. 'People ask me about hotel, Angkor Wat, garment worker strike. No-one ask me about sky before.'

All the way into town the tuk-tuk driver asked Ryan questions as he dodged traffic: where you from? – Australia, very good country; this your first time Phnom Penh? – tomorrow you go torture prison,

I take? They had chatted and laughed.

Since that day the man had taken up a spot outside the Indochine and greeted him every morning, often with a wry comment on the nature of the sky that day. Ryan could almost count the tuk-tuk man as another person that he knew in Phnom Penh. But now that he went back over their first conversation again, the man had mentioned a garment worker strike.

The garment thing is big, Ryan thought, as he eased himself into his beer.

Malee often came home remote and weary. She shared an apartment with her sister Reap and another girl from the village and it was far from the university, near the main road out to the garment factories. There was no money to pay a moto so she had to walk and during this time she would think over what she had learnt during the day, or other things that had happened. Some days she was more deeply involved in her thoughts than others and Reap had learnt to watch her face when the key sounded in the door and she pushed her way into their tiny living room. She could tell when something interesting had happened, but this time Malee curled down like a tortoise pulling its head into its shell and trying to tuck its legs under as well.

The last time Malee had come home so pensive it had been the connection in political philosophy of Mao's Cultural Revolution and Khmer Rouge ideology; she'd no idea the influence of Pol Pot's 1965 visit to China had been so strong. The time before that it was the functions of the liver that still played on her mind when she'd come in from medical school, and while Reap found this interesting for a couple of minutes it wasn't what excited her. In her mind the functions of the body were just there and there was nothing you could do about them, a bit like the Cultural Revolution and Pol Pot.

But she always asked what was on her sister's mind, no matter how hard it was to get anything out of her. This night after five questions Malee revealed the most astonishing answer, one Reap would never have guessed: the source of her perplexity was a man.

Husbands were more interesting than Pol Pot's liver.

'Is he handsome?' Reap asked eagerly.

'Hmmm … fairly, I suppose.' Malee saw the world as composed of many shades of grey that were forever shifting in hue and that would fuse and become new things. She would consider the complexity of every subject, which she would then try to share with her older sister. But Reap was black and white about things, and whatever patience she had was reserved for the ten hours every day she stared at her bobbing sewing machine needle at the Amalgamated Apparel factory.

'There is no such thing as "fairly." There is only good and bad so I think that must make him good.' Reap was strong on this point and as she looked through narrowed eyes at her little sister she saw a faint blush around the ears and heard the softest giggle.

'Aha!' she said. 'I saw that. So, he *is* handsome. And rich.'

Catching the subject of this conversation, Reap's workmate Sophea jumped off her bunk in the bedroom she and Reap shared, and trotted into the living room.

'Did you say rich?' said Sophea, raising an eyebrow as if to say, Not possible.

'He is a teacher so he can't be that rich,' said Malee, not wanting to leave awkward reality completely out of the discussion.

'Your teacher?'

'He's new. He took over from the one who had to leave.' They had heard about the one who had to leave. A girl had had an affair with a teacher – it was compellingly shocking. It was also the kind of precedent that could now drift in an abstract way through the minds of all the girls in the school. The fact that it had happened could not be denied and would not go away.

'You better catch him soon before some other girl,' Reap pointed her finger for emphasis. There were a few boys working in the garment factory but there were no husbands there, certainly no rich ones. In any case, Reap and Sophea were destined to return to the village in three years' time and marry boys their fathers thought were suitable and whom they liked well enough: five years in the garment factory, then the ideal wife and babies. The girls had all recited the poem of the *srey kroup leak* in the early years of school. The ideal wife should manage the family's finances and keep the traditional cultures alive, but she should speak softly and tread silently; if her husband had a foolish thought she should place a better one in his mind, but do it by such power of subtle suggestion that her husband believed the thought to be his own. After two years in the city Reap and Sophea had learnt to speak out and joined in demonstrations for better wages in their factory. This was not the way of the ideal wife, but still they were destined to return to the village and to the old ways.

But Malee was the exception because her life was not so planned. Out of the first five children in the family who had made their way into the world so far, she was the cleverest. Their Pa had almost burst with pride that she was helped by UNICEF and had come to Phnom Penh to become a doctor. His face in the village was high, but it meant he could not fulfil his role of finding a boy for her; when her study finished Malee might work in a hospital anywhere. She would never return to the village to live.

'He might have a barang girlfriend,' Sophea suggested. They waited for Malee's insight on this question.

Malee looked at her sideways and pursed her lips. 'I don't think so,' was her judgement, her first concession to the scheme that the new teacher might, after all, be a prospect.

'What makes you think?'

'Things he said today,' Malee replied mysteriously. 'He is sad. And he's only been here a week.'

'Ah, he's new!' the other girls exhaled in unison. Whether he was sad or not did not seem so important to them.

'Is he nice?' Sophea asked.

'I was wondering when one of you would get around to asking that – handsome, rich, then nice, in that order of importance.'

'Well?' They were impatient.

'Yes. He is nice. He is gentle … and funny, and sad. He has, well, nice eyes.'

Reap and Sophea popped their own eyes at each other in exaggerated amazement. 'Grab him!' cried Reap, whimsically shaking her head from side to side. Their hands grabbed at Malee's knees as if to demonstrate how tight she should hold on. They shook her comically from side to side as if to push some sense into her. When this vaudeville routine and the giggling subsided, Sophea had to dry her eyes, then showed she possessed a more sceptical and serious mind.

'They all seem nice, then they go away. Do you remember Chanti from our village? She fell in love with the French guy from the NGO. After three months she talked to him about babies and the next day he disappeared. One last ficky, then he's gone.'

'Her red-check krama was stiff from tears.' Reap remembered it well; she had never seen another person so disconsolate.

'No-one from the village will marry her now. She's stuck with Phnom Penh guys.'

They were all silent for a moment, thinking of Chanti and the grim lottery which must now befall her with the men of the city, and which could be their own fate too if they made an inauspicious gamble with the wrong man, no matter where he was from.

'But for us, every week, life is just the same as the one before,' said Sophea, propping her head on her hand in a melancholy way. 'Two years already we work in the factory and Malee studies all the time until eleven o'clock at night. At least Chanti had three months of fun.'

'But now she has a broken heart and her ancestors will be ashamed of her too.'

'She will have to light some special incense at Pchum Benh to restore their hearts.'

'Chanti was so forward. She was the one who asked that French guy out, when he came into *Chez Jules*.'

'Yes, it was too easy for him,' said Malee, entering the conversation for the first time in a minute. 'We have to speak softly, and be patient; it is the only way. But I am very lucky. At least I like to study. Sometimes I think I won't like it when I have to stop.'

The other two nodded; when the apartment block was sleeping at night, Malee did two more hours of study. She was as driven as she was smart.

'But,' she went on, 'I think that speaking softly will suit me …' and they waited for Malee to finish, 'in all things.' It was another one of Malee's enigmatic statements, but somehow the other two understood her this time – that it was something to do with the new teacher. 'Put some water on to boil; it's time to cut the vegetables.'

Reap lit a match at the portable single gas burner that was their only cooker, and Malee and Sophea cut the radish and carrots that would go into their noodle soup. Every night was boiled noodle, and whatever vegetable was cheap at the market.

'One day Malee will be a doctor and we will be proud,' said Reap, giving up on the marriageable barang for a moment. She knew not to wish too hard for anything.

'One day,' said Malee.

'One day I will go home, but now we grind. And this week there is another demonstration.'

'Oh yes,' said Malee, looking up again, 'the demonstration.' She looked back down at the radish in her delicate fingers. 'We can't forget the demonstration'.

While Ryan might have come to Cambodia to be away from his family, there was one person he could never ignore, whose heart would break if he did.

He called his sister Janey, his big sister in between him and his brother Dermott. His sister Janey who tied his shoes for him when he was little, who packed him peanut butter, redcurrant jelly and salami sandwiches for his school lunches because that was the way he liked them.

He looked at his phone. It meant retreating in a way; he had Tom, Dith, his classes, even the tuk-tuk man, and then there was the puzzling student Malee. He had come all this way and now he had to think about the Sydney problem again. He looked up the elaborate prefix for international dialling then tapped it all in with Janey's number, took a deep breath and punched the green button.

'I'm supposed to be going without you? To this wedding horror? Where are you? What's happened to you?'

That was how she answered the phone; but it was typical of her – openly acknowledging the problems she had, exaggerating them threefold, and making a joke of them all at the same time. You had to know Janey to *get* her and Ryan knew her all too well. He had been trained over years in the arts of matching it with her. From the airport he had left her a message saying he wouldn't be going to the wedding – that's all he'd said.

'Hi, Janey.'

'Hello. This means I've got just three months to exhume some date and drag him along for company, me an old maid thirty-six years of age. If they last that long, that pair. She's not with foetus, is she?' Janey was always conflating ideas into a bunch of sentences, leaving you to pick which one you wanted to follow, or both – whichever. This conversational mode was confusing to new players, but had advantages for experienced hands.

'You should find someone else, Janey. Someone permanent. You don't think they'll make it?'

'You are telling *me*, and you not over this Amanda. Fifty/fifty I'd say.'

'No chance pregnant. It's been the blink of an eye since I was with Amanda, you've had eleven years – more.'

Janey had fallen in love with a Jewish boy in her first year at uni, in the dramatic society. He was quirky and funny. They shared interests and they got on.

The boy's parents were polite and accepting but, well, a little distant. They didn't think Janey would last but that only drove her on. She upgraded from science to medicine to impress them, and maybe to stretch herself too. She got through ok and ended up in one of those practices where there are six or eight doctors and you never know who you are going to see unless you book two weeks ahead. 'Too bad if you come down with diarrhoea,' was what she said, shrugging her shoulders.

But her success in medicine was not enough for the Adlemans. When three, four, five years passed and she didn't go away, the parents became more and more distant. And then he dumped her.

She was a shiksa.

'I haven't found the right one yet,' she said.

'You're not even going out with anyone.'

'The only men I meet are doctors.'

'So …'

'All married with Range Rovers.'

'Any married with wives?'

'They're the only ones who are interested – very funny. And don't even mention internet dating.'

'You could try going into low pubs by yourself on a Friday night. You know, short skirt, a little make-up – time to cougar things up a little.'

'At least you haven't lost your sense of humour.' Then she had a thought. 'Hey, this was meant to be about you, anyway. What in hell have you been up to these five days since you disappeared on me?'

He still hadn't told her why he wouldn't be attending 'this wedding horror.'

'Oh, yes, that little matter.'

'That one.'

'Um. Let's see. Yes, the wedding. I'm not going.'

'You said as much. Your phone has been silent for days.'

'I won't even be there.'

He heard silence on the end of the phone, then a sigh – all constructed for effect. In the early stages of her brief but notable varsity dramatic career, Janey had been noted for her natural comic timing.

'You said "there," Ryan, not "here." Is that correct?'

'Um, yeah.'

'Um, yeah …' she mimicked. Then her voice came over all cheerful, as if nothing untoward was occurring at all. 'Oh, ok. And just, by the way, just asking but, just where might you happen to be at the moment? If I might enquire, not wanting to be too pushy or nuthin'.'

'Um, let me see now. Just looking down into the street,' and he actually did look down into the street, 'I can see a guy pulling a little rickshaw type thing only they call them cyclos here and there are millions of motorbikes and lots of people in the street who mostly look sort of South East Asiany so I reckon … the place I am in at the moment is probably … ah, Cambodia.'

The silence at the other end of the phone this time was more profound.

'Jesus H Magillicuddy. You're serious, aren't you.'

'I'll be teaching English.'

He could sense her nodding with pursed lips, catching up with the news.

'A very fine thing to do. Do you have any idea how much they pay teachers up there?'

'Enough to live on.'

'Enough for a Cambodian to live on, if he's corrupt.'

'Or she.'

'Pardon me. Women can be corrupt too. Very good. Now, what can I do to dissuade you?'

'I started three days ago.'

He knew that Janey was the last person in the world who would have him walk away from an agreement. He remembered how, when he was a teenager, he had arranged a date with a girl and then had second thoughts. Janey held him by the shoulders and looked into his eyes. 'You said you'd do it so you'd better go through with it. Think of that poor girl,' she'd said, and the date worked out ok after all.

She had been the moral imperative in his life; she chose to see even casual verbal agreements as binding, like a sacred oath or written contract.

'Can I come and visit you?' It was sudden, unexpected.

'Serious?' At the best he had hoped for acceptance of what he had done. 'You want to come?'

'Of course I want to come!'

Ryan could not speak for a moment. Janey had supported him in the past, and especially about this relationship between Amanda and Dermott, but this was a shock.

'I … Well, yes. Janey, I didn't think this was your …'

'Not my what?'

'… not your kind of place. Look, yes. Yes, please. When I am well settled.'

'Well settled could take a lifetime up there.'

'So it could,' he said. 'A lifetime is what it could be.'

'Oh, my God,' he heard from the other end of the line.

That night he was still thinking about his morning lesson. The laptop was sitting on the bed. He flipped up the lid and knelt in front of it without bothering to set up on the tiny table that was there. He typed in 'Cambodia garment workers.' A list of newspaper articles came up; a glance to the bottom of the screen showed there were more than ten pages of them. The *Phnom Penh Post*, the *Cambodia Daily*, socialist weeklies from all over the world, even the *Sydney Morning Herald* and *Melbourne Age* were in on the act. Suddenly it all looked like big news.

Some of the entries were news reports of strikes and demonstrations stretching back a year and a half. Some of them were investigative pieces revealing the shocking living conditions of the workers in huge apartment blocks. The demonstrations had been tense stand-offs between the workers and police to show dissatisfaction at the employers' failure to respond to demands. Workers in the garment industry were receiving around $80–85 per month, the poverty line was $160. One article quoted a representative from the Federation of Friendship Unions who feared the situation could descend into violence. A court injunction had ordered strikers back to work.

One piece showed girls sleeping four to a room in their block of flats. There were pictures of them crouching on the floor, washing dishes in a plastic baby's tub; they had to cart the dirty water down three flights to toss it in a drain; they went the same way for a toilet. Most of the workers were girls who had come in to Phnom Penh from the country and from their $80 per month they sent money home to parents in the provinces. He guessed from what he had heard that even $10 per month would make a big difference to people out there, but it left the girls in the city on subsistence diets, in a weakened state. One story focused on mass faintings – girls passing out at their sewing machines in hot and ill-ventilated factories. There was a procedure called coining, where girls would be rubbed hard with coins to restore circulation and revive them. He shook his head, and wondered what Janey would think of that.

The articles revealed sympathy among the educated class who wrote in the newspapers. But it seemed tentative support, as if testing the resolve of the government: editors and journalists had been bashed in years gone by; one had been shot dead walking in the street with his twenty-one-year-old son. But Prime Minister Hun Sen could not go so far down that road now; it could tempt international disapproval and threaten the flow of foreign aid to his country. On the other hand he had to keep wages down and the flow of capital coming in. Foreign aid and multi-national investment worked against each other's interests to a large extent, but Hun Sen needed both. It was the kind of balancing act that he loved to play, and he knew better than anyone how far he could go at any given time.

Ryan's eyes stopped on a figure. A story from the *Post* said there were 650,000 people in the garment industry. Another story said 700,000 but another would only say over half a million. They were incredible numbers. He remembered the one boy who said, 'garment Cambodia biggest industry.' He was not smiling when he spoke the words.

He piled up his two polyester pillows and lay back on the bed. Was this the first time he had felt he was doing something important? Ever? The feeling that people were relying on him to do his job properly filled him with a sudden belonging. The kids in his class, they actually needed him. And Malee, the scholarship girl: there was so much going on in her mind that he wanted to find out more. And her sister was a garment worker.

He drank a cold beer, looking at the wall in front of him. He checked his emails from home with reports of concerts and piss-ups, of who had fallen down the stairs at the Rose Bay Hotel and chundered off the side of a harbour cruise boat.

Thank god I'm not there, he thought, for the first time. Somehow that meant that at last he could call up Colin. It would have been all too easy to have appeared as a callow and diffident lad before this formidable expatriate, but now he had done something for himself; he had learnt things. He now felt a little less like Alice in the Wonderland of mystery and danger.

Or so he told himself.

Ryan was prepared to concede that he knew less about life now than he had when he was twenty-two years old, which was about the last time he had seen Colin. Then he was just finishing his degree and had a feeling that he could take on the world and win and do it his way. And he had Amanda by his side.

At that time, even though Colin was a friend of his father's (a fact which counted against him), and a user of traditional Aussie sayings (which deepened the negative reckoning), even then Ryan could see that Colin had something: a kind of third eye that saw through what was being said around him, and a native wisdom that kept you honest. There was more to Colin than could be gleaned in a glance. Sometimes Ryan had even wondered whether Colin was being ironic in his use of language archaisms, which were more the intellectual property of the generation before Colin – the returned men of the Second World War. Had he grown up sending up his own parents?

Ryan was ready to meet Colin now, but still wary.

'Where've ya bin? I heard you'd done a runner up here.' Colin answered the phone in his office.

'Took a few days to settle in.' Ryan deflected his first question with an instinct that was self-preservation itself. He told himself, Colin was someone he *had* to visit.

The address was past the Royal Palace on Sothearos Boulevard, on the way to the National Assembly: leafy streets – nice. There was an open space on one side with grass and monuments. Life in a well-established NGO couldn't be all bad. Ryan rang again with a hundred metres to go and Colin came through the rolling glass doors of the modern building as he approached.

'Mate,' he stuck out a hand and gave Ryan's a good grip. The pleasure in his face was so urgent that it was almost needy; Colin was more revealed and open than he'd expected, but still Ryan was careful. He wondered for a second about the life of the long term expat. Colin might be a king in this world, but what about life away from the office? Who did he turn to when the sun went down?

Colin first hit town to help out in the United Nations–run election in 1993. To say he had come for six months and stayed for twenty years would be not quite literally true. But he had found some excuse to return, the way people do when there was something about Cambodia that had ground into their souls and wouldn't go away. For Colin it had been schools. UNICEF had wanted someone who knew how to set up schools and Colin had just split up with the wife. He had met Hun Sen along the way. Ryan asked him about that when they settled down with Angkor Lagers cold from the bar fridge.

'The glass eye is good,' Colin observed. Hun Sen's eye had been taken out by shrapnel when fighting for the Khmer Rouge, before his defection to Vietnam. There's nothing like hearing your name is on an elimination list to get you running across the border. 'You met any glass eyes yet?'

Ryan confessed that he hadn't.

'You will in this country – nearly as many glass eyes going around as blown off legs.' Colin's humour was black. 'They're good these days.'

Colin's NGO was still something to do with schools. That's

where Hun Sen came in. Every second school in Cambodia was named after him; they made for good photo shoots and TV programs, so they had to get a new one going every now and then – the father of the nation cutting ribbons. In comes Colin.

The window looked over trees – twilight, the open park, lights winking through shimmering branches like outback stars in shifting clouds. From that high up the impression could settle gently upon you that life was good. Ryan was unsure whether he should be feeling privileged or whether he was just doing a duty by visiting a family friend. He decided to feel privileged for a moment.

Colin glanced over the view just long enough to make Ryan look out there too and share in his quiet proprietorial pride.

'By the way, I heard what happened.' For someone who only visited Australia once every three years or so, Colin was up on the family gossip. 'What the fuck is your old man doing allowing that shit? Jesus.'

Ryan shrugged his shoulders and tried to seem unconcerned, too cool to be back there in all that stuff.

'Dad's getting old. Dermott is gearing up to be family king,' he said. 'Now he's got his queen; she was a kind of take-over target. That's probably how he thinks of it.'

'And you've run away.' Colin was a tester. He liked to hit you with one so frank and confronting that you weren't expecting it, just to see what you would do.

'There's only so much confetti you can brush out of your suit pants.'

Colin took a huge swig from his beer and leaned back in his chair, narrowed eyes regarding Ryan.

'Good answer,' he said with certainty. 'But it looks to me like you got a bit stuck in your fly.' Ryan stared back at him and made a face, so Colin went on. 'Weddings,' he shrugged, 'fucking hell. Seen a Cambo wedding, yet?'

Ryan shook his head.

'All pink and yellow – hysterical. Big ceremony walking in a circle around the couple, brings good luck. Divorced people have to stay on the outside – bad karma. And noise! Loudest musical racket you ever heard, and I saw AC/DC at the Sydney Concert Hall in 1987.'

'I get your point.'

'She was too normal for you, wasn't she – that girl, Amanda. I mean, she was fucked up but she was fucked up in a normal way. Your fucked up-ness goes deeper than that. Still, she had problems settling to anything, didn't she.'

'You don't have any problems then, Colin – settling down?' It was time to return fire, to refocus this conversation a little.

Colin got up to the fridge and pulled two more Angkors out and plonked one down in front of Ryan.

'You know, marriages are built on a period of intensity that is never repeated and the rules of engagement between two people from that time on are built on that period,' Colin went on philosophically, ignoring Ryan's question. 'Some people are addicted to the intensity, so when it starts to fade they move on. But the prospect is, sometimes two cock-ups can be all right together if they work each other out ok. The devil you know can be ok as long as you actually know him. Problem is, we may never really get to really know him.'

'Or her.'

'Yeah, exactly. *Them* you're supposed to say nowadays, isn't it. But one fuck-up going off and marrying another fuck-up's fucked-up brother is just really fucked up. Problem is,' Colin eased the top off his lager, 'we're all basically cunts, aren't we, fucked up or not.'

'You'd know, Colin.'

'Ha,' Colin threw his head back and laughed for the first time. 'That's the second good answer you've given me, or maybe the third. And I exist in a place where I don't get many good answers. Who's going to dish it to me in this place?'

Colin raised his small brown bottle in acknowledgement while Ryan squirmed in embarrassment. But he could see that he had made some kind of perversely good impression on this strange fellow.

'You know, your dad and I used to hang around in the same

bunch at uni in the seventies. He keeps in touch.'

'Great networker. Always at the parties. Made him sick in the end.'

'In business pissing on can be an occupational hazard.'

'Maybe you should have brought him up here in '93.' Ryan was thinking how that would have solved everyone's problems.

'We could have used him; he *gets things done.*'

Colin was tough enough to make sure Ryan had to hear something good about his dad.

'Sounds like it was a wild time had by all, from what I've heard, and read.'

''93? UN people were running around with allowances of a hundred and sixty bucks a day. In this place! In fairness it should be said that some of them kept a low profile and wired the money home. But some of them ...'

'Gomorrah!'

'Didn't know you were Irish.'

'That's begorrah.'

'You knew that one! You're either smart or just knowledgeable.'

Ryan shrugged. It was from a gag, an old one, one of the old man's. Something about Sodom and Begorrah. He couldn't remember the joke set-up but he would never forget the punch-line.

Colin sniffed and almost chuckled but didn't allow himself quite that much.

'At that time a bottle of whisky and ficky would leave you enough change out of ten bucks for brekky the next morning and a hair of the dog thrown in. You could play up like the Rolling Stones on tour and still send money home to the missus.' He shook his head at his memories. 'Yanks, Dutch, Eye-ties, Bulgarians – the fucken lot.'

'You send some home to the missus?'

'You bet. All of it. I was married then and I wanted it to stay that way.' Colin looked at Ryan quizzically, as if challenging him to contradict. 'With the view of hindsight I may have done some things differently. But experience is something you get just after you really needed it. Isn't that what the man said?'

Colin's marriage had ended back then – old news. But there had been another since and that had gone in the same direction. So what now? Colin had given no hint of his situation, so Ryan had to guess that he was alone.

'We ought to take you out one night – have a look at the town.' Ryan thought of a whole night with Colin, getting pissed with him.

'Sure. I know a bloke might be in it with us.' He could take Tom along as a buffer.

'We'll go to the Heart of Darkness.'

'Jesus. I won't disappear up the Mekong will I? Like Colonel Kurtz?'

'In the totally bullshit film version. No. Not while I'm there to save you.'

Tom had told him about the Heart of Darkness bar: head crunching music system and bargirls with insect persistence. Though he felt a veil of dread dragging over his head he thought it would be interesting to see how Tom was in that place.

'Cheers, old man,' said Colin, chuckling to himself, still assessing the young man sitting opposite him.

'Yeah, cheers,' Ryan replied, crossing his legs and trying to look natural.

We are all acting, fitting in. The central question had plagued him since he was sixteen years old: is there a real us? You may need to go away to another environment and participate in conscious acts of change before you realise that the self you have been so proud of has been wrapped around a core created by anyone but yourself. Even the rebellious lads he had grown up with had templates: Kerouac, Che, Kurt – all icons, poster boys, not hard acts to follow. Sure, you have *chosen* them, and the act of choice works to make them a part of you, but when you turn around and look back it is still just culture.

When you have a new experience, how much of the old should

you keep and how much of it should you discard? When you learn and change, how much of the past do you take with you? Amanda had made a choice. She thought she wanted the kind of success that came quickly; maybe she had jumped to wifedom as a cure. But many things that came quickly could be gone at the same speed – the cool breeze that vanished in the hot afternoon. People who barged their way into your life can barge their way out just as quickly. He had seen it often enough.

In Phnom Penh he was beginning to know where to go. The city was simple with its numbered streets in that colonial grid style. But there was more than that. Feeling comfortable walking through traffic took a few days. On the big boulevards the trick was to choose a quiet spot in the traffic, step out steadily, don't flinch from your course and let them go around you. It takes confidence, but after a couple of days there came a feeling of belonging to a huge team – Cambodians getting through their daily business, and you with them.

During his week of walking the city he found just three sets of traffic lights. Boys on motorbikes slowed down at red lights and looked sheepishly left and right, then charged through if there was a gap and no policeman to be seen. He liked the freedom – people making their own decisions over whether it was right to cross the road. No cops, no lights, no insurance – watch your step. It was an alternative world of ideas. He looked up at buildings, maybe four or five dilapidated storeys high, washing pegged out on strings across alleyways, emaciated figures sitting at windows, waiting for shirts to dry. Who looked after these people when things went wrong, when they got too old to function? He guessed it always came back to the family, people taking up responsibilities – no such thing as a nursing home.

He started going to the markets and dawdling through the fresh food sections. There were types of spinach he'd not seen before. And the meat! Chunks of flesh of varied hues sat out under awnings, attended by women sitting up on the trestles with fans, swishing away the flies, their unshod and dusty feet sticking out between cuts of beef and pork, saying, 'You like?' as he passed. Chickens were crushed up alive in cages, or trussed together by the feet in bunches of ten and twelve, clucking softly. Strange spikey fruits like yellow sputniks and long thin purple and cream streaked eggplants; he began to see them chopped in chunks and winking through the sauce of some lazy slow-cooked spicearama he would make. And mushrooms – where did they get their mushrooms from in this climate? If only he had a kitchen.

Mr Dith had told him he knew of an apartment he could rent, only a kilometre from the school, a good position. He thought about it.

By this time he and Tom would have lunch each day near school, often a bowl of noodles from a hawker's stand with a wooden trestle and some plastic chairs next to its miniature mobile kitchen. It was a bit like a hot dog stand, only about one third of the size, barely wide enough to fit the wok, and could be pushed along the street by hand. The proprietor was a Chinese man named Chin and he was pleased to have customers who could afford $1.50 for lunch any time they wanted.

'No way,' said Tom. 'You don't want that guy looking over your shoulder every day, and that's what will happen if you rent a flat off his old war buddy. He's doing enough looking over your shoulder now.'

'War buddy?'

'Khmer Rouge.' Tom spoke with the dubious certainty of someone who had formed a view based on instinct, and who would be happy to open up a discussion with someone who knew less than he did. He needed his guess to be assumed to be right.

'Khmer Rouge?' Ryan said, startled. 'Do you think? I haven't met one before.'

'Hah!' Tom came back at him, his hands up in mock-shock. 'Compadre, you've met dozens of them.'

Tom motioned with his hands as if to say, they are everywhere.

'I guess so,' Ryan said. 'There was no real purge was there, after the Vietnamese took over.'

'Even Hun Sen was ex-KR if you go back far enough. And he's the man. Bunch of them held out in the jungle and kind of defected and dribbled back over time. After five years of civil war, three or four years of KR, then ten years of the Viets, everyone was fed up.'

Ryan had talked to one of the boys in his class about the times of trouble and what his parents felt. 'As long as killing stop, no worry,' was the mantra the boy had recited. It sounded too pat; it came with a hopeful grin forced up from some hidden, visceral place. He mentioned that to Tom.

'Exactly. They'll gloss over the problem. But the KR are every-where, mate.' He loved to call Ryan 'mate'. It made him sound like an Aussie, or so he thought. 'Go out in the villages and there are people living together – next door neighbours. The KR neighbour may have bashed the non-KR neighbour's uncle over the head with a shovel in Pol Pot time and kicked him into a ditch, but they have to get on with it. It's fantastic. There must be a lot of shit simmering away in a pot somewhere,' he said to finish, showing that even he didn't know everything about it. 'We should go to a village some time.'

'I'd love to.'

'You wanna? Serious?'

'I haven't been out of Phnom Penh yet.'

'You haven't even been to the suburbs, mate. I know some peo-ple; I'll make some calls.'

Ryan looked at Tom now, shovelling noodles into himself with balsa wood chopsticks. He wondered just who his friends might be out in the villages. Could it be dangerous?

'Who do you know?' Ryan asked, as innocent as he could man-age.

'Just some kids who come in to the city sometimes that I've known for a year or so. They're good. Trust me. The thing about this place – it's life without limitations here. You just have to work out where you set your boundaries.'

Tom looked left and right then picked up his plate and tipped the last of the juice onto his tongue.

'Damn, it's good here. But it's not getting you an apartment, is it. Away from Mr Dith,' he stressed.

'And his war buddy. You really think he's KR?'

'I dunno. He's always very careful. You know, the way people are when they have a secret. I worked with a guy once in the States. Just in an office kind of thing. He was the most normal guy. In fact he was so normal he was almost overdoing the normal, chipper act – 'How you doin' guys, what's goin' down?' That sort of thing. All the fucken time; like you couldn't have a talk without this barrage of phoney convo ploys. I left that place but someone told me a couple of years later that he'd been outed as a smack addict. Sad, but it fell into place. He was always covering up his secret – trying too hard. Dith's not like that, but there's something going on in his head that he's not telling about. You know what I mean?'

He did.

In the end the apartment hiring was simple. There were adverts in the *Phnom Penh Post* for apartments and he rang a couple of the numbers while Tom was there. This step was one he had been faltering over, but with Tom there sitting sleek and satisfied after his bowl of noodles, and possessing all the pepper and salt that Ryan didn't have, he began to gain courage. And he kept thinking of those eggplants, the spinach, the chunks of beef – the flies he could be rescuing them from. It was a duty.

He met the owner, Mr Thiounn, at his grocery shop downstairs from the apartment. He was about sixty years old and wore round horn-rimmed glasses that accentuated his puffy face. In the last couple of weeks Ryan had read a lot about the Khmer Rouge years. Mr Thiounn made him think of the Chinese mercantile class who had fled in rightful fear of their lives. Some came back when the Vietnamese finally left in '89.

Around the back a locked gate led into a metre-wide walkway

and a flight of stairs where a little landing looked over a fence of sticks and the back of the block of apartments that fronted the next street. Then there was the shady yard of a small wat. He could see saffron-covered figures, some just lads, moving about in the dappled light beneath the trees. Were they playing a controlled and laggard game of football?

Mr Thiounn directed his gaze back down the stairs.

'That gate must be locked, all times.' He wagged a finger. 'Security.'

Mr Thiounn keyed open the door to the apartment and they walked directly into a kitchen. There was a stove with two electric burners – of course, no gas. The gas under the woks in the market all came from bottles. Still, he could stir-fry from electric plates if he needed to. There was a narrow passageway with a bedroom on the right, a nice little lounge and then a balcony, the door to which, Mr Thiounn recommended, without explanation, should also remain locked.

One month in advance, no questions asked. Electricity? 'Leave to me,' said Mr Thiounn.

'You pay one month advance each month, we have no problem. You want bring girl, no problem. You want girl? Ask me, I get, no problem.'

And that was it. Girl at extra cost – no problem. Thiounn might be a little bit twisted, but no more than average; so Ryan forked over the cash for month number one, without girl.

He went down the stairs and into the street, jingling the keys in his pocket. Back at the *Indochine* the tuk-tuk man who had brought him from the airport was waiting. He still greeted Ryan every time he came in or out, always with the proposal of some inexpensive transport-rich recreation.

'Where are you going, sir? I take you, cheap-cheap.'

Ryan would shake his head because he liked to walk everywhere.

'I take you Tuol Sleng torture prison.' Ryan shook his head. 'Killing Fieeeld, very ni-ice,' the man trilled and grinned, with humour that managed to see how black it was and yet to remain essentially innocent at the same time.

Ryan admired the man and envied his stoicism. Finally he had a job for him.

'Will you be here tomorrow at two o'clock?'

'Yes, boss,' he answered immediately.

'Good. I need you to take me to Street 242.'

'No problem. I be here. I wait,' he said and smiled happily.

Waiting, Ryan thought, as he mounted the stairs, is what they spend nearly their whole lives doing. Upstairs he walked past his room door to the narrow hotel balcony and looked down into the street. The tuk-tuk man was there, sitting in his tuk-tuk, watching the crowd.

The man's eyes caught a passer-by. 'Sir?' he smiled and raised one hand in salute. For a moment his face turned away and his gaze drifted to the river, to the grey brown water inching along to the confluence; his eyes seemed troubled for a moment. What memory had returned to him, survivor of the Pol Pot time that he, like Dith, must also have been – two men that he knew who had lived through it. What violent radical changes this man had been flung around by, and now the social world of capital and tourists that he had to wrap himself around to survive. Ryan thought he briefly saw some tragedy in the man's eyes, as if a veil had been lifted and the true face revealed for a moment.

'Tuk-tuk, sir?' The man's moment of abstraction was broken, the veil quickly dropped back into its place. He raised a hand, picking out a face in the crowd. He smiled once more, at nothing, at faces passing, resuming his vigil, nodding and grinning into the clamour of the Sisowath Quay.

'Ok, if you remember, we came as far as Chapter Six and page two.' Many of the books were already open to the right page in anticipation.

'Now, the conversation we are going to read concerns Sarah who is talking to her friend Todd.' On the page opposite the conversation was a cartoon drawing of Sarah standing outside an American school building; she was posting letters and talking to her male friend. Her dark bouffant hair was swept back behind her head and cascaded down to finish in a point in front of her left shoulder. Her neat jacket was striped purple and green and her shoes and tight skirt matched. Her face was filled with exasperation. Todd was casual, with his hands in his pockets, chestnut hair in an outrageous Fonzie quiff.

'Notice in the first line she says she is going to school now and having trouble "making ends meet." Does anyone know what that means?'

Concerned looks came back across the room. Some looked harder and harder at the page as if the answer would spring out were their eyes to bore into it.

'It's a tricky one, isn't it.' He was going to explain when Thuon put his hand up.

'Is impossible, teacher. When two ends go different way they cannot meet unless they go all way around the world. Then meet.' The tension of the problem had been broken and the class shared laughter. They knew it was not the right answer but it was an answer, and any answer was a good answer.

'This is an expression, which is not completely literal. Do you remember when we talked about what literal meant? Do you remember that?'

Three or four nodded slowly while the other fifteen or so remained wooden. Chi's face brightened.

'Teacher, this is when thing is only true.'

'Yes, Chi, very close.'

'This when is only way.'

'When it can be taken no other way.'

'Yes, yes.' All agreed now; they were no strangers to metaphorical speech.

'When there is no other meaning or interpretation, a thing is then literally true – true to the word. Here, when she is talking about her ends, she means that one end is her expenses, and the other end is her income.'

'Oohhhhh,' the class began to nod together and chant as one, their voices collectively rising in the middle of this extended exclamation and lowering at its end. Every fibre in Ryan's being wanted to talk about Mr Micawber and his own desperate trouble balancing incomings and outgoings, but any attempt to account for the intricacies of the characters of Charles Dickens would be certain to create many more difficulties than benefits, so he decided to leave Sarah's ends to meet of their own accord. He moved on to the most important part of the lesson.

'Now we see that Sarah has two children and has returned to school to get the education she missed out on earlier.'

In the front row of desks Sophy and Chi brightened up and now took even greater interest in the story before them.

'Oh, is like us,' Sophy said.

'Yes, American girl like us,' Chi replied.

They were nineteen and twenty years old and both had children of their own.

'The girl Sarah is having difficulty because she has to pay so much money for child minding that she can't afford to give up full-time work to go to school.'

'Ooooohh,' the class registered its unified interest once more and they looked down at their books again to find an answer for Sarah.

Sophy had it straight away, 'But, teacher, is easy. Just give children to auntie, she will mind.'

'Yes, give to grandfather,' said Chi.

'Yes,' said Thuon, 'grandmother can mind baby and grandfather will play with older one. Is easy.' And the class erupted with good-natured advice for poor Sarah who, though American and rich, must not know much if she could not see her way out of this problem.

Malee now raised her hand.

'Yes, Malee. Can you explain Sarah's problem?'

The class quietened to listen to Malee.

'I think life in America is different. Many people have no family. It is a sad thing.' Malee showed that she had read something of weight, or seen a documentary on one of the better TV channels, and that she had thought about it.

The class remained quiet as they listened.

'Can you add anything more, Malee?'

'Life is hard in Cambodia, but I think life is hard in different places, even though people are more rich than here.' Malee had concentrated hard on a complex sentence that made an advanced point. She looked up and her eyes met Ryan's for a second, then she lowered them modestly. He saw a reddening behind her small neat ears. But the way she looked at him was as if she had seen something within him that he didn't know he was showing, but which she understood completely. He faltered in concentration for a second, then recovered.

'Yes, class, as Malee says, it is different in America, and in Australia too.' They were listening closely now to hear how it would be different in the West. He looked at the clock on the back wall of the classroom. It was five to nine so he thought he might as well talk through.

'In America it might well be that auntie is working and can't mind the children. It might be that grandfather is also working.'

'Oh no, grandfather no work.' The very thought was extraordinary.

'Yes, grandfather may well work full time right through to the age of sixty-five.'

Sections of the class erupted in laughter at the thought of grandfather going to work at the age of sixty-five. Malee smiled at the hilarity around her and could not suppress a giggle.

'Or even seventy.' The howls of mirth increased. 'Either that or they may live very far away. Perhaps even in another city.'

'But then other auntie or big sister.'

He struggled now to explain the way life was in the West. He stuttered in front of his class and was embarrassed. His own life had been full of babysitters as his mother accompanied his father to endless business functions and parties. Eventually Janey had been old enough to be the responsible one on Saturday nights at home, and Thursdays too and Tuesdays; any night the Chamber of Commerce or the Rotary had a 'do' or any business partner or associate chose to blow a bit of the entertainment expense budget. He fought with an inexplicable sense of honour to justify his culture, as if to fail to defend the West was to admit a fault in himself. What had happened to families? The class was silent now, waiting on him. How much of the old culture was he bringing with him, how much was he leaving behind? How should he express all these things, in a simple sentence?

'Well, you see … People, well, people just … go their own way a lot more. People do things by themselves.' Without looking he could feel the eyes of Malee on him; he was giving something of himself away, without wanting to.

In the front row Sophy spoke. 'Where husban'?'

'Well, she may not know where the husband is.' The attention in the room somehow became a saddened silence. 'In America, and in Australia too, a lot of marriages break up. People decide they don't like their husband or wife and they decide to go with someone else and that particular someone else may not like the idea of having someone else's kids around all the time and, and so people like Sarah have to pay someone to look after children.'

'Happen here sometime,' said Sophy.

'Yes, sometime, I mean, sometimes.' He was beginning to speak like his students.

It was almost nine o'clock now and some of them were closing their books already.

'Ok then, pack up for your next class. I'll see you all next Tuesday.'

It had been awkward to have to justify the world he had left, and to go back there in front of these people. He remembered the words of Mr Dith: stick to the book.

Sophy and Chi again were the last to leave, beside Malee, who packed her bag as carefully and methodically as ever.

'You have no wife?' said Sophy, and Chi smacked her arm as if to say that is too far, too cheeky. Then they both giggled and flashed their eyes so he was able to go along with that and the moment passed. When they got to the door Sophy turned again.

'You come to karaoke bar next Saturday night, teacher. We good dancers.' They giggled and bumped their bags into each other to cover the embarrassment they felt at being so forward.

'I don't dance very well, girls. I'm sure you would be too good for me.' They left and Malee was following behind. He had to say something to stop her – any connection with dancing would do, no matter how remote.

'Khmer dancing is wonderful.'

It worked. She stopped at the door and turned, an expression of surprise and recognition mixed together. 'I am going to the classical dancing this week.' He blurted it out; it was the bravest thing he had ever done. 'At the Sovannah Phum.'

She looked at him openly for the first time, across three metres of schoolroom.

'Yes, very good,' she nodded quickly twice. 'Khmer dancing has a place in Phnom Penh once more. It is wonderful.' She smiled, and her cheeks dimpled as she did.

Under the Khmer Rouge all dancers and musicians had been executed. A handful had survived by hiding their identities and working in the fields; others got away in time to Thailand or the United States or Australia. Some of these had returned and were now training young performers to keep the ancient arts alive. They needed an audience.

'Yes, I will go and …' Ryan faltered as he hovered on the edge of asking her outright to go with him. It was not just a wide bridge to cross; it was forbidden. And Malee seemed somehow too good for him, with him so broken, 'and …well, support them and … enjoy the performance. I hope.'

He had become inarticulate. He thought of some film Amanda

had made him watch – Hugh Grant making an art form out of stammering indecision.

Malee did not say a word in reply, but pressed her palms together in sampeah and raised them high to her forehead in respect. Her small feet trod silently on the linoleum, and she was gone.

He went out into the passageway to watch her down as far as the stairwell. He could hear Sophy and Chi, their laughing voices ringing off the metal banisters down a flight or two. The compact figure of Malee stepped neatly behind them, head down.

She was swallowed by the stairwell without looking back.

That afternoon the tuk-tuk man was there in the street, alert and waiting.

'Sir,' he cried, 'I am ready to take you,' then sprang forward to take Ryan's luggage.

Ryan said the address.

'Street 242 …' The tuk-tuk man scratched his head. Ryan produced a map and pointed.

'Ah,' said the man unconvincingly, staring at the aggregation of lines and words on the paper, turning the page in his hands. 'This street, it is not a hotel we are going to.'

'No, this is a flat that I have rented.'

'An apartment, sir!' His face brightened and he turned around in his seat as he gunned the motor. 'Very good, very good. You stay long time!' He nodded in affirmation once or twice. 'You work Phnom Penh now? You NGO? Teacher?'

'Yes,' Ryan said, for the first time feeling proud to be saying it. 'Yes, I'm a teacher.'

'Very good. Very good.' He turned again and their eyes met and they laughed with each other.

A few blocks away from downtown the traffic thinned and leafy trees competed with the massed power lines for command of the street. Ryan began to wonder if he could manage a motorbike in this traffic. The only time his spirit had ever merged with a two-wheel vehicle was in the Greek Islands – the Cyclades. The island of Naxos was larger than most. He had hired a couple of mopeds with Amanda and they tore off into the hinterland. It was easy, the roads were empty, the skies were blue – there were no helmets, few rules.

Freedom. They went across the hills and found a sleepy taverna on the other side of the island, ate some grilled meat and a mound of spinach and drank a bottle of beer, a large one each, then spent the hot afternoon riding back the long way around, by the seaside road.

There had been good times. But when you were away together it was easy. The pursuit of common goals was not so difficult when there was a new experience every day. Riding a motorbike in a Greek idyll compared to surviving these hard streets was like putting a honeymoon next to the dangerous journey of a life together. It becomes like running a business – it takes work.

Ryan and the tuk-tuk man pulled up outside the apartment. On the corner just a few shops up near Monivong there was another tuk-tuk and its driver hanging about and another two blokes sitting on motorbikes smoking under a tree. Next to them a third motorbike stood empty.

'I help you,' said the tuk-tuk man, nodding up the back stairs.

'No, thanks, no room for two of us on that staircase anyway.' Ryan paid the two dollars they'd agreed, then stuffed a few notes of riel in on top as a tip.

'Thank you, sir. Can I take you somewhere now, sir?'

'No, I think I'll be right for a while now.'

'Maybe later,' he said enthusiastically. 'I wait here.' He nodded up to the corner where the others sat.

'No, I won't need anyone for the rest of the day.'

'Ok, is ok.' And as Ryan lifted his bag and took his first few steps up the back way he heard the man rev his machine just enough to join the little group at the end of the street.

'His problem,' Ryan thought, as he turned the key on his new home. But the moment he said those words to himself he knew it was a conscious thought, something sprung from a learned culture of toughness and aloneness that was not really his: a thought that was not worthy of the connection he was feeling for the man and his dark and whimsical ironies, his allusions to the nature of the sky each day. Ryan listened closer. The tuk-tuk man revved down to stop at the corner, the motorbike engine spluttering to a halt, not turning into the deep water of Monivong where he could be swallowed and lost to him forever.

He separated T-shirts and socks into the sparse little wooden drawers of the trousseau. There was a mirror there and he avoided looking at himself. For a year he had not looked at any part of his face, except his hair when he was combing or brushing after the morning shower. He was just not someone he wanted to look at.

He found a piece of dowelling about two feet long and then some string in the drawer second down from the knives and forks. He walked up to the Central Market and bought a piece of material he had seen – royal blue with a motif of caparisoned elephants marching along with their handlers and with ancient Khmer dignitaries in the riding baskets on top. He fitted the material to the dowelling and strung it up to the only picture hook there was in the lounge. The place was now his.

The next big moment was the connection of wifi in the apartment. At the hotel the service had phased in and out of his life on its own terms. His response to that had been to place himself above it. He did not need email – all that needless contact, endless Facebook and Twittering, the egotism of self-referencing posts.

He plugged the laptop in at a little table in the lounge room, by the window. He could see the iron balustrade of his balcony, branches of a tree, power lines – through all that the outline of another small apartment block across the street, towels laid out in the sun to dry. His doctor had said to keep his laptop away from the bed. He needed clarity to sleep. Before he left he had been waking in the night for months. In the beginning he had been on Temazepam, supplied by his GP.

'Be careful,' said the doc. 'They *are* addictive. That's why they're on prescription. I'm giving you one script, to get you through this little period.'

'I understand, mate,' he'd said. 'People top themselves on this stuff.'

'That too.'

Now he would sometimes wake at five a.m. Too late to be taking something to go back to sleep, too early to be healthy. He had Panadeine, with the 25g codeine hit you could get across the counter here. That was all. He didn't even use it every night. Only six tablets left.

He hooked up the laptop and the system came on crystal clear and straight away. Among his thirteen emails one stood out. His sister.

Hi Bubbalinks

How are things settling in up there? Permanently settled yet? I hope Mr Dith is doing the right thing seeing what a valuable asset he has on his hands.

From me I say, Come back I need someone to talk to. Apart from you I only have Jill, Cookie, Estelle, Helen and Bridget. What good are they, I ask you. Oh, and Tim the gay guy you met at little Joey Liebowitz's barmitzvah. He still asks after you. Now all I can do is shrug my shoulders – He never writes, is all I can offer.

Write.

OK, the real and pressing need for this message is that father is ill. I am the messenger. Please don't shoot me. The whole prostate thing is looking curly. So curly that I think it has circled all the way back to where it was last year. And that is 'Terminal.' How long? Maybe six months tops in my GP view, although the specialists of course will not say.

OK, I know this is not as strong a reason for you to come back as is my need for company, but heck, you could alleviate my need to hear from you by writing or even, dare I say, calling!! You could even, gulp, let me have your new number.

Jesus, what an email. How did her patients put up with her? Easy. They liked her because she cared. They loved her because she cared. She always ran overtime but her schedule was full days ahead.

Firstly, there was no little Joey Liebowitz's barmitzvah. It was a joke inspired by the endless round of family events when she was with Joel. From there on any tragically tedious event became attributed to the mythical Joey Liebowitz and his coming of age; it helped to deal with ignoble reality.

Secondly, she referred to their father's health in an oblique and jocose manner – but it was hurting her. She would be visiting and supporting him with every sinew she had. Mother would be doing her duty. Dermott and Amanda she did not mention. And Ryan? He was not blamed for leaving, not by Janey anyway.

Bubbalinks was the name she gave him when he was a little boy; to be used from his adolescence forward only in times of peril. For it to be used at the top of her first message to him in Cambodia, it was a signal of distress.

He wrote back and gave her all his news; he told her about Tom, that they thought Mr Dith was ex-Khmer Rouge. He had taken some time to face up to Colin, but had touched base now. All of this news would be sensitively edited and passed on, he had no doubt. He wished Joey Liebowitz well and hoped his career in computers was coming on; he sent his love to Tim.

He lay back in bed and closed his eyes. She had not said a word about Amanda and Dermott. She was protecting him from the fall-out of his disappearance; he could hear his brother now, 'Ha, too sensitive,' as was the refrain of bullies. He would be derisory and Janey with tears inside her would work her mind through a cache of responses for one that offended no-one.

He had been in Cambodia three weeks now, long enough to have made his point. He could decide not to stay and teach at all, but to go on a tour of the temples for a couple more weeks and then head back home with a fresh head and a bag full of dinner party travel stories. He could fly out tomorrow if he wanted and what could Dith do?

But now he had his apartment. He lay back on his bed and closed his eyes. Images from home came back – Amanda and Dermott, Janey. But he was here, with Tom and Colin, even Mr Dith meant something to him now.

Malee.

He needed a week to find out about her.

He decided to go straight to the market and buy some rice and eggplants and spices – maybe a cut of that beef. He was going to dine at home tonight.

He had been to the Foreign Correspondents' Club to look from their first-floor balcony over the confluence of the rivers. There was a marking line across the waters that could have been drawn by a giant hand unseen, where the pale brown flow of the Tonle Sap met the darker course of the Mekong, and struggled to assimilate. He had always thought of himself like the Tonle, fighting stronger powers, valiant and dignified in retreat. But that was his past.

Now it was time to eat. He had familiarised himself with fish amok and beef lok lak so much in the past fortnight that the zeal of the proselyte was beginning to dim. He could go back to his apartment now and make whatever he wanted, but this was Saturday and he wanted to stay out. The life of Riverside, the anonymity of the crowd, was what attracted him now. What would be the chance of bumping into his student up here, Malee. Zero, he conceded; she was not a Riverside kind of girl.

The place on the corner opposite the FCC was new: polished floor, padded chrome chairs and girls in salmon pink livery out front with matching smiles and welcomes. It could have been a Bondi wine bar. Amanda would have been happy there, drinking and vetching her Sundays away.

Next to that was the Happy Phnom Pizza, ganja herb included. He took a moment to consider the adroitness needed to be on weed in this place; for now he needed his capacities intact just to make his way along the street without upending himself on loose paving stones and crashing into gangs of American college kids on work experience. Past the Happy Phnom was a travel office – internet and bus tickets; Western Union Money Exchange; two shop-house cafés boarded up with galvanised iron shutters and padlocked for the wet season; the Pink Elephant restaurant – Khmer food; then the King's Court Happy Pizza. More pizza and all happy; further up was another travel agent; then the Luxury Boutique Guesthouse and Restaurant – Massage; an Indian place; then the Café Taboo and Islands Massage.

He decided on the King's Court Happy Pizza as long as he didn't have to be Happy if he didn't want to.

It was a typical open-fronted Chinese shop house facing the river boulevard. Two French guys were smoking cigarettes and drinking beer under the awning. The younger one, about forty, was talking with animation – his greasy hair and lived-in shirt somehow suggested decades in Cambodia. His older companion sat pat under a natty straw hat, pursed his lips and nodded quite often. Inside, Ryan glanced at a family group of five and then sat at a smaller table opposite them, just inside, where you could be close to the street but not in it – enough distance to dream in.

The quattro formaggi jumped out of the menu at him: it was the melted cheese he was needing. The dairy culture of home brought sudden remembrances of childhood and making cheese grilled on toast with Janey; watching it rise under the heat of the griller, then laughing as it dropped flat when they sliced it, like they thought a punctured soufflé would.

The woman of the house was at his table and he ordered the formaggi and took a glass of cheap red wine with it – Chilean; sharp, perfect, it would cut through. He could imagine the wine, rasping at his throat, cleansing him somehow, purifying. Mellow wine would not do it.

At the table next to him the little family group went about their business. There was a European bloke, who he placed as an Aussie, with two Khmer women, sisters he guessed, and two boys around seven and eight years old. The older of the women was the Mum and spoke to the boys in Khmer; she might have been forty. The Aussie Dad talked to the kids in English. He was affectionate with them, putting his hand under one of their chins and giving it a little waggle; this only meant that the other one wanted attention too and started crawling over the first one to interpose so Mum scratched out a little rebuke in Khmer and the boy returned to his proper posture with a look that was equal amounts playful and sulky.

Everything was a game. Sometimes Dad tried to make them listen to something serious. They adopted listening attitudes for the length of a sentence, jaw resting on their hands propped up with an elbow, then they wriggled and giggled. They were cheeky tykes. The dad kept a sleepy look around his eyes, a narrow pallid face and then a mouth that was an ironic gash between his nose and chin. Mum drank quickly from her own glass of cheap red then ordered another. She seemed just a little frazzled by those sharp and precocious boys. Dad gave no hint of being either happy or sad. Beneath his dreamy eyes there was a benign sort of acceptance of all that occurred around him. This was what he had chosen.

He was a stoner.

The younger sister was quiet, looking on, an expectant smile like someone waiting for a call, addressing a word or two to the kids or her sister – a night out with her family who were all so very familiar to her, nephews that she probably shared a room with. One of the kids was pale and looked more like his Dad in features while the other was darker and favoured the mother.

But they were a family. They lived and breathed together.

When he pulled a slice away from his pizza the blue cheese oozed off like lava and he bent forward to catch it, still hot and almost scalding, in his mouth. The two boys watched the strands of cheese and the hungry man risking scalded lips. As he reached for his wine he caught the eye of one of the boys, and winked. Without hesitation the boy slid under the table and came across to grin at him between the horizontal wooden slats of the backing of another chair at his table. He was about to say hello but the mother machine-gunned a rebuke across the space between them and the child returned straight away to his place – his family. The younger sister spoke softly to the boy and then smiled shyly across at Ryan, nodding approvingly at his interchange with her nephew.

After a while the family group rose to go out to a tuk-tuk that mum had arranged a couple of minutes before. She handled the cash and paid for the pizza – the keeper of the keys. She guzzled the last of her wine, then all five of them piled into the tuk-tuk and their driver kicked his motorbike into spluttering life and they merged into the Sisowath Quay traffic.

There was something about the unexpected equilibrium of the family that had drawn him in – something about the open quiet smile of the younger sister, the tranquillity of the stoner. If he had come in a half an hour earlier he could have watched them longer, maybe he would have spoken to the boy, met them all.

They had something that was good.

He felt that he couldn't really say he had been there until it rained. For three and a half weeks each morning he had pushed aside the curtains, inspecting the sky. Wispy cirrus drew away to the north and moved little, threatened nothing.

But that morning the air felt different. He had never been in a tropical downpour or known the romance of standing in the warm rain, soaking without cold. There was a build of tension or relief or excitement in all faces at school as black clouds collected like a warning and the flaps of tuk-tuks blew up in the gusts. At four o'clock it came, at the end of school; a pit-pit-pit on the roof, like dry rice grains popping in a hot skillet, then faster and faster until the sounds came together and formed into a roar. He could hear the girls outside in the street screaming for fear or joy, for the crazy simulation of both together, and he went to the window to watch them cling to each other under plastic ponchos, making clunking pantomime runs across the street. The deep gutters were full almost at once; it was a world of grey cloud and deep rain and people bent, stumbling, running, splashing bikes through lakes.

The rain pounded the startled city for an hour and a half. Even though the roads were uniformly mounded in the middle for drainage, still there was no dry place to walk. To cross the street meant shoes and socks being soaked and pants drenched halfway up the shin.

All week it continued, off and on. The day would begin with dull high cloud and sunny bursts, then in the afternoon the wads of black-sheep wool came together and the wind blew up in spasmodic gusts. The signs were not hard to read: tuk-tuk men hurried to tie plastic covers on their vehicles; the café people brought their chairs inside; people ran for home before the gathering storm. Then an hour or maybe two of thundering rain and it was over.

And the rivers rose. The rains had begun in the mountains the week before and the swollen Mekong had already hit Phnom Penh and shoved itself into its confluence with the Tonle Sap. As soon as the school closed up on Saturday afternoon he walked over to see the sight. He followed some tree branch debris and it went with him at walking pace all the way up the quay away from the Mekong; the Tonle Sap River was in retreat. He stopped for a moment to watch the branch of crooked twigs and leaves flow upstream and against the common run of nature. The grey skies stretched all around opaque and low, and the sun glowed dull and flat somewhere up there behind.

The moment he paused to look, a woman approached him and began to talk, asking where he was from. Her skin was dark and sweaty and she wore no shoes; the soles of her feet were cracked, and dust and dirt were ground in so deep it seemed no simple bath or wash could ever erase the stain. Her blue dress had been slept in – perhaps on the quay itself. 'Where you from? You touris'? Where you wife?'

'No. I don't have a wife.' He found himself answering her in spite of the unease he felt.

'You see,' the woman said, raising a finger, bidding him, perhaps, to wait for a moment. She turned back to two young girls who were sitting on rugs, playing at cards. The woman may not have slept on the riverside at all; she could have brought her girls, her neighbour's girls, someone's, to the river to pass the time. From her voluminous shoulder bag she drew a small notebook and tore a page from it for him. On it in huge letters that filled the page was the word 'Leang' and underneath it a phone number.

Ryan furrowed his eyebrows into a puzzled look and narrowed his eyes. 'Tha' my sister. Speak goooood English.'

The children would be her sister's.

'She sleeping now.'

He stuffed the note in his pocket as that seemed to be what she wanted and he smiled and nodded to her as if he understood and would be a happy conspirator in her plans. He broke away and she did not follow him. He looked back at the children. This could be their playground, or just one of them. He had been too polite to ignore her when she approached and now he had her sister's number: a stranger, but now somehow not, a contact far from the world of school and Dith. What had happened in the cities, since Westerners and their money had arrived? He knew that not everyone was engaged in following the trail of dollars, but still he wondered that the presence of capital had turned the nation backwards; an essential and ancient purity of social order had been breached and replaced with a form of controlled chaos.

Rivers flow backwards. He resumed his walk, more quickly now. There was something biblical about the Tonle Sap. More than that, there was something arcane that ran through the whole Khmer world that he was trying to grasp but did not understand yet. The Tonle would now carry its waters hundreds of kilometres to the lake and drop silt that would act like fertiliser when the dry season came and the rivers and lakes went back to their most-of-the-year shape; it was the same elemental force that had born the Egyptian civilisation five thousand or more years before. For all its conflicting forces the river proceeded with a vaguely harried dignity; its disquiet ran beneath the surface.

He walked back to his apartment. All the way he thought of Malee, and of the riverside woman's number burning in his pocket. It was Saturday and the night of the classical dancing had finally come around. He wanted to see the dancing but the street number was distant and he felt like he had already had a long week. Still, he might see Malee and learn more about her. If not, at least he would be able to say that he had been there; he could engage her in conversation on the topic and that could lead somewhere. The same tuk-tuk man was waiting on the corner with his group of mates, so he spoke to them about the dance performance that night.

'Tonight I go to Street 484. Do you know it?'

The three of them bent their heads in discussion that went on for a full half a minute. 'Is far,' and he pointed vaguely down towards the south-west of the city.

'Yes, is far. How much? You take me there tonight? Seven o'clock.'

'Oh, I think,' he said, rubbing his chin, 'bring you back ten dollar. Yes, I be here.'

The guide book said it was the Classical Dance Association of Cambodia. He had glimpsed it before: girls with their fingers stretched, tortuously deliberate portraits of mythical stories, outfitted in silver and gold and jewels, elaborate headwear, perfect balance: Apsara dancing.

Later that night they pulled out into Monivong and headed south. It was a broad avenue with three lanes in each direction; Saturday night and there was excitement in the air – people going places. Lads in bunches, girls three on a motorbike, giggling over ice creams as they sped along, waving at the barang in the tuk-tuk.

A night-time office block facade was punctuated by windows lit up here and there; it seemed to him like a blaze of starlight, the Milky Way anchored for him up there on the east side of Monivong. Surely it could not be cleaners working Saturday night? Above him trees, as high as the second level of the buildings, were strung with electric lights. And past these trees, that looked like someone had plugged them into a socket and had blown their hair, they drove along at a smooth easy rate that was itself a novelty. The close quarters combat of the city grid was behind.

They swung right at a big roundabout then turned left again and entered another part of the city. Darker – narrow streets were lit by single bulbs every hundred yards or so; the tuk-tuk man slowed to look at street signs etched onto corner stones that were so rounded by weather that they could have been from the middle ages. Street 420 – nowhere near it. They drove gingerly up to the corner and turned right and right again – Street 422. Then left and left again – Street 424.

He checked his phone: 7.21, nine minutes to show time.

He motioned back to the long street they had turned off; they must go further up there to find 484 – surely that was it. But the tuk-tuk man was alone in his thoughts and seemed not to see or hear. Up and down they went again and made it as far as 428. The driver was hesitant and uncertain now.

'Go down the other street,' Ryan shouted and signalled with his arm, meaning the cross street that would go past all these side streets. His man began to look desperate now. He was lost.

There were little shops at corner places – old fashioned corner stores. They passed a small group of girls standing outside, some squatting on low plastic stools, knees together to save the view of what was beneath their short tight skirts. But this was not a social gathering; these girls spoke little or nothing and sat as if waiting, smoking cigarettes as if they really meant it – down here on a Saturday night.

And a little epiphany struck, a light and gentle awakening that had descended on him from the expectant, lazy attitudes of the girls: the man might think I am here for sex. He sat back in his seat to think, not caring about lateness now. The tuk-tuk man seemed to care for him, to see something in him. It may have been only Ryan's inexperience or even fear that the man had responded to, but since his first hour in Cambodia the tuk-tuk man had been close to him, almost as if he was giving care or protection. Yet there was a distance. If he was looking for a brothel surely it would not matter much which place he went into, so why bother to find Street 484?

'Street 484,' he said firmly.

'Yes, I find.' He looked worried now.

'It's the place …' and Ryan waved him over to the side of the road to talk. 'It's the place where they do dancing.' The man looked back blankly. Ryan held out his hands in mimic of apsara dancing moves and fashioned his eyes in the bewitching style of the classical dancer.

'Dancing?' The man did not seem to know the word.

'Yes, dancing,' and Ryan moved his shoulders and arms in a lingering rhythm for the man, hands still out with fingers stretched engagingly.

Slowly, so slowly, a look of recognition came over the face of the tuk-tuk man. His mouth and eyes came open in the appearance almost of awe.

'Sovannah Poom,' he cried. 'Sovannah Poom!'

'Yes, yes,' Ryan nodded furiously, a jolt of hope bringing him to life. It was the Sovannah Phum Classical Dance Association of Cambodia. Ryan had never guessed that the man would know it by its name. He had underestimated him.

'So sorry. Sovannah Poom,' the man said again and gunned his machine to vibrant life, executed an abrupt U-turn; the tires squealed as they bit into the rubble and potholes of the dim suburban street, then raced away. The girls at the corner shop turned their heads to look.

Now they hit a more generously lighted street. He looked at his phone – 7.29. At least they were going to get there now, he thought – late perhaps, but it would happen, and there would be no more apsara miming.

'Sorry, sorry,' the tuk-tuk man turned around and hit his head quite hard with his open right hand to indicate how stupid he thought he was. 'So sorry,' he looked at his own watch and sped his machine ever onward.

Malee and Reap waited at the door of the Sovannah Phum Classical Dance Association. Malee turned around to check on Sophea in another little group of girls from their village in Kampong Thom: two cousins and three others who were friends of theirs or friends of friends from the village, and an older woman from the factory who was their supervisor.

That was the way it worked when you came to Phnom Penh. The network of village girls who had preceded you would get you a test for a job at their factory, would pay the bribe that got you in, would feed you while you waited a month for a position to begin. Without them you would be dead, or on the bus back home and losing face for your family.

When they had done their four or five years in the factory – the air stifling like a mask, the work mindless with repetition – they would return to the village, most of them, as virgin brides. It would be disgrace to become enamoured of the modern ways and the make-up and gold jewellery, to be walking out with boys after dark, to keep money for yourself. To fit in as a modern person in the city, and to remain a dutiful daughter who upheld the moral certainty of the village; it was a balancing act they performed each day.

It was 7.30 and all the girls wanted to go to their seats, but they waited for Malee. There were no secrets in a group like this and everyone knew there was a rich barang who was interested in her. He had said he was coming to the dancing tonight, but some of the girls were sceptical. Married barang couples sometimes came to the dancing, or genteel girls in pairs or small groups, but not a man, not alone. The band was in place by the side of the stage and they could hear a crash of cymbals and a whirl of oboe-like horn music as the musicians warmed up for their performance. The cousin of one of the girls was dancing tonight and they had special seats beside the band.

'We have to go now,' said Malee, softly to her sister.

'I want to see him,' said Reap, jumping up and down on the spot. She was the same height as Malee but stockier, she seemed built closer to the ground and she had an intelligence that was feisty, where Malee's was thoughtful, contemplative. 'He is handsome and rich; he will be my sister's husband.'

The disappointment was in Malee's eyes too as she took hold of her sister's arm. 'Come on,' she said. Reap was hard to move when she had her mind set on something, but tonight she was outnumbered seven to one.

'Huh,' Reap's eyes flashed in anger. 'They are all the same. They say they're good, but then they do something else. He is a no-good husband for us, just like that French NGO for poor Chanti.'

Indeed, Malee had wondered, could he really be what he seemed to be? How could she ever know? The feeling swept over her that her daydream was really as crazy as her rational side had said it was, and she winced within herself at her own foolishness. The problems and risks with barangs were the reality of the night.

She smiled at her sister and smoothed her hair. Reap smiled back at the touch of her sister's consoling hand; it was almost as if she was the sister waiting for the man and not Malee. 'Come on, sister. We have to see Sonith. He will be a great dancer.'

Arm in arm the two girls made their way to their seats. As they let the canvas flap of the performing structure fall behind them Reap took one last glance back at the empty forecourt and Malee watched her sister look, and felt inside her that it was hopeless.

They turned off the main drive and into another small street, but this time the tuk-tuk man knew exactly where he was going. There, all at once, was an old house that sat among sheltering trees, a wonder among the blocks of flats. They turned through an open gate into a brightly lit courtyard where they came to an abrupt halt.

'Sovannah Poom,' the tuk-tuk man said, turning in his seat. 'So sorry.'

'Nothing to be sorry about. You've done brilliantly.'

The man's face was filled with joy. 'I wait,' he said. 'I wait.'

There was a card table with a couple of kids still selling tickets. On one side of the courtyard a door opened into a lit room that looked like a little gift shop. Opposite that was a low barn-like structure that was enclosed by dark curtains that billowed out like sails and around which you could see the backs of the heads of the people inside. He could hear a man talking into a microphone, probably introducing the show.

In the dim light inside he could see that half the audience of about twenty-five people were Western: young couples in their twenties or thirties and a couple of girls who could be Northern European. A Khmer father was there with his four-year-old daughter and a young mother with a little girl too.

There was a group of young women in a corner. They sat next to a band of Khmer musicians nested beside the stage: a clarinet type of instrument that would not have been out of place charming snakes from baskets in a market in Bombay; also a xylophone of wooden bells hit with drumsticks; and two drummers, one seated at a nearly full circle of gongs and another with two large drums beaten with the hands – plus the host with a microphone who was just taking his seat.

Ryan found a place on the hard bench seat and there came on to the stage, not poised and elegant apsaras, but a bouncing troupe of young men. He had quickly glanced at the paper program handed to him and it had said something about the Reamker which, he could see now, was a Khmer version of the Ramayana.

Tonight it was the Ponhakay Story.

The five boys on stage seemed all under twenty-five. The older man with the microphone, the master of ceremonies, watched from the side as if he was the holder of the deed and title to the whole business; a little smile played on his lips. He must be one of those who got away – a dancer or singer from the old days who'd run away before the Pol Pot time. Or he had hidden his identity, his smooth dancer's hands, and made out to be a working man.

Unlikely. This was one who got away – one who had returned. There was something serene about his attentive smile. He had not the cloud that lived on the countenance of so many men who had survived the horror, or who had been conscripted in its perpetration and had buried the memories inside them. Memories that would explode back into the human system when a car back-fired in the street, when unexploded ordnance was detonated in a field nearby, when the most careful system of defence was pierced by a word, or a picture, or a name. This musician was a free man.

Four of the boys left the stage and the principal dancer did a solo piece. He was impressive. Stripped to the waist, his sinewy musculature strained as he leapt and writhed. Then, crashing through the spell of the performance, cries were heard from the courtyard and the audience turned as one to watch as eerie face-shadows were played from outside the pavilion onto the long silk sheet which was the back 'wall' of the theatre. Outside, the other four dancers were now holding torch lights behind flat puppet frames held up on a pair of wand-like sticks. The shapes danced around and fought each other and there was a great deal of hallooing to accentuate the mystical conflict. Then the shapes were brought through the silk into the theatre in procession and the four boys jumped up on stage with the light now thrown on another silken sheet up there.

The band on the side of the stage raised the level to a crescendo and the elder with the microphone had begun warbling, crying out the story. The clarinet wailed over the top of it all and the xylophone of wooden bells crashed to the thump of drums as the host wailed on and on. Suddenly, all vanished from the stage and the band was abruptly silent, the audience frozen in rigid attention – the stage was bare.

After a pause of no more than ten seconds the dancers came bounding out again, scratching and tumbling as the army of monkeys which is conscripted by the hero Prince Preah Ream, who is searching for his abducted wife. Their monkey routine was good; it was time for some comic relief. The stage was cleared again and one dancer stood poised behind the silk screen with arms outstretched while the light played on him from behind so he appeared as just a shadow. He waved his arms for a moment; then another set of arms appeared from his side, then another and another. Clearly there was a row of dancers back there not visible to the audience until their arms rolled out, but the trick was made to portray one of the many-limbed Hindu deities. The effect was magnetising. The performance had ended.

When the clapping was over, Ryan turned to see the tuk-tuk man standing at the side. They had let him in to watch the second half. He also had a ten-dollar round trip fare to collect. He was very happy.

But Ryan could see that he was pleased by more than just a fare and a show. A new layer of respect had been laid, not sprung from wealth or social position, but from something deeper and more real; when the tuk-tuk man realised they were not making for a girl bar in the suburbs, but for Sovannah Phum.

'You saw the show,' Ryan said. 'I am glad.' The man nodded many times in pleasure, but he was already turning for the door. 'OK, let's go,' Ryan said.

It was then that he saw her, from the corner of his eye, and he stopped on the spot, without knowing he had done so, while his man walked on a couple of metres before him. She had left the little group of women who were in the corner next to the band. She was standing a couple of metres away, facing him.

It was Malee. She pressed her hands together and bowed her head so slightly.

'You are here,' he said, then thought, how foolish, for she was obviously there.

'Yes,' she said, and seemed to be fighting between embarrassment and a desire to speak. 'I … came. My cousin,' she waved back at the stage and the musicians, 'he is a dancer.'

'Oh, how marvellous,' Ryan said, not able to conceive, in that moment, of anything that could possibly be more wonderful.

'Yes,' she agreed, and pressed her palms together once more. 'I thought you were not coming.'

She has been looking out for me, he thought. A long forgotten Christmas morning childhood thrill went through him.

'Oh, yes, we had trouble finding the place.' He motioned to his tuk-tuk man who grinned and nodded furiously in acquiescence.

'Yes, it is far from city.'

'Indeed. All my fault really. I knew the name of the place and only gave him the street number and …'

'Oh,' she smiled. 'I see. The street numbers are confusing in this part of town.' She nodded sympathetically to the tuk-tuk man.

They had spoken; it was enough for them both. She had seen that he was really there – had truly spent his Saturday night at the classical dancing. For him, it was a step, and any footfall in the direction of Malee was an advancement that he simply had to take; he had lost his power of choice.

The tuk-tuk man was waiting.

'Yes,' he said, 'I'll see you next week.'

And she was gone and then he was outside. He wanted to stay for a minute to savour the moment, but the drizzle had begun again and the tuk-tuk man had already tied the plastic covering around his vehicle and started up the motor. They were soon headed towards the Foreign Correspondents' Club.

Had she really come to see her cousin? Or for him? Whichever way it was, he felt a glow of possibility settle over him.

They drew up at the FCC and he handed over the ten dollars. The tuk-tuk man was still happy.

'Do you have a name?' Ryan asked. 'I mean, that I can call you.'

'I am Chean.' The man nodded and grinned in appreciation.

'Thank you, Chean.'

And as he hopped on his driver's seat to take off, Chean turned one last time.

'Soon,' he said, in his singsong voice, and paused a moment as he gunned the motor, 'you will have a girl freeennnnn.'

Chean chuckled happily. He pulled some blue plastic over his head and was lost in the quayside traffic.

The night came when Colin and Tom were to take Ryan out to the Heart of Darkness bar, a semi-legendary place in the Phnom Penh fabric, famous for many things in the old days including gun battles between the hot-headed sons of elite families; throw in crooks and drugs and the picture is complete. But what he wasn't used to was the 'bar girls.'

He had always found it difficult, even a little unfair, that men, or boys for that matter, had to be the ones who did the asking out. It was the man's role to take initiative, to cross the dance floor, so to speak, and risk embarrassment. Social media had changed some of that, but in his teenage years it had been known that girls would flirt to encourage risky offer-making on the part of males, only to then turn it down when the whole peer group was in earshot. Asking a girl out could be a perilous business.

But in Cambodia the rules were all different. Since the days of Angkor good village girls like Malee would be approached through a third person known to the family, with an offer of marriage. Many girls now would have a say – a limited negotiated form of veto that could be different in every family. But once an arrangement had been confirmed it would be a serious affront for a man, for a family, to renege. For her part the girl was expected to be untouched, gentle and softly spoken. And clever. The perfect wife would always know what to do, and would guide her husband to the best outcome for their family.

But the moral unity of the nation had been altered forever by the delayed arrival of dollar bills and factories around the turn of the millennium. Now, for the first time in history, girls left the village on motorbikes for an uncertain but maybe profitable life in the towns and to support their ageing Khmer Rouge–survivor parents from there. Factories and tourist cafés swallowed them. Some made it into universities. Others who fell through the cracks found themselves in other forms of casual employment. Bar-girls had become like the water in the tap or the air in the sky. They were simply there, and their idea of relationship could take many forms.

Ryan, Tom and Colin had had enough to drink over dinner to get the three of them just humming. Colin led off to the Heart of Darkness and Tom pretended that all he knew about the place had been gained from hearsay – reports from a third person. Colin and Ryan threw each other a look and a raised eyebrow.

As they approached the place a boy in a black jacket reached across and the big copper doors opened before them. Noise – Phil Spector's Wall of Sound had nothing on Korean pop music.

Inside there were hot red lights, suspended from the ceiling, that glowed over tables but barely illuminated, like hellfire suspended in Chinese lanterns. Lasers stabbed through the darkness around the tables, strobing blue and white flashes on the handful of dancers. The music switched to a disco beat throbbing through – *Can't Take my Eyes Off You*; not the Chris Montez version but a disco group with three girl singers – a seventies treatment of a Western sixties song, probably recorded in Asia somewhere in the nineties.

'Hello, handsome man!' Straightaway there was a girl by Ryan's side. She wore hotpants and raised platform sandals of iridescent silver, plus a tight red T-shirt that nearly matched her lipstick but was more crimson where the lips were caked in deeper fifties film noir red, the sort that stuck to collars.

'How can you tell I'm handsome, you can't see the nose in front of your face in here.'

The girl looked blankly at him for a moment, then her face

creased up in a grin.

'Ha, you're funny.' She slipped her arm inside his.

'You don't know the half of it.'

The music throbbed into another number crackling over the same beat: he caught the words 'Never gonna let you go' echoing over and over.

'You come dance me.'

He now saw that there were two more like her, one at each elbow, awaiting the outcome. One wore a pink headband with a little rosette at a jaunty angle on the side – something she might have longed for since her kid sister's baby photo. She might have been sixteen or twenty-seven, hard to tell.

Colin leant forward, 'You come back later. We have drink now.'

He waved them away, and the girls melted into the shadows.

'The good thing is that they're all freelancers in here. If they bother you too much the boss gets pissed off and they kick 'em out.' They took a place at the bar. Tom was trying to keep track of the conversation, but his eyes were everywhere.

'Why do they let them in?'

'You buy them drinks; that's good for the boss. Other reasons too …' and Colin waved his hand again to signal the end of that topic.

'Are they prostitutes?'

Colin shrugged. 'Depends.'

By the dance floor was a podium about three feet high with the figure of a woman carved in wood; like a Cycladic figure, or a Modigliani – staring, unnerving. A soft light played up from below, accenting its other-worldliness – some jungle spirit up for appeasement.

The music changed from disco beat to something that reminded him of the song *Fame* ('I'm gonna live forever'), but the words went more like 'Say that you'll love me forever'. It was a rip-off where the melody line must have been just different enough to pass the laws of copyright.

The girls drifted under the arcs of light and began to dance in the most desultory fashion, their arms and legs barely moving. The one who had spoken to him glanced across for just a second; her eyes narrowed and she managed to pout and smile all in one seductive movement of the mouth.

'They can't come here just for drinks.'

'They like you they take you home, or your place much better, or down the lane will do. Some of them work…'

'In the day?'

'Do a shift in a café somewhere, maybe. Then if they pick up ten bucks from you it's a goldmine. She'll be back in five minutes.'

'Why not just give her five bucks and say keep off – not interested.'

'Ha! If they think you're a soft touch you'll *never* get rid of them. Pay them for nothing and they'll want a lot more of that action. They'd want to marry you then because they know you're not only rich, you're pissweak as well – perfect man!'

Ryan thought of the money he'd put together before going up there – three thousand dollars in the bank. He'd worked reasonably hard for a few months to get it, but that would be a lifetime's savings for these girls. What would an amount like that mean to them?

Another girl came up to the bar and brushed her shoulder against his arm. He turned to her and she smiled, 'Hello, handsome man.'

He put his hand up and motioned no; she raised her eyebrows in that 'maybe later' way that they seemed to have, and moved back to her group.

He turned to Tom, 'I know where to come if I'm ever lonely.'

Tom's eyes had been all over the room. 'No shortage of company, muchacho.'

After two beers they got out of there. Ryan soon was sick of raising his voice to out-decibel the screaming pop-noise; Tom decided to save it for another time; Colin had seen it all before.

The Pattaya Bar on the next corner was like a regular pub by comparison. The 1970s West Coast rock they spun there was back-grounded. There were two pool tables and on one the girls played each other and two girls played with two guys on the other. One of the girls at the first table said a friendly 'Hi' as they walked in and they said 'Hi' back and went to a table; a stoic grimace was passed to the other girls, signalling their dud status.

'Don't they ever play Khmer music in these places,' Ryan said.

'Never,' said Colin. 'They think *Hotel California* is hip.'

'But no one listens to this sort of thing anymore. Do they?'

'You don't listen to enough FM radio, man,' said Tom.

'Only in supermarkets.'

'And there you can't help it, right?'

'It fouls up my shopping. How can I concentrate on the choice between smoothy and crunchy with *Crocodile Rock* and *Piano Man* in my ear.'

'You're a hard case, man.'

'And *Back Off Boogaloo* on a good day.'

'I think Ryan needs to relax a bit more,' Colin put in.

'You take me to the Heart of Darkness bar, to relax?'

'All right, dear, it is a touch noisy in there.'

'The girls here leave you alone.'

'If they think you're interested it'll be different. And if they like you they'll want you for boyfriend, but yeah, they're not so, what you'd call, pro-active in here. Not too many girls, or the lads for that matter, will sit at home twiddling their thumbs in this city. You got to be on the make, all the time; but still, if they don't like you they won't take you.'

'Ok, so they choose.'

'If you look like trouble they'll only take you if they're really hun-gry.'

'They might only get a customer every two or three nights but it'll still pull more than a job in that garment industry you've been talking about. Eighty-five bucks a month don't go far if you've got the old folks back home to support.'

Ryan tried to imagine eighty-five dollars a month, even here. But there was genuine sympathy in Colin's voice as he dropped the knowing tough guy approach for a moment. He nudged Ryan gently. 'Poor bitches are probably saving up for English lessons.'

'English lessons?'

He checked out the girls more closely.

'I already checked, mate,' said Tom, 'none are in my classes. You should do the same, wherever you go.'

'Jesus, what if I ran into Sophy or Chi out here.'

'Don't call me Jesus.'

'What about this Malee you keep talking about?' said Colin.

'Not in here, no way. Not that kind of girl, Colin.'

'Oh, I see, she's the nice one is she – the truly "nice" one.' He went into the exaggerated tone of the documentary voice-over – 'The moral certainty of the village untrammeled in the poly-temptational big city.' He was poking for a reaction.

'Yeah, she's smart, is Malee,' said Tom, picking up on Colin's line. 'Nice, truly interesting, but she plays the long game for sure. She's just smarter than the others – high stakes.' His voice turned into a rasping whisper as he leaned forward to Ryan's ear. 'She wants to take it all.' Then he laughed and slapped Ryan's back in a way he could not tell was playful or pitying.

Still, anger rose in Ryan. Why did Malee have to symbolise something to these guys? As if Khmer girls were just for bonking the loose ones and ignoring the nice ones. Malee didn't play games of any kind.

Still, they had him thinking. Malee had come up to him at the Khmer dancing; he hadn't had to do a thing. She knew he was interested. She *knew*. Ryan became annoyed for a moment but he couldn't show up his interest in her to them; that was probably what they were waiting for. Luckily the conversation drifted off into loosely related matters.

'Your Malee might be into the long game but these girls couldn't even spell it,' said Colin, flicking a hand towards the pool table.

'In which language, Colin?' Ryan wanted to get him back.

'Yeah, good point, buddy,' Tom put in, slapping his thigh. 'If they have to spell it in English, you have to spell it in Khmer, Colin. Ha, ha, ha.' Tom was pissed by now.

'Ah, ha ha-ha.' They joined together in mocking Colin; Tom motioned for a high-five and Ryan reluctantly complied. He didn't go for all that basketball team celebration thing. Girls at the table turned around and smiled encouragement – the boys were starting to have a good time.

'You fucken pricks,' said Colin. 'All right, my buy.' He signalled for three more. 'The problem with your argument there, though, is that I probably *could* spell it in Khmer.' The other two just looked at each other and grimaced acknowledgement.

'What would Dith have to say, if we were reported out in such dens of disease?' Ryan ventured.

'Ah, the enigmatic Dith,' said Tom.

'Aren't they all enigmatic,' Ryan returned, 'according to the stereotype? That's what you guys are into, isn't it. Half good, half bad – never saying what they think, all that stuff.'

'They don't have the disadvantage of a Christian background. We have to pretend that we're being good all the time, especially when we're not; always giving false reasons for doing shit. Big cultural difference. We're always supposed to be working to raise ourselves in the world. They can just say, "Eh, karma, whatever. At least I'm not a fucken cockroach." You know what I mean?'

Colin bought into it at last, 'Everywhere people tell you what they think you want to hear. But in this place it's subtle. You have to listen closely. To press an opinion on you is a display of ego, and that's not the traditional way. So there are rules to follow. Rules are good; at least that's the traditional way – the way it was.'

Ryan thought of the woman on Riverside with her sister's children. The family was working together all right, but the sister was certainly sleeping in late. The woman had seemed full of cares; the earth was in her feet in any sense of the term. Of Western pretension she had none. She wanted something for her sister – a date, a boy-friend, a husband … five dollars. She had asked for it.

'They want to know where you stand, they just don't want you to know where they stand,' Tom put in.

'Not sure that's true,' said Ryan. 'There might be less double-speak in this country.' The others looked at him, urging him to go on, but he kept his silence. If he told them about the woman on the quay they would ask if he still had her sister's number in his pocket, and he did. He could almost feel it now nestling against his thigh, burning almost. She had been so direct and earthy that she had fright-ened him.

'Maybe. Who knows? I've been wondering about that since 1992.'

'Like Dith and his questions. You've met him.'

'Years ago,' Colin admitted.

'Was he Khmer Rouge?'

Colin was quiet for a moment. As he did from time to time, he simply turned the question around.

'Would you have been?'

'What? KR?' Tom answered. 'Would we have been Khmer Rouge?' He turned to Ryan. 'If you'd been brought up in the jungle with no education, or even if you were in the city looking at Sihanouk and his court lounging around with about a hundred dancers and concubines, going to Paris for holidays every year. If you had the Buddhists telling you that ambition was evil, that any education bar the old folk stories was bad, that you had to love your work in the fields or in the factory. If someone then shoved a gun in your hand and said, "There lad, now you have power. We will change the world – the Chinese are on our side." Wouldn't you have been tempted to say, "Fuck it, I'm in." Huh?'

Ryan had to admit that, yes, he would have been tempted to be in. What red-blooded ox-rider would not? The fact that things had gone terribly wrong – that could not be attributed to the farm boys, the followers. Even a lot of educated people in Phnom Penh welcomed the KR, not guessing what was going to come next. But the idea of Mr Dith, reserved as he was, taking up a gun at any age, was hard to take to. It was too much of a figment that their boss could once have been Khmer Rouge.

'Who knows,' said Colin. 'You can never tell in this place, and forty years on, people will change. Your Mr Dith could have been a lad's lad in his day. But whatever you do, don't ask him. It would be unspeakable rudeness. And your little Malee, don't ever ask her what she's after either, because she won't say.'

They had turned it back on him. Were they teasing, or were they not? Were they as hard to read as they said the Khmer were? He decided that neither of these guys had met a girl like Malee before – she was different.

At the end of their next class Malee packed her bag as carefully as ever and left at the tail end of the crowd.

If Tom and Colin had been trying to turn him off the idea of Malee they hadn't succeeded. When he wrote an email sometimes his fingers stopped moving and his thoughts trailed away. When he read a book he stared without comprehending, the pages not turning. When it came to their next class together the tension rose within him and the prediction of Chean the tuk-tuk man kept singing away in his head. 'Soon you will have a girl freeennnnn.'

But if he was going to see her again outside of school he knew a million nods and winks would not do it; he had to take a risk. If he was sacked he would not get another teaching job, in Cambodia at least, unless he lied on application forms. It was a slope he did not really wish to travel down. So far in life his jobs had all been honest simple work and he had left on his own terms.

After the first class of the week he had complimented the dancing night to her. Malee had smiled happily but the conversation stilled and went in no other direction and she left for her day at university. The next class she had smiled and he had bid her goodbye, but they didn't talk. After that she smiled goodbye and left with her lips compressed.

Was she showing exasperation? Saturday was his last chance, or the week would be over and the joyful impetus of Saturday night would all be lost. It was all up to him for the code in which Malee had been raised would never allow her to initiate anything with a man.

He wrote a note including his phone number and asking her to lunch on Sunday, at the Blue Pumpkin, a bright and noisy upstairs café overlooking the river. Having written something down his anxiety was lessened by one degree, but still he felt so lame with a note. He was meant to be confident, to just go out there and get what he wanted. Rules? Huh, no consequence. But there could be an embarrassing scene with Mr Dith around the corner, other teachers coming by. He was breaking the rules he had agreed to. But the note sitting in his pocket somehow gave him strength, as if it meant that the decision to act had been made – it was in writing.

She could even turn him down and tell the class that he'd asked her out. That would be the worst disaster.

She finished her packing and moved to the door.

'Malee,' he blurted her name and then did not know what came next. She stopped, backpack in place, two books under her left arm, and squared up to him as if to say, 'Ok, out with it'.

'I … I,' he began to hand her the note. She leaned forward and peered at his hand, as if to read from a metre away what was scrawled on the little sheet that was there.

'I'd like to see you,' he said. Once he'd uttered those words it mattered not – Dith or no Dith, walls with or without ears. He handed her the note. He thought now that it would be ok to do it like that because the note had his number and that was required information, wasn't it? George Clooney could do it that way – talking to a girl then handing a note with his number. Simple.

She read the note. The place was silent except for muffled noises from the stairwell down the hall.

'Sunday … I can't,' she said in a broken way. 'I will tell you …'

Then she broke away, through the door and down to the stair-well. He stood in the corridor. Her calf muscles sprang like coils under the weight of her pack as she broke into a run. He had never seen a Khmer girl run before. It was something they simply didn't do. She trotted quickly down the stairs and as she made it to the turn, where he could still see her face, she gave him an open, frank, meaningful look.

And then disappeared.

He exhaled heavily and turned to look the other way up the corridor. There was no Dith. The space was empty and quiet. He had an hour off before his next lesson. He packed his bag and locked the door of the room.

When she said 'I can't' he'd felt hope, that she wanted to come with him but could not. When she dashed from the room his heart sank – he had gone too far, too soon; perhaps he had broken whatever spell had been created so far between them. But when she looked up at him so calmly before disappearing he returned to a state of expectation.

And now. Who knew? He had fifty minutes to prepare for his next lesson and a pile of tests to mark, and Malee's would be certain to be the top one.

He didn't have to wait long in the end. At the end of lunch time he received a text message from Malee. It was as if she had taken the morning and the lunch time to consider her answer, and then had been decisive.

'Tomorrow at lunchtime I must go to demonstration with my sister so I cannot come to lunch. I am sorry but another time it will make me very happy. Malee.'

To the demonstration! Of course, there was a wages strike on and there would be a demo on Sunday in support. He turned to his computer and searched 'Cambodian worker garment demonstration' and found the details. He was immediately compelled by the idea of the protest – the justice of the cause. It would take place in the industrial sector in the south-west of the city at midday. He had never been there. He devoured what information was available on the net and then went to the corner shop to buy the *Phnom Penh Post* and *Cambodian Daily*.

As he walked his steps quickened with urgency and certainty.

On Sunday Chean was waiting at 11.30 as they had arranged. The day before he had cheerfully accepted the ride, but once he heard the address he was worried.

'You go garment place,' he said. 'No good, boss. Plenty trouble.'

'I'm just going to have a look.'

Chean shook his head and gunned up his motor.

'Ok, boss. You careful.'

Ryan didn't know what else to say. He knew what he was doing but not exactly why he was doing it. He just had to go, at least be close to the place. He had to see. He had to be able to talk about it with her sometime. He needed to be closer.

'Could be OK,' Chean turned around to speak. 'Could be danger. Big people in Phnom Penh no like garment strike.'

He had already got that impression. TV reports had shown garment workers at previous demonstrations with angry faces, blockades of trucks trying to leave a factory, police in lines with shields – but it had all been stand-off, a placing of stakes in a union bargaining game, no action.

They went south on Monivong as they had on the way to Sovannah Phum, then hung right at a huge roundabout onto Sihanouk. The plane trees and office buildings had lost their happy protectiveness now in the light of day. No lights winked in the buildings; there were no crowded motorbikes with excited girls – garment workers on parole. There was just the grey regretful Sunday morning and uncertainty in the air.

They swung left into a long dusty road pocked with roadworks, signs, diversions. It was confusing to Ryan but Chean negotiated it all; swinging onto a crumbling footpath to get around trucks, through a corner petrol station. The city-scape flattened out to ragged-looking shops with just one floor of accommodation above them. Half-fed brown dogs sniffed about, fossicking with the crows for scraps. The street had an unsatisfied and derelict air. In places blocks of flats poked out of the rabble, strings of clothing lining little balconies. Sunday was the day for all practical matters: shopping, washing, visiting – the day for protest too.

This is where Malee and her sister live, he thought: in these blocks of flats, out here surrounded by wasteland being measured up for more factories and more blocks of flats – a short ride to work six days a week and the same ride on the seventh day of protest. That meant thirteen days without end these girls came down this road, to this grim and desolate place. After years it would eat into your soul; and if garment profits stayed high, in ten years this place would be packed with blocks – girls supporting their families. And what would happen to these blocks – grey ghosts with a hundred eyes – if the industry collapsed and girls returned to their villages?

Large buildings began to appear with eight-foot fences and large gabled gates big enough to accommodate trucks of any dimension, the places where buses and open tray trucks dropped herds of sleepy workers not long after dawn each day. Inside was tarmac that would have been packed with a shock of motorbikes during the week, but now they were parched and lonely spaces. In some places a truck was backed up to a loading bay, a fork lift vehicle running up to one of them, then back in, like some messenger from the dark side. There were factories all the way up the street, and outside one of them was a huge group of people; even from a distance he could feel their energies focusing inwards to a huge pair of gates. Ryan felt something sway in the pit of his stomach.

As they came closer he guessed five hundred people – quite a crowd. Chanting came to their ears. Three girls wearing dust masks carried a placard sign in Khmer with just one thing understandable in English: $160 – the amount they were asking for, a doubling of

the Government legislated minimum wage. An open-topped truck
rolled up with another thirty demonstrators crammed on top; they
all jumped out together in a swarm and merged into the crowd. There
were two young men with megaphones and as Ryan arrived one began barking instructions. The noise was great and as he stepped away
from the tuk-tuk Ryan could tell this was not a five hundred crowd,
maybe double that. Some men were there but mostly girls – baseball
caps and T-shirts and jeans with thongs on dusty feet; but some were
dressed up, rose pink rouge on their cheeks, lipstick – Sunday best.
The air was electric with excitement and possibility.

A woman about seventy years old had set up a rice stand by the
side of the road and grinned at him with yellowed stumps of teeth.
Her frailty seemed at odds with the mess of committed and agitated
youth that heaved around her, with her tiny stall; but who would
harm an old lady? Not any of these demonstrators. Her trust in those
around her filled him with warmth and hope. Another man sold corn
and bananas grilled on open charcoal. He looked up in hope as Ryan
jumped out.

It was a grimly festive and expectant atmosphere. On the opposite side of the road at least two hundred motorbikes were parked.
Under a twenty-foot rubber tree with pink flowers there was already
a small gathering of tuk-tuks and their drivers, interested in the outcome, anticipating a return fare. Chean joined them and Ryan began
to skirt around the outside of the crowd, looking for a face he might
know.

People were still arriving on motorbikes, some crowded with
three and four people on board. A tuk-tuk came up packed with
seven passengers who all bundled out with the kind of glee that
comes from novelty, the kind of apprehension that comes from uncertainty and danger.

It was quiet inside the factory. The crowd stood outside, and
waited. The men with megaphones circulated, encouraging the
chanting, keeping spirits high. There was a fire engine in the street
on the other side of the group of protestors, then a handful of police

came out of a side street and formed up in a loose rank, shields held in their left hands, batons in their right. Ryan walked in through the crowd, checking faces. A few people looked at him twice – a Westerner, not a garment worker. They may have thought him a journalist. Some smiled, welcoming him to the cause, as if he could help to give them strength.

He saw her, with a girl who just had to be her sister – neat as Malee, stronger built, but somehow worn as well. And then he lost them, he had seen them for just three seconds. He waded into the crowd to where they had been, but could not find them. He stood on tiptoes, towering now above the crowd. Then, again, he saw her. This time she was watching him, staring at him – it seemed as if she was the only still person in the whole crowd, a look of wonder on her face. She nudged her sister and then her face broke into a wide grin and she waved at him as it dawned on her that he had come there for her, for no-one else and for no other thing, but for her.

They pushed through the crowd toward each other. When they met there were no hugs, no episodes of drama. She raised her hands quickly in sampeah and so did her sister; he did the same.

'This is my sister, Reap.'

'Hellooo,' Reap grinned so wide her face might break open.

'We must listen for instructions,' said Malee. They turned their attention to the young man with the megaphone who now spoke, longish hair flopping over his eyes; he wore thongs, a white shirt and blue jeans. He must have been no older than twenty-two. After a few words the crowd began to move forward and to press together into a tighter group in front of the iron gates. A loaded truck was moving up from inside and the gates were opened inwards to allow it out. At this point people could have spilled in and rampaged through the factory had they wished, but this was not the plan. The crowd tightened and linked arms, presenting itself as a phalanx of solid flesh to the truck. Those at the front abutted the metal grille of the monster. If Malee and Reap had not moved up to talk to Ryan, they would have been down there, facing the machine. The crowd pressed forward against the truck and the truck moved so slowly it was barely perceptible. There was much heaving and shoving and in a full minute the truck had made about a metre's progress. The face of the driver of the truck showed fear and stress; his duty lay in getting through, but here were a thousand people in his way. The face of the young man with the megaphone was contorted with imprecation to greater effort. Then he too confronted the truck, placing his own body weight in with the rest of the crowd, shouting into his megaphone all the while. There was a scream, as if a woman had lost her footing and was going under.

Suddenly the driver lost patience and his foot went down on the accelerator and the truck lurched forward just a foot, but that was enough to crunch down eight or so of the girls who were pushing, and the boy with the megaphone too. Those who had fallen were screaming in panic as they scrambled to their feet and pushed back into the turbulent crowd behind them. One voice rang out over the rest, a yell of pain as well as of anguish. Had the truck run over her foot or leg? There was a hubbub of shouting and real anger now. A hundred protestors screamed at the driver and megaphones were adding to the confusion of noise; the smell of sweat and fear was in the air. The driver stopped his truck and put his head out the window and shouted back, his face anxious. He was just another worker after all, caught on the opposite side in somebody else's war. Guards from the factory now joined in the shouting and began pushing the crowd back with batons held in both hands, swinging at heads.

The situation was a war of clubs and fists and scratching and pushing when the game changed in an instant. From the side that the fire truck had been standing, there came a cannonade of water so fierce that it was knocking people down, right off their feet. Strafing from left to right and back again, it mowed down people who tried to rise and were hit down hard again. The three of them were wetted through by the spray off other bodies, then Reap was smacked down by the full force of the cannonade. Malee and Ryan pulled her up and they all held to each other for support. A sharp crack of sound snapped over and over again. Police were firing above the crowd.

'Jesus, bullets. Come on,' he cried out to them and grabbed their hands.

All around people were panicking and running, picking themselves up, falling down again, slipping over. The three of them ran for it, back towards the clump of trees where the tuk-tuks had been. They were in the clear, away from others, doing better than average. Ahead of them the drivers were revving up their engines and turning around for the road. Was Chean there; was he gone? Ryan saw a bright red tuk-tuk U-turning in the street, pausing, waiting.

'Chean!'

'Boss, jump in. Come quick.'

They all leapt into the tuk-tuk and were away. Malee and Reap looked at each other and then at Ryan in amazement.

'You have a driver!'

Chean turned around, 'Hellooo, I am Chean,' he said, and turned back to the road.

'How did you get here?' Ryan asked them.

'We came on Reap's motorbike.'

'Oh, hell,' he said.

'We can come back later,' said Malee.

As they revved away into the regular Sunday street Malee's right hand held her sister's hand tight, and her left hand held on to two fingers of Ryan's hand, tight.

Part Two

'H ome, boss,' said Chean, as they watched Reap and Malee run into their block of flats. 'Garment people bad thing sure, but is trouble for you.'

Ryan watched them push through glass doors then disappear. 'Rubber bullet,' Chean went on, shaking his head. 'Next time real.'

Next time? The way he saw it he had just survived a once-in-a-lifetime experience, but for all the garment people it was part of their routine. 'Rubber bullets – Jesus. How do you know they were rubber?'

'Sound different to real one.'

Ryan shook his head. What doesn't this guy know about?

'I was a soldier.' Chean shouted over the rev of the motorbike engine.

'You were?' The main road traffic was thick with motorbike fugitives from the demonstration. Some were wet; most were not. It was difficult to read the faces. Many still carried an air of excitement about them, as if the truck blockade and water cannonade had elevated their lives, as if their day had become more a mission than a duty. But mixed among the animation there was the discomposure of resignation and weariness.

'After Pol Pot run away to the jungle. I fight him there, with the Vietnam army – six years.' The traffic thickened and the tuk-tuk slowed.

Ryan wanted to ask him more about the Khmer Rouge days, but couldn't bring himself to do it. For a start he was still dripping from his assault by a water cannon, and he had just held hands with a girl who was his student, and whose sister worked fifty-six hours a week in a garment factory for eighty-five dollars American per month. That was enough complication for him at one time.

He looked back at the pale-grey concrete Soviet-style apartment blocks they had left behind. Was life better for Reap now than it might have been before the Khmer Rouge? Leaving the family and village behind … for this? The old world had been replaced so suddenly for those like Reap who came to the city. Her fate had been to stay in the village and to be the centre of a family. But this – he looked back at the grey ramshackle apartment block – this was prison.

Chean revved up the engine and took off into a gap in the traffic. He drove hard when they found clear space and angrily barged through tiny spaces in the traffic. It was as if some bad spirit had taken possession of him when they talked about Pol Pot and the Vietnam army; as if only distance and the piercing overburdened whine of the tuk-tuk's little motor could drive it all to another place.

Later Ryan walked from his apartment to the quay and back again to settle himself, but he was still feeling wired. He rang Malee – no answer. The television news showed protest images of angry faces and megaphones, but the rifles and water cannons had been excluded. He took some codeine and in his fitful sleep he dreamt of holding Malee's hand: her fingers lying in his palm were delicate, so much more tiny and fragile even than her real ones. Reap was there, and Chean, but they were remote, outposts in the purview of Ryan and Malee. Some other person he could not see took Malee's hand and was shaping as if to snap a finger off. The finger was crooked at him in a beckoning way, but all it did was remind him of the delicate handle of a porcelain teacup. And then he started up in bed awake, and could think of nothing but Malee.

The Pchum Benh holiday of the ancestors began on Wednesday. Everyone who was in Phnom Penh from their homelands went back on their motorbikes or clung to whatever overloaded vehicle they could grab; the city would empty. He only had two days to talk to her, one if they were leaving on Tuesday to escape the crowded roads.

In the morning he sent a text message: I must see you at the Blue Pumpkin at 4.30. Ok? He waited and waited through an endless minute before the reply came in: Ok.

He picked up the electric kettle to test the water level then tipped the switch to get his day going. The little orange light on the top always pleased him – flick, and there it was, one tiny control thing that never failed him.

Then he noticed a sheet of A5 paper that had been poked under his door, neatly folded over once. He picked it up, and read:

Mr Davey, You must come and see me first thing.
7.30 in my office.
Mr Dith

Good god. Dith.

Ryan looked closer at the clock than he had bothered before: 6.50. He had time for a cup of tea and some biscuits.

He stopped and talked to Mr Thiounn about security. Someone had come through the locked gate all the way to his apartment – this was a serious matter.

'Oh, yes,' said Mr Thiounn, grinning. 'I put note.'

'You?'

'Yes,' he confirmed, bowing and smiling.

'But how did Mr Dith …?' But he gave up trying to understand. Somehow, somewhere, there must be a connection between Thiounn and Dith. Or perhaps when he told Mr Thiounn where he worked, he had contacted Dith, hoping to establish some sort of patron relationship. He could only guess, but if he asked the reply would surely come as obscure as the Delphic Oracle or couched in terms of a haiku. Or more likely, quite simply: 'Mr Dith very good man.' Make of that what you will.

All the way there he thought about his last twenty-four hours: Chean, Malee and Reap, the demonstration, Dith – the note, Mr Thiounn. After weeks of idling his spare time away his life had sped up so suddenly and it was his connecting to Malee that had done it. Matters were suddenly out of his hands and he began to hunt for associations between all these factors and people. But with a Dith meeting forced upon him, the only connection he could solder together in his head right now concerned Malee and Dith.

Malee was his student and Dith was his boss.

The door to Mr Dith's office was ajar, as it had been on his first morning. This time his boss's lips were compressed and his nod of greeting was quick.

'Ah, Mr Davey, good morning. Good to see you. I like to catch up to you after two weeks or so to see how things are.'

'Of course.' Ryan glanced up at the clock to emphasise the fact that it was close to lesson time, without risking an impoliteness by saying as much.

'That's ok,' said Mr Dith, noting every non-verbal move of his young teacher. 'Just want to say, you are a good teacher. Students are very happy with what you are teaching them. We hope you are happy here.'

'Oh, yes, certainly.' Ryan was still wary. 'I can't complain.'

'The test results from your first fortnight are very good, I think.' He had the tests in front of him, in the middle of his desk.

'I'm so glad you are happy. I have had Tom here to help me out and get me settled. His advice has been very useful.'

'Ah, yes,' said Dith gratefully, as if the mention of Tom had opened a side-door to the message that was seeded within this conversation. 'Mr Andersen is a good, experienced teacher now. With us for more than a year.'

'Nearly two he says.'

'He has talked to you about the way …' and here Dith's eye-brows came together in a frown, 'the appropriate way to be, with the students.'

Danger.

'Is not good to be so close. I mean, in this job I hear many things. Sometimes true, sometimes not true.' Dith stopped and looked at Ryan, almost appealing for him to fill in the gap that would make this conversation easier; but Ryan only stared back at him, alert and uncertain. 'In this country, Mr Davey, it is very different. I mean, the way people behave may be different to Australia.'

'I've noticed one or two things.'

'Yes. The people with the power work in a different way.' He placed his hands together in front of his mouth, not in a sampeah, but tapping the ends of his fingers together, meditating his next words. In Cambodia direct speech is seen as intimidating and a way through a problem should be found so that no-one loses face. Dith was looking for a way to imply to Ryan what should have been understood without the need for words. But now Ryan changed the subject away from the nudging and prodding.

'Mr Dith, do you think the garment workers should do what they have to do, live the way they have to live, for eighty five dollars a month?'

Dith's head and shoulders straightened like a sentry on duty when the captain walks past. He seemed to hold his breath for a moment. Through his first couple of weeks at the school Ryan had listened in to the obscure circuitry of Khmer communication. But this was confronting directness, and it changed the question between them from the simple matter of what was allowable or appropriate, to the more complex and demanding issue of what was proper and moral.

Ryan knew that Mr Dith's private views counted for nothing against the responsibilities he had to the owners of the school. His position may have seemed powerful from the view of the classroom, but to those outside who had the money, he was another employee – an important one, but still expendable. Ryan knew that, but he was burning to find out how Dith really felt.

Dith sat back and rocked in his chair, fingers still pressed together. It would be a rudeness to make no answer at all.

'In this country many people work for very low pay,' Dith said. 'Even teachers receive low pay. It is not good. In some schools teachers resort to corrupt ways.' He was struggling now. He dipped his head in respectful acknowledgement that Ryan was doing a very good job for very little money.

'Even in this school some teachers sell to students books that they have been issued free by the government.' Mr Dith bowed his head in sorrow, as if this was simply the way of things. He looked up again in confusion: Why must you take sides, his face seemed to say, you crusaders? Western ideas: human rights, unions, NGOs – they all were blunt instruments against the old ways of his country, where people knew where they stood in a system of patronage, and where power was not questioned like this. The question put to him was one of morality and rights, almost hypothetical, and as such could have been easily retired from the conversation, but Dith seemed compelled to go on. There was something in him which connected with the garment question.

'There are many things we cannot control – many things that could be better in this country. Some students have siblings in the garment industry. I think things are very bad,' he nodded again in acknowledgement. His own view had been glimpsed; he seemed to waver on the edge of a rare personal disclosure.

Dith looked distantly into the air above Ryan's head for a moment, as if choosing his next words carefully. 'I too have a relative, a worker in the garment industry. I try to help her, but there are many in my family.'

So, Dith was working into his old age to support family members. But there was something else Ryan just had to know, and he managed to overcome his usual diffidence to ask.

'Mr Dith,' Ryan leant forward in his chair, closer to Dith, 'do you have a wife?'

Dith stiffened. Ryan thought he was about to call an end to the interview; for a second Ryan thought with dread, I've gone too far.

'No, Mr Davey,' Mr Dith finally responded. 'My wife died. I understand that it is very difficult to live without a wife.'

He was struggling with his memories, or with what he had to say about them. But again he turned to what his profession and his position required. 'But you should not have a close friendship with a student.'

These words were forced from him as if squeezed from a towel that had already been wrung dry by stronger hands, such an effort did it seem to be. Mr Dith looked up to Ryan's face for half a second and then dropped his gaze and half closed his eyes. Though this had begun as a discipline meeting, it seemed there was now a small bond between the two of them – one of loneliness that was shared but rarely spoken of, and of family absent, for widely differing reasons perhaps, but absent nonetheless.

'I think is time for lesson now.' Mr Dith raised his hands in sampeah, as high as his nose this time.

As he walked away Ryan locked in his mind that Dith had said that he should not have a relationship. Not 'must not' but 'should not.'

Reap pulled up another piece of material to her sewing machine and folded a hem for stitching. It was the last day before the Pchum Benh holiday, when even the garment factories would be closed. For three days they would light incense sticks in temples, bring food to monks in the wat and offer gifts to their dead grandparents and uncles and aunties. Special appeasement went to all those spirits who had died violent or unexpected deaths. Nearly forty years after the fall of the Khmer Rouge, there was a great number of those.

Malee and Reap would go, with Sophea wedged between them, on Reap's motorbike, all the way one hundred and seventy kilometres to Kampong Thom.

In her factory Reap sat working – turning the hem under, pinning it, feeding the material through the machine. Her back was bent as she watched the bobbing needle closely so the shirt went through perfectly every time. Her head and neck were fixed like that for five hours from the seven a.m. start until lunch time when she would sit on the tiled kitchen floor and eat from bowls of rice and spinach, and then on through the long hot afternoon.

It was thirty-six degrees inside the factory and humid. The walls were like high fences of iron and above them were opaque windows that never opened and through which emanated the dimmest outline of cloud and sky. Two girls had fainted as that morning ground on towards lunch time. But Reap would not faint. She had never fainted. She was strong and steady; she had one of the best completion rates in the factory. She had that to be proud of, that and her clever sister and the money they sent home. Reap had become the solid rock of the family, but some days the rock felt weary. She anticipated Pchum Benh as a blessed and even euphoric time to be with her family, and three days without a sewing machine.

At lunch time she was able to check her phone and there was a message through from Malee.

'He called me. He wants to meet today.'

As she read the message Reap's heart lifted for a moment in hope. From her pay she could manage English lessons for Malee and help out Ma and Pa. But what of her, Reap? If she wanted to leave this place, to pay for English lessons for herself and to try for a job in an office, the only way was to have a rich barang in the family. Then he could help Malee and Pa and then perhaps, for once, she could help herself. She closed her eyes and allowed herself the only three seconds of the day that she imagined herself to be anything other than a garment worker. She saw herself nodding acknowledgement to her well-groomed colleagues as she tucked a folder under her arm and pressed the button on the lift – all the way to her office on the fifteenth floor.

But it was not her place to dwell on selfish thoughts. She turned the phone off and put it in her bag where it belonged, along with her comb and smog mask, and the baseball cap that would keep the hair out of her eyes on the motorbike. It was news she had been waiting for, but she could hardly dare to dream.

The Blue Pumpkin was modern and plastic, upstairs looking over the Sisowath Quay, the street and the river. Downstairs there was a bakery bursting with French pastries, breads of sourdough and walnut, and little sausages in flaky wrappings. Upstairs it was blue and white and noisy with clanky tables and chairs; on one side there was a vast open lounge like an endless futon that ran along one side with giant pillows for hipster travellers to prop themselves with their laptops. It was a place that young Khmer people could go and snack among NGO-class Europeans and expatriate Australians. To be taken there by a respectable Westerner was special.

'I didn't have time to change,' said Malee, looking around at the other girls there.

'You look wonderful,' said Ryan. Malee relaxed as she saw the other girls were wearing nothing that special. The waitress brought the plastic menus and smiled generously.

They ordered tea and fish amok, light creamy curry built around turmeric. The moment they ordered food she was settled.

'My father was a fisherman,' Malee began. It was time for life stories. 'On the river.'

'Was that the Mekong?'

'No, another river. Smaller one. Goes into the Tonle Sap – other side of the mountains from the Mekong.'

'I am going up the Mekong to Kratie for Pchum Benh, with Tom.'

'Tom?' she wore a puzzled look.

'Mr Andersen.'

'Oh, him.' She didn't get that carried away by Tom, but it wasn't the time to say why not. 'Anyway, I have a first brother, then sister

Number Two, Reap, then me Number Three.

'You're the baby of the family!'

'Oh no,' she laughed, almost screamed. She was a different girl here, away from the school – talking about her family; anxiety had seeped out of her. 'Then there is Number Four and Five and Six all the way to Number Ten.'

He put down his fork.

'Ten of you! I don't believe it.'

'Here, I'll show you my bong pictures.'

She pulled a wallet from her bag and out flopped a concertina of photos, about twelve of them.

'Bong pictures?'

'Bong – my brothers and sisters. And my very good friends. They all bong,' she laughed. 'Here is the little one,' she said proudly over a photo of a boy about ten years old, grinning up at the camera over what looked like an iPad.

'My God.'

'He is going to be a lawyer one day. He has already decided. My oldest brother Chamroeun, he works for Samsung in Phnom Penh. He brings home his iPad sometimes and Number Ten just plays games all weekend.'

'Oldest brother works here?' said Ryan looking out to the Boulevard below them, as if the brother could come past any minute. The idea of a brother had never occurred to him and somehow made things awkward.

'He don't like the city so much. He works for the big company run by foreigners. I think he had a fight with someone and he isn't getting any more promotions. He keeps his life a big secret these days.' Malee raised an eyebrow and gave a mysterious look.

'Can't he go back, to the homeland?'

'Aaaahhh, when he was thirteen he was going to be fisherman, like Pa, only he was always making jokes, always fooling around. One day he fell off the water buffalo and broke his arm.'

'Water buffalo,' said Ryan flatly, as if he didn't quite believe it.

'Yeah, sometimes those guys are crazy. Arm was broken in two places and it took many hours to get him to a doctor, so then he can't pull in the net with the fish and he stayed at school, so my sister and I became fishermen.'

'You?'

'Yeeaaahh …' she said, drawing it out as if to say, why not. 'We get up at four in the morning to go to the river with my father. Then we come home and have a wash from the bucket and get on bikes and ride to school seven kilometres to be there at eight o'clock. Then we ride home at lunch and back again seven kilometres for afternoon classes.'

He remembered her legs that had sprung like coils as she ran to the stairway. Her arms, at that moment lifting only a tea cup, held a wiry elegant strength.

'That's twenty-eight kilometres each day,' he said. And that's without the fishing, he thought.

'My father was brought up in Phnom Penh and he was going to school in 1975.'

'Khmer Rouge.'

'The Pol Pot time. They took him to Kampong Thom.'

'And he's still there?'

'Uh huh. We will be going home tomorrow,' she smiled, captivated with the prospect, it seemed, thinking nothing of the inconvenience of the three-hour trip on the back of a motorbike on muddy, pot-holed roads.

'Your father didn't come back to Phnom Penh?'

'Oh, yes. He came back to look for his family. He went to his old apartment where they used to live, but there was someone else there. Another family living there. He went everywhere to find them but they were nowhere. His father was a teacher.'

'Oh no.'

'Yeah, so he was probably killed by Pol Pot.' She said the words dispassionately, as if it had never occurred to her that sympathy could be attached to such a thing.

'When they were taken away my father had to rough his hands to make it look like he was a worker, so they wouldn't kill him too. My father smart; he is always thinking. So when he came to Phnom Penh he can't find his family and he is homesick for Kampong Thom. He was in love, with my mother.' She covered her face with her hands and giggled at the thought of her parents as young lovers.

'Before he left he went to the message wall and told them where he was going, but we never heard from anyone.'

'Message wall?'

'Was a big, big wall,' she swivelled in her chair and pointed over her left shoulder, 'about one kilometre away. Everyone left messages for their family in case they turned up alive. One woman saw his message and came to tell him that his sister died in childbirth. They forced her to marry Khmer Rouge man and when she gives the baby they put hot coals under her bed to make her blood work better.'

'What? The Khmer Rouge did that?'

'Uh huh,' she shrugged, as if to say, who else.

'They make her drink rice wine too. Lots of it. That is the old custom. She died an agony death, baby too. That baby my cousin from a Khmer Rouge man.' Her eyes went still, seemingly focused on a distant point somewhere past Ryan's left elbow. 'That is why I become a doctor. No more of that.' She looked up at him, into his eyes, so swiftly, and returned to her fish amok. 'I am a scientist,' she said proudly, 'no superstition.'

Ryan was overcome by the speed with which these revelations had been delivered. And the look she had given him was an enigma: it had lasted one second and had been full of knowledge, pity, suffering, purpose, strength. Was it? Or had it been nothing, empty? A cup half-filled with his projections. He returned to the story of her father.

'And your Pa became a fisherman.'

'And he farmed rice sometimes. My father was brought up in the city and he knew about education. So he made us go to school. Then UNESCO sponsor me.'

It was the first time he had heard of the United Nations doing something good.

'Did they pay you money?'

'No, no,' she shook her head, 'they gave me a new bike to ride to school. It was much quicker,' she said, with real excitement in her voice. Ryan wondered for a second what the old one must have been like. 'And pencils, and books of paper to write in.'

'Paper?'

'Yeah, you know, writing down what the teacher says is very important.' She looked at him with quiet mockery and raised an eyebrow again.

'Yes, yes, all right. But didn't you have paper before.'

'Hmm … not much. We wrote over old things all the time. We wrote in between the lines of old books.'

For a moment he couldn't speak. The image came into his mind of young kids writing in the spaces between lines – perhaps first ruling through what had been there before. 'Good grief,' he said.

'When bong Reap came to Phnom Penh she brought me here to go to school. My other sister, Number Four, she married and has a chicken farm in Kandal. She sends money home too.'

'How many sisters do you have?'

'Seven.'

'What?' he squawked like a cockatoo. 'Seven sisters!'

She laughed until she almost doubled up. 'My parents wanted another boy after first brother so they kept trying but no good – eight girls in a row.' She tucked her thumbs behind her palms and held up all the other fingers to give a graphic illustration of the number one family joke.

'The little guy in the photo? That's him?'

'That's him.'

'He thinks he's the king of the family?'

'He *is* the king of the family.'

'Eight sisters doting on you.' Ryan thought of his own family and the positioning for power, his brother taking up with Amanda –

win/lose techniques that could never happen here.

Malee looked at him with a questioning little frown. He realised his face must have turned serious and he wondered what Malee might have seen there.

'It's all right,' he said. 'I just realised I haven't called my sister.' He tapped on the table with his fingers. 'I'll do it as soon as I get home.'

He had changed the subject. Cambodia had been brutalised, but the family, at least, still clung together. If they didn't support each other, no-one else would.

'I will see all of them, except Kandal sister,' she said, tapping the table a couple of times herself. 'She will stay with her chickens. Reap will place incense at the temple to say hello to our grandfather.'

'Your grandfather is still alive?' He could hardly believe it.

'No,' she laughed again. 'He died long time. That's why we go to the pagoda. But I am lucky, this year my uncle and auntie that I have never seen are coming from France, and my cousin Cris.'

A bowl of fish came, swimming in a yellow sauce, with a side dish of tomato and cucumber chopped in lettuce and a drizzle of Kampot pepper dressing.

'Yes, I am lucky,' she repeated. 'But in two weeks' time there is another demonstration. I must go.' There was no faltering in her voice, but her tone suggested that the demonstration was a duty, not a pleasure.

Another demonstration, he thought; the things she must do to keep herself, her family, her life together. Only then it occurred to him that her grandfather had died, been killed, in 1975 – Pol Pot. She had passed over that fact, not milking it for sympathy.

And now she must go to another demonstration. If she must go, he thought, I must go.

The road to Kampong Thom sat on an enormous dyke that ran through flat rice fields that in this September flood time were sub-

merged in coffee-coloured river water for hundreds of metres on either side. Even Malee and Reap, who had grown up within the annual
downpour cycle, were wide-eyed at the magnitude of this year's
floods. With one hand clasped on either side of the motorbike seat
Malee stared out over the swollen river that was now a lake. She
rested her head on the shoulder of Sophea in front of her and Sophea
laughed but Malee did not hear her. She was wondering about the
odd barang and his quiet smile, and his silences that did nothing but
draw her further into him and made her talk, even about herself; and
when he spoke, the things he said made her laugh or made her wonder. Up front Reap was fixed in concentration on the road ahead and
swerved or slowed to avoid vehicles coming at them on the wrong
side. But for Malee the ride was a rare time when she could daydream
and drift.

They turned away from the river and up along the secondary
road to Kampong Thom City and slowed through the traffic there,
then pressed onward. On the outskirts of the village someone
shouted hello and they waved, then they fell to wondering what the
river that came up to their own house would be like.

In the village ducks quacked past and the girls cried out greetings
to them; a buffalo was guided across the main street by a small boy.
Every person knew them and when they stopped at Sophea's place
many came up to greet them and to exchange small gossip, so their
progress was slow up to the branch road that took them away to their
house. The two sisters were respected in the village because Reap
was sending money to her family, and Malee would one day be a
nurse, perhaps even a doctor. They were both bringing excellent face
to their Ma and Pa.

Away from the village street, the road was firm in parts but
patches were soft and muddy as cake batter, so they crawled up towards their house slow and careful, but bubbling with anticipation.
Flooded reaches lapped right up to the side of the road. Boys jumped
from the back of their homes into five feet of water in places that
would be firm ground ten months of the year. Girls splashed about

in the shallows and some paddled little canoes, whether running errands or for recreation it was hard to tell, as it was made into a game either way.

Chickens scooted away in groups of five and six as the motorbike came by and on the side of the road some families had set up temporary sties for their pigs, the flooded river having taken their usual homes under the stilt houses. One brooding sow was lying in the mud and was nuzzled by six or seven little piglets. At a corner shop some boys played pool and drank cokes. A man bent over some ageing farm implement and made sparks with a welder; he stood to watch the approach of the bike and waved as the girls went by. It was quiet season for the farms and everyone was catching up on odd jobs and taking their ease.

The last section of the road was long and straight and Malee felt her life blood flooding into her as they drove. She had gone to the city to study and to be a success, but here she did not have to think in English, she did not have to walk the hard streets of Phnom Penh or breathe the petrol fumes that swamped her in that place. Here the whole world knew her and she knew them.

Their house was a wooden one on stilts and there was a steep gangplank of a ladder to walk up. For twenty years it had been a struggle for Pa and Ma to feed their enormous family. There had been little else to do, after the Pol Pot time, but to go back home and make children who would one day be your only security. Now four of the children were out in the world and they were holding their own, but Pa was worn out from work.

As they rode into the small yard at the front of the house, their Pa came outside and stood to watch them. He was dressed in culottes and sandals and wore a faded washed-out singlet. He grinned and nodded amiably, as if the sight of his girls had assured him once again that his life's work was safe.

But as they stepped up the gangplank to the house the girls could both see that their father's joy was not complete. He was showing them at once that he was so happy to see them but also that something had happened, and when he placed his arms around their shoulders – one arm around each girl with his face in between – he hung on to them too long and squeezed them tighter than his modesty normally allowed.

'Pa, what is it?' Reap was the first to speak. 'Is Cris here?' She wanted to see her cousin.

'Cris is here.'

'And uncle Meach and auntie Kim?'

He looked at the ground and his face turned sorrowful. 'Ma will tell you.'

'What's happened?' cried Reap. Malee gasped a little and held her hand to her mouth as she could tell that some disaster had struck. Ma came running out at the sound of voices. She had put on weight, at last, thought Malee. She grasped at her two oldest girls. 'Thank the Buddha, you are safe.'

'Ma, what *is* it?'

'Meach and Kim. They went onto the river this morning.'

'Oh my god,' Reap gasped, 'the river is huge.'

'And fast,' Malee put in.

'They have not been here since Pol Pot time. They took the canoe this morning before any of us were awake. Last night they were talking about the old days, about going out on the river and pulling in the fish. They were talking as if the river is like heaven or a beautiful afterlife. But it is not like that everywhere. It is dangerous. And yesterday an hour after they came to the house the ravens came.'

'Aaaaahh no!' Reap gasped.

'Oh my god,' thought Malee, and looked at the ground. The belief was that if the raven came and sat on your house and made its cawing sound, then someone would die within three days. Malee was trained in science. She had completed a three-month placement in a hospital in Phnom Penh and she knew the reasons that people died. But still, still she felt herself shiver at the story of the raven; they were messengers from the other world.

'Two raven came to the house and sat on top and made their noise.' Malee had never heard Ma speak so much. 'I went out to throw stones but when I did the ravens only flew up and then sat back on the house. All day they keep coming back. I tell Meach and Kim don't go out on the river, but as soon as it was light they went out. You know where the water goes around in circles, can take you in.'

'We should have gone with them,' said Pa.

'But when we got up they were already gone. We waited for an hour for them to come back. Then we went to borrow the neighbour's canoe and Pa and Chamroeun went out to look for them.'

At that time of year the river rushed with whirlpools and eddies from sudden mountain rains.

Reap for once was struck dumb, with fear. Malee could not believe it. 'The ravens come, and they are dead,' she said, almost to herself. She shivered a second time and held her hands to her chest, as if to warm the heart that beat within. 'The ravens,' she repeated, in a whisper, to herself.

'Pa found them. Kim was stuck in tree branches from a little island and Meach was floating in the shallows. The achar is coming.'

'They hadn't tried to swim in forty years,' Pa said sadly, 'since before Pol Pot.'

Suddenly a wailing began from Reap that started low and threatened to burst from her, but was contained by her as she fought to keep her anger inside. It was not fit to wail at fate, at karma. It was something that had happened to her uncle and her auntie in another life that was brought to bear on this day; they all knew that. But still, there was crazy rage in Reap. Malee felt it too, but kept it boiling inside. At least Meach and Kim had returned to their homeland and would be cremated there.

'What about Cris?' said Malee.

'Cris is here,' her mother replied, and she stood back and there indeed was a childlike boy, standing shyly in the doorway, looking much younger than his fourteen years, with deep dark eyes set in

Maleee's bird-like frame, and with elfin ears that seemed to have grown ahead of the rest of him. His Adam's apple showed up and down as he gulped nervously. Behind him was Number Ten brother holding an iPad and looking up at his French cousin. Ma held her arm out to Cris and he came forward to join the little group. The faces around him were by turns sorrowful, pitiful and filled with tears. He looked around them and in his moment of grief and alienation he spoke in the language with which he was most familiar.

'Bonjour,' he said quietly.

Malee and Pa looked over the two bodies laid on biers at the back of the house, and listened to the lapping of the waters of the river that had taken them. Two monks in saffron robes shook incense burners and mumbled prayers to frighten away the evil spirits and to keep the souls of the dead couple pure until the day of cremation, when their remains would be stored in the village stupa. A handful of older men and women from the village had come to remember Meach and Kim and to keep their merit building right up to cremation day. They stood well back away from the monks and clasped their hands in front of them. These people had known Meach and Kim in the Lon Nol days, before the Khmer Rouge. Some had been children together and had only the day before relived their past adventures on the river in a joyful reunion.

Perhaps, it was thought, the joy of the day before was too much for the returned couple and they had been unable to stop themselves from pushing out in the canoe the next morning. Maybe there had been more to it, said some. Perhaps they had come home to die; they were at journey's end; they had brought Cris to his family, and then the river had simply been there to receive them. They knew the risks, they had not forgotten everything. It was meant to be this way. There would be much speculation in the village and yes, said some, they had come home to die – for that reason and for that reason alone.

Malee and her Pa were alike. Even with a tragedy in the family, and with all the emotion that surrounded them, Pa was looking ahead; he had no choice but to think. And Malee was doing the same.

There would be three days until the cremation; Pchum Benh would start tomorrow. This would be the best possible time to dispel bad spirits. The temple would be full of monks and incense and kind offerings: the presence of family and many villagers would help to create merit for the deceased.

But there was still the problem of Cris.

Pa turned away from the monks and motioned to Malee. They went outside to the gangplank and sat down. Malee's legs dangled in the air over the seeping waters as Pa squatted on a stool and took a rolled-up cigarette that he had stuck behind his ear, then flamed up a disposable lighter.

'Cris, he is a Frenchman.'

Malee cocked her head in an ironic way that said 'He is?'

'He looks like us but he is a Frenchman,' and Pa pointed to his head as if to say, in here. 'I can keep him in the village with us, but he will be unhappy. Your Ma and I are very worried about him; we don't know what to do.'

The first time Malee caught sight of Cris, emerging from behind the skirts of Ma, she already knew what to do. But she could not to say it to Pa, not yet; the idea would have to come from him.

'Does he have people in France?' she said.

'He has nobody. Meach and Kim had him very late in life. He has no brothers or sisters. There may be Khmer people in his city …' and he shrugged his shoulders as if to say, but what will they do, what guarantee do we have?

'Poor Cris.'

Pa held the cigarette carefully between his thumb and forefinger, took a drag and then spat out a speck of tobacco. There was a pause as they looked across the road, past the neighbour's house and through the treetops to the river beyond. Malee waited to hear whatever was on Pa's mind, as the ideal Khmer girl should.

'Your sister told me that you have a friend.'

'What did she tell you?!' Malee's voice rose higher than any ideal

girl's should, then she checked herself. She was suddenly frightened
or even a little angered because under normal circumstances it was
not permissible for her to have a boyfriend. A girl should wait until
her father found a boy. In three years in the city Malee had been a
good girl, like the others from the village that she knew. She had
never had a boyfriend. But Malee was the first girl from the village
who would not return; her future was uncertain.

'Reap tells me you are a good girl,' said Pa, holding up his hands
to silence her. 'But there is a man who likes you. Your teacher.'

'We have had lunch together. That is *all*, Pa.' Malee felt her voice
rising again and she had to sit with her head held back to stop a tear
running from her eye. Must every step she took be reported back to
the village?

'That is good. Is very good.'

Malee looked up in surprise. 'That is good?'

'Teacher is good. Very good. He is Australian, yes? This is a very
good country.' Then Pa's eyes narrowed and he rasped out the question that was on his mind.

'Does he speak French?'

'French? Pa, I don't know that. I don't think so. He speaks English. He teaches English.'

'Might speak French too?' Pa's eyes narrowed again.

'Pa, I really don't know. I really *don't* know. Would you like to
ask him?' said Malee, with as much sarcasm as she would ever muster
against her own father.

'Yes,' said Pa, 'you ask him if he speaks French.' He spat out
another speck of tobacco. '*You* ask him.'

The bus pulled up outside the Heng Heng Hotel in Kratie and Tom
and Ryan jumped out to stretch their legs; the three days of holiday
were before them. The Mekong had been in flood but the waters had
eased back now and people were cleaning up and beginning to get
on with business, the last night before Pchum Benh. A week before
it had all rushed through the town, sinking shops and cafés three feet

deep in the brown river and whatever it brought with it. Ryan could not imagine the level of chaos that a flood would bring.

Decayed French colonial buildings surrounded the covered central market. A handful of cafés led up to the foreshore where a string of hotels lined the river – no doubt stylish places in the 1960s. A man trotted over from the hotel to collect their bags and in five minutes they were checked in.

Tom had said they would meet up with his friends and they turned out to be two girls, one each. His girl was beautiful, sexy, and nice enough. She wore make-up and that surprised him in the provinces, where the vanity of adornment seemed so incongruous with the struggle and poverty they had witnessed from the bus window all the way up from the city.

Tom didn't seem to care whether his girl was made-up or not. He greeted her with a familiar caress on the cheek then drew her to him with his arm around her waist. They eased back on the lounge in the hotel bar and Ryan tried to take on some of the sprawling body language of his friend but ended up sitting on the edge of his chair, within easy arm's reach of his beer. Tom talked up the virtue of their trip.

'A few hours on the bus, compadre, but it's all worth it.' He was speaking as a man who was trying to persuade his friend that their efforts would be rewarded, but who was trying to convince himself that this wasn't one trip too many to Kratie. He all but slapped his stomach in that conscious gesture of self-satisfaction. 'Not that much to do here, I guess, but we make our own fun.'

After a couple of beers at the hotel lounge the two of them disappeared with a giggle and a grin, Tom stretching as a man who had still not shaken the bus out of his limbs and needed a good lie down. Ryan was left alone with his girl and suddenly it was not so easy to go along with other people's plans.

He had to decide. His instinct was to defer, so he complained of being tired from the five hour trip and said he wanted to pack it in early. His girl pursed her lips and frowned and then seemed to become upset, on the edge of tears. He said something about tomorrow but then stammered on about going to see the dolphins, the Irrawaddy freshwater dolphins that inhabit the Mekong River downstream from Kratie. They were the town's number one attraction, still hanging on, a couple of hundred of them, in a bend on the river twelve or so kilometres out of town.

He thought the dolphin idea would turn the girl off but she bewildered him by jumping up and down on the spot and clapping her hands in excitement. She would settle for no action tonight if they could go to the dolphins tomorrow. The guy who had commandeered their bags came over to claim the fare the moment he overheard the conversation; his tuk-tuk was waiting outside. Everything was arranged in one minute and Ryan could hardly say no – ten o'clock tomorrow.

The road out to the dolphins that next morning was long and straight, under a canopy of jungle trees that held hands above them. A soft breeze of possibility whispered at the leaves and the tunnel of foliage induced not only their visit to a threatened species, but a new phase of opportunity with it. Around them brown water licked at the stilts of houses and all along the way villagers went unhurriedly about their business.

So the scene was beautiful and his girl was happy. She had greeted him that morning with such a squeeze that her feet left the ground for a second or two, as if the cement that would bring them together that day had already begun to set.

To say she relished the sights on the road away from the town would not be strong enough. She yelled out and pointed to the pigs and chickens; she *called* to them. A rooster cocked its eye and followed her with it. She watched closely the corner shops and their little groups of idlers. Women in pyjama suits of melodramatic pink and green and yellow gossiped and watched over children running around naked – the girl waved to all of them.

He wondered about her.

'Do you live in Kratie all the time?'

'Oh no, Phnom Penh some time, Kratie some time.'

He remembered: Tom had said that if she liked someone, she might come to the city to be with him. She could be in Phnom Penh next week if he wanted. He felt her lean into him as she spoke.

'Did you ever go to work in the city?'

She straightened, and concentrated on her sentence.

'I work the garment some time,' she smiled, 'but too slow.'

'Do you mean you were not fast enough on the machines?'

She smiled and nodded. He thought of Reap, who seemed almost superhuman: to work in that factory and to sew the same hem of the same shirt ten hours each day for a year, or two years, or five. He could not see this girl toiling ten hours, not for a single day. She would always be a country girl, even in the middle of the city, but to have failed at garment manufacture would have meant a loss of face for her family.

'Your family live in Kratie?' She shook her head to say no, without any expression. So, he thought, they live in a village and she cannot go back there.

'Do you come out here to see the dolphins very often?'

'Huh?' His sentence was too complex – too fast.

'You see dolphin some time?' He motioned ahead of them, up the track.

She shook her head again; her eyes went wide for emphasis.

'Never?' He could not believe that. Never?

She answered very deliberately, 'Not one time,' and smiled again.

He sat back for a moment. The tuk-tuk fare was eight dollars, a day and a half's pay in a garment factory, and for a girl who could not keep a job, unreachable.

'You like to see the animals?' He motioned at the pigs and chickens they were passing.

'Uh, huh,' she nodded. Her grin came back, unpleasant factory thoughts gone. She would live for the day, for the hour if need be.

They bought two tickets at a little sentry box and walked on planks placed across a boggy open space that led to the trees by the river where there waited an old dark-skinned boatman with crooked teeth, wearing culottes and a singlet that may once have been lilac in colour and was thin and frayed from years of wear. His face lit up at the sight of them and he motioned them into a solid wooden boat with a little canopy for the sun, then cranked a big old motor to life and pushed her out with a pole. They putted along about thirty metres out from the bank.

The girl pressed her shoulder gently into him and closed her eyes for a moment, all dreamy and appreciative about being taken out on the river. She had taken off the make-up and left just a little pink around the eyes. She had guessed that he did not like it and today she was more natural and relaxed; she had read him. Her lips were thin and perfectly shaped. There was a puff of breeze and her hair flapped in her face and when he reached over to brush it away for her he could not stop himself from touching her cheek. She smiled, her eyes still closed, and buried her head further into his shoulder, both arms around his arm now.

When they swung out into the river there were whirlpools and snags everywhere, chunks of debris swirling and circling, but the boatman steered easily around them. Little sandbars and banks appeared; tree foliage poked out above the flood-level waters as if they were the emaciated hands of unappeased Pchum Benh spirits, wandering Pol Pot victims with no family to remember them.

But, crossing to the other side, there was so much space that the river seemed half a kilometre wide and there descended upon them the kind of elusive peace that you don't find anywhere on land. It washed over him in the half a minute it took to get right away from the bank — the water lapping against the prow, the low chug chug of a big old outboard. He closed his eyes for a moment and then he felt the girl's hand close over his. He was now inside the dreamy peace of the river, as if he was living within the instinct of the girl. Was this where he could find his place? If he truly wanted exit from all that brittle selfishness of Western life, this could surely be the end of the journey. He looked at her again; her eyes were closed, she laced her pretty fingers inside his.

He turned around to see if the boatman was noticing, but the man's whole face was lifted in pleasure at the river, as if it mattered not that he had made hundreds of trips before, for each one was extraordinary. The romantic vignette before him had barely flickered in his consciousness. He acknowledged Ryan with a couple of nods and he said, 'Aha, aha.'

Then the boatman flicked a switch and the outboard chugged and coughed a couple of times and was silent. They drifted in to a scrap of tree that was reaching up from a submerged sandbank. The boatman tied up on a long rope and the feeling was of drifting weightlessness. In this elbow of its course, the river had no need to show its strength; it presented as a kind of elemental and eternal lake from which, as in some creation myth, he could be made again. While the whole nation around him was in the shock of its forward spasm to modernity, he could ease himself back into the mud of the banks of the Mekong and sit, with this girl beside him.

They waited for six or seven minutes, eyes wide open now, but there was no dolphin. The boatman showed no concern. The girl sat on the edge of her seat, intent and mesmerised by all that surrounded her, watching and waiting.

Then there was a ripple on the surface sixty or eighty metres away. A short dorsal fin and a grey snub-nosed shape, a soft snort and an atomised puff of Mekong water and it was gone. The girl grinned and petted his hand again.

Then three broke the surface together, a mother and her pups, on the other side of the boat this time. All the while the boatman watched and every now and then he raised his arm and made a soft low noise to show the motion in the water and the lazy grey bodies breaking the surface. The dolphins returned to their rhythm of life, languidly appearing and then returning to the deep. Ryan tried to take a picture but he kept taking snaps of water where they had been a second before, of ripples on a surface.

After half an hour a long low wooden boat appeared, crossing the river, its piercing modern outboard whining away as its master held on to an iron upright and steered with his foot while he smoked and talked to his mate. They made rapid progress in their trip from one bank to the other and were soon gone. But the dolphins had disappeared too. Ryan fought hard to resist rising annoyance. These people in their boats have business to do, but why obtrude the dolphins' home, this placid bend of the river? It was their one place of refuge, where they could breed and live. After five minutes the boatman's arm shot out again – the first sighting after the boat's intrusion – then another and another. They stayed like that for twenty minutes more, the three of them out on the mighty river, silently watching for nature to battle its way back.

The girl held Ryan's hand all the while.

'Back now,' said the boatman, the only words of English he seemed to know. Their hour was up. He cranked up the outboard again and the dolphins disappeared once more, to their homes in the deep, to the distant shore, away from all of them.

When they got back to Kratie, Ryan had asked the driver if they could go visit a village the next day. The man scratched his head. 'Is no good. Road is mud.'

'Why you want go village? Stay here town with me,' the girl's lips pursed into a moue and her eyebrows drew together into the tiniest frown.

Ryan again was forced to consider the expectations that went with a trip to a bar with the girl, the implications of sex; he was innocent of the way to progress these matters. What kind of commitment would she want? Any? And where was Tom? For a moment he envied Tom his simple approach: come up to Kratie for the weekend, have some fun, go back to work: or so Tom was presenting it to him – consciously, too consciously maybe.

She was nice, lovely. He could imagine the next hour easily enough; he had thought about it nearly every minute he had been with her. It would be certain to be wonderful, but what of the hour after that, and the next, and the next day or week after that. Malee was in another province only a hundred kilometres away, across the mountains, with her family.

'Look, I'm tired,' he said. 'I didn't sleep so well last night. I'm going to have to go and, and rest up for a while. Perhaps I will see you later on, with Tom and your friend.' The words came out of him haltingly. He could see the tears in her eyes.

He was what she had wanted.

'Ok, I go,' she said, and turned and walked away towards the market, where the cafés were. He watched her walk to the corner. Her golden legs were perfectly shaped. She turned and showed him one last hurt look.

And then she was gone.

This year's Pchum Benh temple gathering was different as everyone dressed in white to remember Meach and Kim. Older ones sat on cushions in the front, with small children curled in their laps. All of Malee's sisters were there, except Number Four who had talked to all of the family on the phone the night before. She had chickens to feed and her own baby to support as well as Ma and Pa.

People from the village had sent bunches of white flowers, and those who could attend had pressed little clumps of riel and some American dollars into Pa's hand, for they all knew that it was Pa who must now take responsibility for the orphaned Cris.

The bodies had been set out in open coffins for viewing, in order that the mourners would be reminded of the impermanence of life; and as they moved away they bowed their heads humbly in affirmation of the lesson learnt. Cris stood by the side of Pa and received the consoling attentions of these strangers. He lived now in a strange land, full of people who looked like him but whose customs, especially here in the province, were bewildering to him for their remoteness from his own experience.

When all were settled the achar stepped forward and intoned a chant in Khmer. For twenty minutes the mysteries were repeated and in time the thirty or so who had come to show their respect began to file away.

Malee took Cris by the hand and led him out of the temple. They sat in a little grove that was by a small stream, a tributary to the river.

'We will be all right here for a while, Cris.' Malee spoke the simplest Khmer expressions she knew and in the few words of English that she thought Cris might know. In this way they edged forward, she watching closely for his nods of understanding. 'They will take your Mum and Dad away to be burnt now.'

'The bodies,' said Cris, in what English he could. 'Their spirit gone, into the river.'

'The achar and the monks were asking them to come back home, into the house, to live here forever.'

Cris nodded his understanding of this aspect of the Khmer ways. His parents had told him about spirits living on after death, but he had not seen a Khmer funeral before – and now, his own mother and father. 'I've watched them for three days. No want to see more.'

His eyebrows were knitted in a frown. Malee too was challenged by what had happened. She had brought a medical book with her to study, but into that scientific space of her mind had come the ravens and spirits of Pchum Benh to fill her world with the old ways; she felt herself slipping back into her childhood spirit world with every day she was in the village. She held Cris's hand and he let her do it.

'Cris, in France do people think they will return in another life?' It was a question that Reap would never have thought to ask.

'Some of them do. Some Khmer people do.'

'Do you believe what they believe?'

'I don't know. I went to a school was Catholic. They say if you are good you go heaven, but boys at school don't believe. Maman and Papa, they try to be church, but people don't want them there.

Better be nothing.'

'School. Of course, you must go to school.'

'I don't want school.'

'If you don't go to school, Pa will kill me.'

Cris looked up at Malee. 'I don't want that to happen,' he said, deadpan.

Malee laughed and Cris smiled. He hadn't lost his sense of humour. Somewhere, sometime soon, they would have to find a school for him.

'Cris, do you like Reap?'

'Yes,' he turned to her, his face brightening. 'And you. You are my cousins.' He crinkled a smile. 'I never had cousins before. This is cool bit.'

'Cris, when the ceremonies are all over and Pchum Benh is finished, I will have to go back to Phnom Penh.'

'Yes, I know. But I want you to stay,' said Cris, for he had truly felt that, with his parents gone, his fate was to remain there, in the village, to go to school with the villagers, to eat Khmer country food, to become a Cambodian peasant and to work in the fields. They would never send him back to France alone. He had no return ticket. The savings of his Maman and Papa seemed to have been enough to get them to Kampong Thom, and that was all. There was no more money.

'Cris, when Reap and I go back to Phnom Penh, would you like to come with us?' The words were out before she knew it. She could do nothing else.

'To Phnom Penh!' He had spent a night there in a hotel and had walked along Sisowath Quay and looked at the dark river and felt the frantic movement of the city all around him. He had been excited by it. 'With you and Reap!'

'Yes, with me and Reap.' Malee was gladdened at the sight of the hope that had sprung up in the face of her little cousin and knew that what she was proposing was right. There would be trouble, but it was right.

'Can we go on your motorbike?'

'Yes, yes, my friend who came with us will go back on the bus, so there will be a seat for you.'

Cris's hands grasped his knees, tight. His eyes widened and then moistened, then he blinked three times and held his tears in. And Malee knew that, although some things were impossible, they could still be done.

Pchum Benh was over and it was the morning for all to return to the city. The family was gathered to discuss the problem of Cris.

'How are we going to feed him?' said Reap. 'What will he do in the day when I am at work and you are at university … in our little place.' Reap and Sophea shared a room and Malee slept in a little broom closet that she also used as a study. The other girls all went to bed early to get up at six o'clock for the factory while she slept sometimes as late as seven thirty after studying late.

'He can sleep on the couch,' Malee said hopefully.

'He will not sleep on a couch,' said Chamroeun. 'What kind of place will he think Cambodia is? He has come from the West and you want him to live on a couch when he is used to his own bed and his own room. I am the first brother so he must come with me. He stays at my place.'

'Bong Chamroeun, we respect you as first brother, but you have friends come to visit you on motorbikes and stay up late at night,' said Reap. Since moving away Chamroeun had lost face in the eyes of the village. He had not been successful and was not seen as a proper successor to Pa. Now that Cris was an issue it was a chance for him to regain his place by providing for him. If the girls got Cris, Chamroeun lost face again.

Malee spoke with her eyes respectfully cast down and with words that she had weighed. 'Yes, we respect you as first older brother, but still it is not the best place for a boy to be living with grown men, even for a little while. You and your friends do things we are not allowed to do, things that would not be good for a boy. Because he is a boy and we are girls, the place for Cris will be with us at first. Then he can stay with you later on.'

She looked at Cris and he nodded his head minutely forward in assent. But even the most minute of nods said to bong Chamroeun that he was not gaining the respect that was his due.

'Later on. What do you mean by this "later on"? Now you are making me for a fool. I will look after the boy now.' His voice rose. 'He wants to be in the city and he will be with me.'

Pa had been silent through this exchange and the polite and consensual ten minutes which had preceded it. He had wanted time to think about it and to talk to Malee more about her friend in the city, the teacher. But in a wood and bamboo house where twelve people were sleeping there were few opportunities to talk. Pchum Benh was over. Everyone must return to Phnom Penh and a decision was needed. He knew it was his time to speak.

'Chamroeun,' he said, and bowed in his direction, 'we respect your help to Cris. Your house is a very good place.' He raised his hands in sampeah. 'Reap and Malee's house is also good. Malee is a student and she speaks very good English.'

'But the boy speaks French, Pa. There is a difference.'

Pa bowed his head in response to the urgent and disrespectful tone of Chamroeun. 'Yes,' he said, 'but the boy speaks some English that he learnt in school. And' – here he faltered and his eyes were cast down – 'sister Number Three may have a friend who speaks English and some French as well …'

'You talk about the teacher friend … the barang! What is she, a prostitute? You let her go with the foreigner? You let our relative be taken care of by a stranger?'

'He will be with two cousins all the time.'

'You come and visit us all the time, bong,' said Malee.

'Yes, we want you. Cris wants you too,' said Reap. Cris nodded enthusiastically.

'We don't need barang in this house.' Chamroeun picked up his helmet with a swipe and walked out of the room; Pa had spoken and his cause was lost. Around the room all heads remained bowed in silence. Malee's hands covered her eyes and she sobbed; her brother whom she loved had called her a prostitute.

Since he had gone to the city to live, Chamroeun's temper had become short. In a few moments they all heard the whine of his motorbike engine at high speed come from the side of the house and out into the road, there was a panicked cluck of chickens scattering, and the motorbike roared away down the dirt road to Kampong Thom City.

Pa remained focused on the floor in front of him. Cris was alert, waiting for whatever happened next. Ma was praying silently. Number Ten sat next to Cris, hoping this meant that he could visit Phnom Penh now. Reap stood and went over to Cris.

'Come, cousin,' she said, holding out her hand. 'We must pack and go. Bong Chamroeun will be fine in a day or two, you wait and see.'

Cris rose and went with Reap to pack his things. As they left, Pa allowed his gaze to lift to Malee, who had remained sitting opposite him.

'I'm not so sure, Pa,' she said very quietly. 'You know what he's like.' Chamroeun would take defeat very badly.

'Give him time,' said Pa hopefully, knowing within himself that time, sitting on a question unresolved in Chamroeun's mind, might only make things erupt again.

Tom and Ryan took the mini-bus back from Kratie – fourteen people crammed into the ten seats and a cage of a dozen chickens shoved in with some baggage behind the driver. Not many Westerners went for the crumple and compress of the troop carrier and they were honoured with two seats saved for them at the back – not one single person sitting on their laps.

The twisting river disappeared from view as the road made a straight run to the south through rice fields with water buffalos, damp stacks of hay on higher ground, tarpaulins slung across them, stilt houses lining the road. It was the first time they had been able to talk about Kratie and the new type of relationship that had been dandled before Ryan there – the sort that some people came to Asia to find. But they were both silent.

After half an hour the driver slapped a video into the slot and a show flickered to life on a small TV. There was a comedy pair in a live stage show, a husband and wife team with a five-piece Khmer band behind them and a lively audience loving what they did. The wife was berating the husband with a wagging finger and he was giving back as good as he got in an exasperated, hands-on-hips, I-simply-don't-believe-this fashion. From time to time he appealed to the audience while his wife's back was turned, with a gesture or a raised eyebrow. They must have all been on his wavelength because they laughed uproariously. The comic timing was good; they were a great team. Even without knowing the language it worked – a husband and wife situation where the arguing and complaining is squeezed out of a bedrock of affection and respect.

The bus loved it. The boy next to Ryan was totally tuned in. Old men were comically associating with the beleaguered husband; they slapped their knees. A mother and her child were both giggling, the four-year-old girl holding her hands over her mouth and looking up at her mum to share the joke.

There was a close-up of the woman on the comedy team. Beneath her arched eyebrows and huge O of a mock-shocked mouth she was caked in make-up to look younger than she really was – this team must have been going for years, decades, so there was a purpose for the cosmetics. But it made Ryan think again of the girl Tom had set him up with, and it must have made the same connection for Tom.

'You are one weird man, man,' said Tom. 'That was one gorgeous honey of a girl back there.'

There was a long silence as Tom looked out his window at the rice fields, more hay stacks, the occasional phlegmatic water buffalo, houses lining the road. 'But … but,' Tom raised a finger for emphasis, then pointed it at Ryan, 'sometimes I wish I could be more like you.'

He went back into a bundle of himself, folded his arms over his chest and made out to be dozing. He had the look of a man whose short holiday had not been that satisfying either – someone who was not just going home but was already at the end of something.

Then he opened one eye and came back with a question. 'Ok, so something happened, but you were holding back on that girl. You got another fish to fry?' There was curiosity, concern and envy mixed up in his voice. Tom did not look directly at him very often but Ryan could see right now that the eye that he had cocked open was veined with red. He had lost the look of the resilient one, the guide, the man in control. Now he seemed self-conscious, even contrived.

Ryan said nothing for a while. Then, in a spasm, 'I dunno. Maybe.'

Tom sat up with more interest awakened now. 'Malee?'

'Maybe.'

'Oh, Jesus,' Tom groaned and flopped back in his seat. 'That's complicated.'

Ryan shook his head and would say no more, as if the question was too hard for him at this time. The skies were dark, the fields passed by and the rain came again. The bus tore into the weather without flinching. Another small bus coming the opposite way came straight at them in the rain and ducked in front of a tractor, missing them by half a metre. Tom's eyes were shut but he had the look of a man not resting, but thinking.

'I had a wife once.'

Tom spoke, both eyes half open now, peering through the rain. It was Ryan's turn to sit up straight.

'You're kidding me.' Until this time Tom had given out a reading of his life that was just enough to answer questions and cover patches. He hadn't taken it anywhere he hadn't needed to.

'In St Paul, Minnesota. We were good together, for a couple of years. So good that we got married. Just seemed like the right thing to do at the time – to make the big statement and all. But it ended up being more than a symbol. Everything changed straightaway, overnight. It all became so serious. My life was planned out for twenty years ahead, more.' Ryan simply nodded with interest. 'I became a civil servant: Motor vehicles – Registration.' He looked over at Ryan and then said very seriously, with even narrower eyes, 'I could have been a team leader.'

'Jesus, you gave up that chance.'

'I had the right stuff. Mate, you can't live with a noose around your neck.'

But Ryan wasn't having the subject turned back on him so easily.

'Married, government job. Kids?' he joked idly.

'Yeah. One.' Suddenly Tom's fingers went into action, as if some decision had been made. He pulled his wallet from his back pocket and snapped out a picture of a blonde girl, about four years old, with a cute smile and a gap between her two front teeth. He held it up for about five seconds and then flipped it away back in his pocket.

'Daddy's girl. There, now you know.'

Ryan was shocked but somehow not surprised. He was shocked because he hadn't thought deeply enough about Tom to even consider the possibility of child. He had accepted as much of Tom's story as had been implied by Tom and that was all. It had probably taken Tom months or years to wrap himself up in his gown of hardiness, but he must have gone through his own first month here once, alone and running, just as Ryan was doing now.

'Be careful, man, is what I want to say; it's harder than it looks. Since then I haven't even been able to think of settling with anyone. They say you're more secure in a relationship. I say you're not. I say you're only secure if you have three relationships. Then,' and he turned to look at Ryan and held up a finger for emphasis once more, 'if you lose one you've still got two left.'

It was faux cynicism, from a man who was needier than most.

'And you can look for another one to top up to three again?'

'Exactly.' Then, peering ironically, 'I don't know why they say you're so dumb.'

'Those girls?' Ryan tossed his head back in the direction of Kratie.

'Or someone like them. Each of those girls will have three or four on their own team. Your girl has one guy comes from Sweden every year for three weeks, just to smoke weed and fuck the ass off her. Next to him you were looking real good.'

'But she still would have kept him?'

'Sure, until you ask her to marry you. Then he gets the flick pronto. But are you going to do that?'

Ryan shrugged as if to say, well, not right now.

'That girl of yours probably has three different Sim cards in her purse. You know, a little juggling … Until she gets what she wants she's a professional girlfriend. She'll be in Phnom Penh in two weeks. You gonna see her?'

Ryan thought of the woman in the Happy Pizza Bar and her stoner husband. He was one who had accepted the deal. They had found a way to communicate with each other. They had two boys and they were as quietly content as he had ever seen a couple; he was a man who had some pressure off him. No-one was asking him to work in a factory, or warehouse or office; society did not compel him to be a success in The City. She had gone out to arrange the tuk-tuk while he had stayed in his seat and stroked one boy's hair and talked quietly to the other.

Ryan shrugged his shoulders. He felt a new empathy for the girl back there. She wasn't getting what she wanted but she was surviving, trying to improve her lot with whatever was available to her. The dolphins had retreated before the sound of the motor boat, but always came back to the surface to survive. But he was not so overcome by the metaphor that he couldn't see that their own boat had frightened the dolphins to the deep as well. Would he be pushing that girl down too, like the garment factories might be, or bringing her up?

At ten o'clock the night of the dolphin trip there had been a foot upon the stair, soft and purposeful – hers no doubt. Then a knock on his door. She had stood there, three metres from where he lay. He could hear her exhaling breath from the exertion of two flights of stairs. She knocked a second time, insistent, as if she would rouse him from the most dead of sleeps. She knew he was there. To not answer the door would be ridiculous, a rudeness. More than that, he would feel shame later for his inability to act. He was an observer of the world, an outsider perhaps, but he could not look on forever.

Had he been judging her? Against Western standards that were, what? … prudish, wowser – hypocritical, maybe. Steeped in churchy ideals that he did not even consciously believe in?

When he opened the door she put her arms around him in an expression of the kind of wordless relief that would accompany the restoration of some primal normality and which gladly shoved away the madness of the ninety minutes since she had last seen him.

She felt him growing against her hip bone and she gently rubbed herself up and down against him to encourage his erection. She lifted her head up to him and he kissed her and she worked his hand underneath her shirt to touch her breast. He gently stroked her nipples, first one side then the next.

And then they were inside his room and she pulled him on top of her and her breasts were in his face and mouth. There was a tube of jelly from her shoulder bag and she rubbed him slowly, slowly until after three or four minutes he began to groan and then he came and she had tissues and mopped at him and then lay down with him and put her head on his shoulder and kissed his face.

'Next time everything. You my love-me man,' she'd said.

Ryan tried to shake the thoughts from his mind and return to his talk with Tom.

'Did you ever think it might be easier with just one?' Ryan knew now that Tom had tried the regular married way in the past, but still.

'Not if everyone plays by the rules.'

'Yeah, but who makes the rules? Not them, that's for sure.' Ryan tugged his head back in the direction of Kratie and the girls there and all their forlorn hopes.

'I guess I do.'

'And why is that?'

'Because I have the money. Same as everything else that happens in this country. Same thing as happens in any country as far as I can see. Still, they're better off with me than without me.'

'Sometimes I think they might be better off without all of us, just living in the old ways.'

'Sometimes I think you think too much.' It was Tom's way of deflecting attention from himself, but sometimes Ryan thought that Tom thought much more than he ever let on. 'They're never going to get the old ways back, not in the cities and towns anyway. Even in the village, you know, people go to the city to work and bring back ghetto blasters and game stations and all that – Khmer village lads listening to hip-hop.' He shook his head. 'But it's a life without limitations here, for us – a matter of structure, isn't it.' Ryan turned his head to Tom with interest, to watch the man's face as he spoke. 'Life without limitations, the journey without end, is kind of exhausting, brother.' He had never called Ryan 'brother' before. 'But the life of wife is … I dunno – determinative. There you go, do you like that one?'

'Did you ever do any philosophy, at college.'

'Just enough to screw me up forever. I dropped out.' He raised an ironic eyebrow. 'It was too structural.'

'Is there much else you haven't told me?'

'Probably.'

'So, what are you going to do with yourself?' he said to Tom.

'Don't know. Stay here until the end of the year.'

'Dith wants you.'

'He does? You been talkin', you two?'

'Hah,' thought Ryan. How could he explain? He hadn't told Tom he'd been in the demonstration and had had rubber bullets whizzing around his ears. They had both been reserving parts of their stories, feeling each other out. 'We had a chat. I got the impression your job is good.'

'I dunno, muchacho, I dunno. I still talk to her sometimes, the girl.'

'Leaving the door open?'

'You ask a lot of questions.' Tom had probably never shown this much to anyone in Cambodia.

'I guess I think people should just share things more often.'

'Well, to share I guess you have to trust.' Ryan began to think of how he himself had probably only ever really shared with Janey and was wary of everyone else.

At that moment Ryan's phone buzzed and there was a message, from Malee.

Hi. How was Kratie?

He wrote back: Fine. How was Kampong Thom?

Too much to tell. Q: do you speak French?

French? He'd done five years of it in school and could still use quite a bit.

I can get by Ok in French. Why?

Talk later. On motorbike now. See ya.

Ryan switched off his phone and wondered about the mad place he was living in.

Do I speak French? He rubbed his temples as if to massage thoughts and solutions into himself, but nothing came. All he could feel was that there was some force moving around him now that was not of his making or in his control. Life seemed equal parts escape and surrender; when you let one thing go, did you absolutely have to take up something to replace it?

Back in class Ryan saw Malee but he had to watch her go out with the rest of them and down the stairs without a nod or a glance. On Friday they went to the Blue Pumpkin and before Malee went home to study she told him about her boy cousin and about his parents who had died in the floods. He could barely believe that she had another burden in life, a mouth to feed. Malee told him that Cris was a joy to her.

After two more weeks Ryan asked her if she really had to study on Friday nights. She told him that every day she spent as a student was another day that Reap had to work in the garment factory. If she did an extra unit every semester she could finish her Science and Medicine course in the middle of next year instead of waiting until the end.

'How much do you get for working in the café?'

'Seventeen dollars per month.'

'Seventeen … but that's just four bucks twenty-five a shift: a five-hour shift.'

'Uh huh. Reap gets eighty-five dollars a month and we send twenty to Ma and Pa.' He did the arithmetic: eighty two dollars a month between the two of them, before paying the rent.

'Nurses in a hospital are paid much better, like, five times more. Then I will be able to help Pa and Ma and the kids.' He couldn't immediately find an argument to counter that; to climb out of the well of poverty involved a life of toil for all of them.

He could see her handling more responsibility even than a nurse. In his mind there was a stethoscope around her neck; she was listening, making decisions, speaking quietly but with authority – weary but satisfied at the end of her day, coming home to … to what? To an empty apartment in Battambang or some other provincial town big enough to boast a hospital; perhaps she would be there in the capital.

'They say that sometimes it is important to have a little time away from study,' he said, 'so that you go back to it with a clearer head.' She looked at him quizzically. 'You know, get away from it all – go to a movie, something like that.'

'Yeaaah,' she smirked with irony. 'Got it. You like Hong Kong film or India film?'

'Both.'

'No you don't.' She kicked at him under the table.

'I do now.'

She picked up a spoonful of food and looked down at it, and a smile spread across her face.

'Maybe you could come and meet Cris one day. We could go for a film then or kick a football with him.'

'Sure, love to. He sounds like he could do with a big brother.'

'He likes Hong Kong films,' she stretched her hands out in front of her face and did a couple of karate chops, 'er … just like you do.'

The day after Ryan put the idea of the movie to Malee he received a text from her.

Pa is coming to town to go shopping. He wants to go to lunch. See you at the Pizza Company at 2pm

It turned out Pa had been watching TV the night before and had seen the ads for the pizza franchise; he wanted to try the barang food and he put two and two together. As Malee said, Pa was always thinking.

Ryan arrived ten minutes early but they were already waiting for him, crammed into an American diner-style booth. They hadn't ordered anything; they knew nothing of the menu and in any case they were afraid that if they ordered they would have to pay up front and they were waiting for him to do all that. Pa grinned broadly. His teeth were nicotine-stained but that fact seemed to bother him little. His hair was a thick shock of black, flecked with grey and his face was rounder than Malee's, more like Reap's; Ryan decided there and then that Malee must follow the Ma that this man fell in love with. Pa's grin got wider on Ryan's appearance and he kept ducking his head in acknowledgement, but he didn't get out of his seat or sampeah or make to shake hands.

As well as Pa there was the boy, Cris, who seemed to be anticipating Ryan's arrival quite intensely. He addressed him in French, '*Bonjour*' and thrust out his hand to shake.

'Bonjour, monsieur,' Ryan replied, 'ça va?'

Pa's face lit up in pure delight.

'Aha, aha, aha!' Pa repeated and looked around at them all; there was vindication of his judgement that Ryan and Cris were a made pair. There was a sister there as well, must be Number Five Ryan thought, and also another man who had come from Kampong Thom to go 'shopping' too – a semi-retired mate of Pa's whose name sounded something like Tommy. He was tiny, as if he had been stunted of growth in childhood years; his face was lit up with excitement on being introduced. It seemed that meeting the barang was quite an occasion.

When pleasantries and introductions were completed a plastic menu was pushed in front of Ryan. The list was nearly as confusing for him as it would have been for them – what to order for people he didn't know, who had never been in a pizza place before.

The whole table was looking at him with cheerful, expectant faces, wanting to see how it was done. Malee seemed unpractised in the art of hosting a social occasion; there was watchful silence all round as he looked over the extensive menu.

'Reap could not come today?' he asked.

Malee said something in Khmer to her Pa and then she replied, 'No, Reap has to work until six o'clock.'

'Ah, of course.'

He turned the menu over and there was more on the back. It appeared they did toasted sandwich things that were slid into an oven with cheese sprinkled on top, and macaroni cheese bake and fries as well. He thought about the idea of pizza and fries on the side. Pa looked like he would devour pizza, fries, the plastic menu – anything. He grinned avidly at Ryan, waiting for the moment of ordering. This was getting difficult.

'What about Samsung brother?'

Again Malee said some words to Pa and he shook his head decidedly and said some words that were like 'Nah, nah, nah.'

'First brother Chamroeun working too. Number Five has the day from school to come to the city for the first time,' and Number Five grinned and looked down modestly as she realised she was being referred to.

He could feel that the conversation had been changed quite deliberately away from the subject of Chamroeun, the Samsung brother who had had trouble with barangs. A girl appeared wearing a white plastic apron with green and red vertical stripes and a little paper hat with the words 'Pizza Company' written across it. With her Khmer looks and American outfit the girl embodied a bizarre, incongruous cuteness and, as she held her order pad at chest height and pertly poised her pen ready to take the order, she seemed to know it.

The pressure was on. Pa was watching the way he handled the situation. He went against the macaroni bake and straight for middle-of-the-road tradition, with one Sicilian pizza and one ham and cheese, all to share. Green tea was on the list but he decided on soft drinks all round. When he completed the ordering everyone leant back with pleased looks on their faces. It was as if he had made a great success; he half expected a slap on the back, such was the impression he had made, such was the goodwill at the table.

They talked about this and that. Ryan referred to things that Malee had told him about Pa's life, avoiding the Khmer Rouge years out of delicacy. Malee asked Pa questions in Khmer and he replied, looking at Ryan all the while, and Malee replied to him in English. Meanwhile Cris listened intently, as did Number Five, but did not speak. Tommy continued to respond ecstatically to every utterance, without making one himself.

They loved their pizza. Pa went back to the ham and cheese time and again and they all laughed when he bit in hard then pulled back greedily and the cheese fell on his chin and he needed to stuff it in with his fingers. It was the most hilarious thing. Pa took it in good spirit. They all laughed together without hesitation or mitigation; the family was as one, and Tommy was treated as a member of this gang.

Conversation slowed to a walk and Ryan began to worry what would happen when the eating was done. But after about an hour it was all over quite suddenly. There was a glance at watches and nodding to each other: they had seen what they wanted to see. Ryan caught the eye of the waitress and he paid the bill in cash. Pa's eyes widened and he nodded happily at the wad of notes and keenly watched the money change hands.

Then they were out in the street and Pa and Tommy and Number Five all piled into a tuk-tuk, which had arrived by arrangement, and with a quick chorus of waves they went back to the bus station – a four-hour bus trip in the morning, then a pizza, then a four-hour bus trip back, then Number Six would probably pick them up at Kampong Thom City and drive them to the village, all four of them on one bike.

Ryan was left on the kerb with Malee and Cris.

'I guess that's it,' said Ryan.

'That's them all right. Pa says you should take me shopping now.'

'Shopping?'

'To buy me something nice. But it doesn't matter.'

'*Je voudrais un téléphone portable*,' said Cris. Then he looked up and saw the look on Ryan's face, 'One day – *ça ne fait rien*.'

'Ok,' said Ryan hesitantly. He thought he understood, but there was unease stirring in him. Colin and Tom had said that he would be expected to take his Khmer girl shopping, and how that would be only the start. They had said it was best to be clear what the boundaries were. The problem was he had no idea what the boundaries should be.

Cris went to the nearest public school. As Malee took him in for his first day he eyed the hungry lean dogs in the street; they nosed around in piles of rubbish and competed with ravens for stray scraps. He was introduced to the class as the new boy and took his seat in silence as all faces stared, even the teacher's. The story had already got around that he was from France, that he spoke French and didn't know a word of Khmer (which wasn't true), and that people in France were lucky as there were lots of frogs and snails to eat there.

At morning break-time he filed out into the corridor with every-one else and wondered what would happen next. Would he sit by himself while the other boys played with their friends? The girls melted away and the boys gathered around him, looking, staring at him; Cris was their property, at least at first.

Then the first question was blurted out, 'Do you really speak French? My grandpa speaks French.' 'Where is France, is it close to Israel?' 'What colour are the frogs there, are they green or brown?' 'Did your parents really die in the flood?' 'Have you seen Ronaldo play?'

At lunch time a football was produced and he was first picked. Everyone wanted him on their team. He said he normally played in defence but they put him in attack anyway. They fed him the ball, until he scuffed a shot at goal and they decided that he knew his own game best after all and he was eased back behind the midfield and did a fair enough job for his side, just booting the ball artlessly up-field when it came near him.

Before class went back in he told them about his two cousins who were so cool and how one was going to be a doctor; about how he slept on the couch in their little lounge room and no-one told him what to do; but most of all he told them about his friend Ryan who took them to the Pizza Company and was like his big brother and who came to visit all the time and who he spoke French and English with.

Most of what Cris said was true; only a little was exaggerated.

They did go shopping.

Malee possessed only four shirts: two white and two pale blue. She matched these up with one knee-length skirt that she wore to school and university, and one pair of trousers that she wore to work. She washed every third night and hung the shirts on a line from the window, except in the wet season when they rolled the shirts up in a dry towel to extract as much moisture as possible and dried them inside, or gave a hundred riel to Mrs Leang on the ground floor who had a washing machine with a drier.

Ryan had never bought clothes for a girl before and it felt strange; it felt … serious. He had been brought up in a place where women had their own money from the time they were seven years old – some before that. Or at the very least had parents who would materialise every item on their child's birthday or Christmas list as a biannual right of passage. Buying clothes for Malee seemed so old fashioned, so pre-feminist, that a part of him rebelled. On the other hand it would bring them closer. And it had nothing to do with Pa. Malee was so unjustly poor; but even in Australia there were people who were unjustly poor. And what had he ever done for them? And he was in a foreign country now; he could adopt local customs or just stick to the mindset he had brought with him, as if he could pretend that the state of Western culture right now was the high point of all-time world civilsation. That would seem overbearing and he didn't want to be like that.

Such thoughts were circulating in his mind and colliding with each other in a tangle. But events soon overtook them and cleared the space; they were almost at the Sorya Mall already.

They entered and strolled past the glitter of jewels in a sea of display cabinets. Malee did not even glance at those; it would be im-modest of her to even think of appearing anywhere near her village in jewellery. If she wore such things only in the city, the news would be heard back in the province before the sun went down and the disgrace of selfish vanity would be upon her for life. To be appropri-ate a gift must be nice, but tasteful, and practical too.

They rode the escalator to the higher levels and rummaged through the clothing stores; it was an experience for both of them. They found a shirt and a pair of pants of a silky lavender colour; when set against her jet black hair and her glistening light brown skin the suit was beautiful for its simplicity. He waited while she ducked behind a screen. She was just a metre or so away, changing clothes. He listened to the old white shirt rustle from her shoulders and drop to the floor, the new one slipping over her and then silence as she

looked at herself. He felt awkward, but excited. When Malee
emerged, she seemed even tinier than she had been before. She
stroked the smooth and flawless fabric; it would be reserved for the
very best occasions.

'Can I really have it?'

He saw how she tried to restrain her joy.

'Yes, of course you can have it. If it's the right thing to do.'

Malee briefly pressed her palms together in sampeah, and raised
them to the level one does for a respected friend or equal. He
stretched his hand out to her, and stroked her hair once.

The suit of clothes had cost him just fifteen dollars.

By the time they emerged from the Sorya Mall darkness was closing
in and he took the first tuk-tuk that was waiting outside. In her street
the concrete apartment blocks were ghostly grey against the evening
sky. Stray pips of light escaped from their towering walls like random
half-closed eyes in a giant disfigured modernist face.

When they arrived at her building he paid the man and told him
not to wait. He would walk her in and say goodnight properly, whatever the cost. At the glass door that led inside he stepped close to her
and stroked her hair again. She did not stop him. He drew her to him
and he kissed her lightly on the forehead. She leant in to him. The
light was dim beneath the shelter over the doors, and no-one was
coming in or out just now. He held her in his arms for a minute and
they stayed there without speaking. He would not try to go too far
too soon, though every sinew in his being wanted to place his hands
under her shirt and touch her, to go down the back of her pants and
caress her buttocks. He thought of Kratie. There the embrace had
been hers. Here it was his; or rather, it was theirs. In Kratie he had
given in to it because it had seemed the right thing to do; here he
fought it because it was the right thing to do.

He could have stayed holding her forever, but it was time to go
and so they released their embrace and he bent to kiss her goodnight.
She responded to him with her mouth closed, but with her lips

pushed out searching for him as if enquiring after something but not knowing where to find it. It was a beautiful small kiss, but peculiar. It occurred to him that she had never kissed a man before.

He laughed, or rather smiled and chuckled together at his epiphany about this girl. She heard him and recoiled.

'What's wrong,' she said, in horror that she had made some irreversible mistake.

'Nothing's wrong,' he replied. 'It was just the most beautiful kiss I have ever had.'

She relaxed again and exhaled a sigh of relief.

'Me too. I must go.'

And she went, as abruptly as Pa had left that afternoon, scampering up the stairs. There was just the faint odour of her sweat on his face, and as he stepped out into the night he still felt her hair on his fingers and he remembered the caress of the silky shirt against her taut shoulders as he held her.

He was in a strange place. He should have got the tuk-tuk man to wait for him; that's what they preferred to do anyway. He just hadn't wanted anyone around when he was saying goodnight, but now practical concerns swept back.

There was a pole with a light up on the next corner, and others at intervals that diminished into the distance. They were like candlelight spots in a harbour that showed the direction for a ship to take, but shed no light on what laid below; walking in between them could be awkward, even dangerous. In the other direction it was five hundred metres or more to the main road. There would never be a tuk-tuk along here; no-one down here could afford one except him. He would have to walk up to the main road and flag someone down. And then he remembered – Chean! He had Chean's number in his phone but had never had to use it.

'Yes, boss,' Chean answered brightly. Ryan told him he was at Malee's flats.

'Oooooohhh,' said Chean, 'danger place. I come for you. Ten minutes. No worry.'

Ryan stepped into the empty street. There was a convenience store a little way up the road but it was quiet now. It was eight o'clock at night and this was not what anyone would think of as a party part of town.

There were some low bushes behind him next to a broken paling fence that had strips falling off it, some lying facedown by the bushes. Then he froze as he heard a rustling around the branches. Could it be rats? He hated rats. Then there were the quick steps of humans. He froze for a second as a shudder of fright went through him, then he turned around to face whatever was coming and walked straight into a blow on his forehead from a solid stick of wood, and then another and another. There were two men, it seemed, piling into him. He slumped away and down from the blows and as he did he grabbed the arm of one of the assailants and tried to pull him down. His other arm grabbed the man's shirt and he tried to push him into the path of the other one to make him stumble. But the man evaded his grasp and, off balance as he was, he swung another blow at Ryan that missed and while he was open Ryan went in with a punch that connected with him on the lip or nose. The man reeled back for a second then righted himself and came back harder. Then he felt another crack on the back of the head from the other one behind him and Ryan instinctively flung his elbow back to go for that one's nose as well, but his arm was grabbed and pinned and then a kick came, aimed at his genitals but scuffing only his thigh as he turned to protect himself. Then they pushed him down and smacked him time after time with the flat side of their paling cudgels, then they threw the posts away and both of them kicked him three or four times in his ribs and on his arse.

And then they ran. When they had taken a few steps one of them stopped and said in a darkly sibilant, raspy way, as if he was trying to disguise his voice.

'Keep away, barang.'

And then running, running, until the steps disappeared and a street away there was the sound of a motorbike revving harshly and whining away into the night.

He had been hit many times, but not hard. They had been using palings of wood, but nothing like a baseball or cricket bat. One of the kicks had connected hard around his perineum and he could feel it as he rolled up onto all fours. He felt his mouth. There was a split in his lower lip. He was not ready to stand for a little while so he stayed there on all fours, spitting blood out of his mouth, trying to remember whether he knew the number of Malee's apartment.

And then there was the whine of another motorbike motor and the tinkle of a caravan behind it. The tuk-tuk stopped and then he heard a couple of scuffling steps.

'Boss?' Then some more steps and again, 'Boss, boss.'

Chean was feeling his arms and legs for breaks and then his head and lastly he touched his mouth and felt the split.

'You ok, boss. Nothing broken. You come with me.'

Chean helped him gently into the tuk-tuk and laid him down on his side. And as they drove away Ryan began to wonder why first brother Chamroeun had not come along to lunch that day, when the rest of the family had taken such trouble to make it all the way from Kampong Thom to the city.

In the several minutes between waking and opening his eyes, the scenes of the night before were played out over and again in his mind.

The fight, if you could call it that. But no, you couldn't. He had been surprised, taken advantage of, beaten; he was paling-smacked. He was no fighter, but he surmised that the others were not really such practised exponents either.

If they were criminals they would have taken something from him. He had fifty dollars in his pocket – half a month's wages for a garment worker, about a week's worth for someone in an office. And the weapons, they were just sticks of wood picked up off the ground, no planning.

He had light bruises all over his arms and around his buttocks. There was a small split in one corner of his mouth. The blows had seemed to be aimed at humiliation, not physical hurt – a pressure valve of steam going off in someone's head.

When he turned over he felt his arse; that was where it hurt the most, the final kick.

Chean had brought him up the stairs the night before, had laid him out and taken his shoes off, then fed him four Codalgen with a glass of water – that's a hundred and twenty mgs of codeine along with masses of paracetamol. As they came in to the flat together Chean had looked around the place in awe of the bountiful space it afforded just one man. Ryan thought now that the look Chean had given him had said: 'She will want this.' He didn't whistle softly like some people might, but Ryan now swore to himself that Chean had pursed his lips to do so, but had then thought better of it.

He sat up in bed, his eyes still shut against the light he could feel searing through his window. Jesus – no! He would not go to work. What did it matter if he did or he didn't? What did anything matter now? No-one had ever hit him before. Not like that. And he had never hit anyone either – ever; but when he'd had a chance he had socked one of those blokes a good one. He was a bit proud of that. Hey, I'm a fighter, he said to himself. I'm a tough guy. He had to tell himself that, no-one else would. He felt his right hand. It was ok, just a bruise on the middle knuckle.

Of all the things he remembered from that whole day there were two that came to him now: the look on the face of Pa as Ryan counted off the bills to pay the Pizza Company girl, and what Malee had said: 'Pa said you should take me shopping, but it doesn't matter.'

As if it didn't matter. He could see now how much it mattered to one of them. He could see that there was conflict in the family, over him. He felt now that Pa had sprung a honey trap around him. They said that once you had been sucked in to the family all the way, the demands for money became greater and greater until you were paying for the wedding ceremony of sister number six and held responsible for the successful marriages of all the rest of them: pink and yellow bunting, roast chicken feasts, deafening Korean pop music, the monk and the civil celebrant.

Suddenly Ryan felt like such a tourist, and with that thought there returned to him the second memory of his day. At the end of the Pizza Company experience, in the street when they were seeing Pa and the rest of them into their tuk-tuk, a man had ridden past on a pushbike: a kind of goon, a Westerner, with an open-mouthed staring expression on his face. Ryan had thought of the look he imagined on Coleridge's ancient mariner. This idiot had taken particular notice of Ryan, it seemed, with Malee's family and, as the tuk-tuk carrying them took off, the man did a U-turn in the street and rode past on the other side, all the while his pop-eyed, leering face focused on Ryan. And then, again, he turned to come back up on their side of the road and as he passed once more he caught Ryan's attention with a twitch of his head and he cried out loud in a sing-song trill, 'You'll never be one of them!'

And then the man had given a quick high laugh and pedalled hard on his bike and he was away, happy, merry almost, at the delivery of his telling line. When he arrived Ryan had been a tourist. But what was he now? If he was a stayer he guessed that made him what they call an expat. It had the ring of a stereotype that he didn't like. Could he ever be more than that? Expatriates brought dollars and disturbance dressed up as help, but on the other hand no nation can remain in isolation for ever, even though Cambodia had seemed to be trying to achieve that for forty years.

Ryan had thrust that memory away then, but now it was harder; he had bruises all over his body and the memory of this prescient idiot savant stuck fast in his head. He forced himself up on his elbows and turned from the light. He peeped one eye open at the clock: five past seven. He had to send some texts. It was Friday so at least he would only have one day to be covered at the school before the weekend. He sent almost identical texts to Dith and Tom, a simple message saying he was sick and suggesting that Tom fill in for him on Saturday. Then he turned the phone off.

He went to bed again and dozed and dreamed and imagined things. Even Reap now seemed sly. And then he saw her in his mind, sitting in the garment factory, sewing up sleeves, pushing the fabric under the needle; over and over again she pushed a T-shirt through the machine and then she began to laugh maniacally. He looked down and there was his face printed on the T-shirt and Reap was pushing it under the needle and there were stitches all over his face, like some Frankenstein's monster that had been in a knife fight: 'You'll never be one of them' the face croaked at him in a voice that was not his own. He sat up in bed. He was hot; he was awake.

'Jesus fuck,' he said out loud.

He did not know what to think. He went to the fridge and took a cold drink of water. He poured some on his cupped hand and washed it over his face. He thought of Janey – he still had not called her. How many days had it been? Perhaps that was the one constructive thing he could do with his day.

He turned his phone on again. It was ten o'clock. There was a message for him from Malee: *They said you are not at school today. What's the matter?!*

He thought for a minute and went through a series of wordings for his answer. He wanted to suggest that he was being taken for a ride by her and the family, but he didn't want to say it outright. He spent five minutes composing a message that said he would call off their friendship. That would be the easiest and safest thing, but then he deleted it. It was a delicate thing and he could not decide, but he had to do something. After three or four versions and twenty minutes he wrote: *I got beaten up last night. Welcome to the family.*

It was simple. It hinted at bitterness, but not blame. It suggested her fault as a member of a family, but not as a person. Some girls would drop a man for a text like that; perhaps he was tempting the issue of fate, so Malee would end it for him. He thought of the girl from Kratie, her look of hurt as she walked away, her knock on his hotel room door. He could be with her next week. It would be easier – the stoner …

He turned the phone off and dozed for a while. He decided to make a Skype call to Janey at three o'clock; by then it would be half past five in Australia and her patients would have left and she would be at her office writing up her day, finding things to do to stop her going home.

By two o'clock he was ready to do something and he made himself a coffee and checked his phone. In the first minute of lunchtime the answer had come through: *Beaten up!! What!! Aaaaagggghhhhh!! What do you mean??* And then five minutes later: *What do you mean??!! Help, tell me!!??*

He rang back. She would be back in class at the university by then and he left a message: 'Uh, yeah, when I left your place last night I was beaten up in the street by two guys armed with sticks of fencing wood. They kicked me too, ah, and one of them told me to stay away from you. I guess that means someone in your family doesn't like your new outfit. Perhaps I should count myself lucky there weren't any nails in the fence palings because I might not have an eye now, er, or a brain I suppose. Um, I guess that's all I need to say. Bye.'

As he pulled the phone away from his ear and paused his finger over the red button he thought his message was good on the factual side but needed something editorial to round it out. 'Um,' he said, 'I thought we might have had something. Bye.'

It was meant to hurt. It was meant to say, 'We could have been good but for your stupid brother. And sister. And father. And the whole rotten family thing.' The girl from Kratie would be in Phnom Penh next week and he still had the phone number that the child-minding woman from Riverside had given him — her sister, the one who slept late. As Tom had said, there weren't many rules for guys like them, only the rules they dictated to themselves. Then again, perhaps he could have stayed in Australia and accepted his own fate; should have gone to that wedding and accepted the humiliation, to be with his sister Janey if nothing else, to be best man at his brother's wedding if need be. In mythology, wasn't it always those who tried to avert their fate, to defy the oracle, who met the most grisly ends?

These Cambodians would *never* have left home – anything for the family, don't rock the boat.

He sat down hard in his TV chair and his arse hurt sharply from the kick he had received. He winced and rolled over onto one cheek.

'Fuck,' he said out loud, in exasperation. And then, after thinking about his situation with a cool head for a minute more, he repeated the only word that summed up his situation perfectly.

'Fuck!'

'What on earth?'

'What do you mean "on earth"?'

'What happened to you? Tell me now.' His sister Janey was using her sharp voice, the one that was meant to show him that this was a situation that entailed the suspension of the standing nicety orders that governed their relationship in all but exceptional times.

Ryan squirmed in his seat but his arse hurt again and he screwed his face up into a wince. Janey's face leaned forward for a closer look and her eyes were narrowed, a sure sign that no amount of banter would deter her from the answer to her question.

'I fell down the stairs, out the back here.'

'Oh Jesus, pull the other one. Stairs don't hit you on both sides of the head. I'm a doctor for cryin' out. Do you forget this fact?'

He made a mock-thoughtful face, 'Oh yeah!' he said, as if a lightbulb had just been snapped on. 'So you are.'

'Bring your face up to the screen.'

'Oh, come on …'

'Bring it up to the screen!'

This was the woman who had been his mother as well as his sister on all those lonely Saturday nights when their parents were out schmoozing money – the only person in the world he would take this from.

He leaned close to the screen.

'Jesus, your eyes are like a cross-section of the red cabbage I cut open last week.'

'You been making sauerkraut again? You know, the one you do with the …'

'Don't change the subject! Have you been to see a doctor?'

He shrugged his shoulders. Really, what was a doctor going to do?

'What happened?' Short, blunt, demanding.

'I got beat up.'

'By whom?'

'It was dark. I don't know.'

'You know. I can tell that you know.'

He asked himself why he had called Janey, when she was always going to see through him. But he knew on another level that he was calling her *because* she would see through him and would then force him to confess. We play these games with ourselves, he knew. And by the time all that had happened he would have shared it with the only person he *could* share it with.

'It might have been Malee's brother.'

There was a silence of some seconds and then. 'Oh … my … god.'

Silence. They looked at each other. Janey's face was showing the signs of her characteristic overthinking, where very often two plus two was equal to five. He awaited the outcome.

'If you have a cucumber take two slices and put them over your eyes. I will be there in two days.'

'What! You can't—'

'I can.'

'But your patients—'

'Are like your classes. Someone else can do them. Do you know, I haven't been away from this place in three years.'

'I thought you loved it.'

'I do but, Jesus, there's a limit. The reason I haven't been away is because I haven't had anything to do with myself. Normally I find holidays stressful because there's no outlet for my nervous tension; now they're all making life stressful for me here by telling me every five minutes I should have a holiday! Nowhere to go except to join some tour group full of old people, god love them, and go to Ephesus or the Pyramids or, or …'

'Stonehenge?'

'Or some fine place like that, but to do it in such style and in such company that I feel like my life is over some thirty years too soon. And now my baby brother has conveniently gone to the tropics and got himself into bother and he needs his sister. There is a flight goes every night to Singapore. Then I get whatever connection there is to Phnom Penh. I will be there the day after tomorrow. I might be a fucking wreck by the time, but I will be there.'

And Janey began fossicking in her bag right there and then.

'What are you doing?'

'I need my card; I'll score handsome frequent flyer points for this. Now get off my screen, I want to book a ticket.'

'Ok. Bye-bye, sis.'

She reached forward and the screen popped to grey. Ryan sat back in his chair and wondered. Whatever had happened or was going to happen, Ryan's day had just swivelled on an axis. A little of his energy had returned, and whatever had happened to him mattered a little less.

Before Chean brought him home, Ryan hadn't had many visitors in his three weeks in the apartment. Tom had come over the day he rented it and pursed his lips and nodded his approval. 'Bene hacienda, muchacho,' he'd said, murdering, Ryan thought, his Spanish and Italian together. Still, it sounded good.

Colin had bought two cold beers from Mr Thiounn and come up saying they'd better drink them before they warmed up, even though Ryan had a fridge already. They'd cracked them open and clinked tins and Colin had told Ryan he was proud of him – something Ryan had taken a day or two to think about. He was still not certain what would make Colin proud.

Apart from these intrusions and his Skype sessions with Janey, the apartment had become a stronghold of solitude for him and just now he was glad of it. He decided to let things go and not think again. He could let Janey do all that for him when she arrived. There was a sudden release from decision and worry. He went over to the Kandal market and bought some eggplants and mushrooms. He already had some chicken from the Sorya supermarket and he cooked them to-gether in a wok with some pad thai sauce; he boiled noodles and tossed in some spinach at the last minute. He sat in front of the tel-evision and avoided the BBC and the Asian English language news channel and the Australian and American ones too. They were start-ing to seem foreign to him and his remote control dwelled on the local section of the channel numbers instead.

There was a game show with a yellow backdrop and all the wide-eyed contestants were wearing pink make-up and flapping their hands up and down in excitement. Then a news channel and for a while he tried to work out the Khmer words that were being spoken. After a few minutes his head began to hurt from the effort and he switched again. On the next channel was Hun Sen – giving a speech! He was famous for his long rambling speeches that attacked his po-litical foes and made claims about them that were outrageous and impossible to validate, but which would sink into the minds of who-ever watched.

Hun Sen was sitting at a long desk in an auditorium full of peo-ple, and alongside him on either side of the desk were generals in their full regalia topped with khaki hats with red bands. Hun Sen spoke very seriously for a minute – there was something terrifyingly magnetic about this man with so much power, the survivor who be-came a dominator. Then his face lightened into a crooked smile and he uttered what must have been the joke conclusion to some long story. Along the line of generals and colonels everyone broke out on cue into grins and nods. But their grins were squeezed out of their faces like lemon juice from a mangle. Hun Sen went back to his speech and in a minute he broke into another leer and began nodding at his own joke again and the grins and nods were squished up again from the cavalcade of generals. On and on the speech went, each malicious joke eliciting a more pained and forced response from the brass up there, each joke perhaps presaging the political or earthly demise of the person who was the object of its intention.

After ten minutes Ryan almost felt sorry for the elite up there on that stage behind their leader, their boss. It became embarrassing to watch. It was all about money and power; it was a bullying game in which no-one had any rights – none. The followers, even the powerful ones, had to abase themselves to stay in the gang of thugs. What a place, he thought, and decided he had seen enough of it.

At that moment there came a knock on his door. It was a soft knock but a sound that carried and which demanded an answer, almost proprietorial. He started at the sound. Hun Sen continued smirking on screen, but the spell of his Machiavellian and demoniac presence was broken. Ryan went to the door.

Malee was there. Her eyes were pleading and angry.

'Where have you been?' she said, then started. 'Oh my god.'

What would he say? Could he say what he thought, or just relay the facts, that he had been beaten up.

'I was beaten up by a couple of guys. They had sticks.'

'Aggh. Sticks! But …' she immediately began to examine him with her nurse's hands.

'There isn't any cut. They were fence palings, from outside your place.'

She stood back, confused.

'My place?' she gasped. 'It was there?' Her eyes widened as she considered the possibilities.

'Anyway, er, why don't you come in.'

She was distracted, thoughts racing as they sat.

'Who was it? Did you know?'

'Hard to tell in the dark, but I don't think I'd ever seen them before.'

Malee was silent and thoughtful as she sat.

'Ah, one of them told me to keep away and called me barang. It seemed he was saying to keep away from you.'

They sat like that for a few seconds and then Malee's head nodded in recognition. 'Ah, I see,' she said. 'Bong Chamroeun. I should have thought of that straight away.' And she relaxed her shoulders and sat back in her seat as if this meant the problem was resolved.

'Ah, I see? What do you mean by that? He's just assaulted me. Isn't that against the law here?'

'The law? Oh, yes, the law,' she nodded as if to say, good point. 'Chamroeun is angry about many things, not just you. But you take the blame. He wants to take Cris away from me, and you especially. Cris can't wait to see you again; you are his hero. Bong Chamroeun has lost face.'

Ryan thought for a moment about how he could achieve a pedestal position with a boy, so quickly, without any intention of doing so. And Chamroeun …

'But bong is even now,' Malee finished.

'What do you mean by even?'

'He has his face back.'

'You mean he lost face, so he gets a mate and waits for me in the dark and hits me with fence palings. He smashes my face, so everyone respects him again?'

'He had to do something and that was about all he could do.'

'You mean, you're just going to leave it at that?'

'It's in the family, so it's over. If it had been someone outside – different story. You still have power, with us.'

Ryan flopped back on the sofa, his mouth gaping. The whole thing had been dismissed, just like that! He had expected a little more attention, maybe some outrage. He *had* been beaten up after all.

But somehow, for the first time, he could feel the power of her desire for him. The clash with Chamroeun had brought him more deeply into the family and if he was so important to someone else's face that meant he had more consequence than he had figured before. And such was the power of the person of Malee that when she had said it was ok, that somehow that made it ok. Ten minutes before he had been drawn into the leering power of Hun Sen and had thought about leaving Cambodia. But now …?

She put her hands to his head, gently feeling the wounds again. 'I want to do something for you.'

'But there's nothing really to do, is there. Just wait until it heals.'

She felt his mouth. 'I will bring some cream.' She came close to him, as if to examine him very closely; she was in his arms. Her cheek touched his cheek and her mouth moved to his and they were kissing. She was tender, with loving small kisses, her mouth more open this time, sexual.

He lent forward and laid her on his couch and knelt on the floor in front of her and stroked her hair and kissed her right there, kneeling in front of her, bending. Then his hand was underneath her shirt and she shivered and her whole body twisted as he stroked her stomach. Her skin was smooth to touch. His hand came around her back and unhitched her little white bra. Her breasts were so small that, but for the sake of modesty, such a bra would have served no practical purpose. He stroked her nipples and then lifted her shirt and applied his mouth to them, first one then the other, kissing and licking, back and forth until she began to moan, not low but a high gasping open-mouthed pant, as if in complete surprise at the sensation she was experiencing. He felt at the soft fur between her legs and felt the wetness there. Her arms were around his head and her legs twisted together as he kissed her and she writhed three or four times. Then when he kissed her on the lips and their tongues came together her body gave a little shake and her eyes were wide open for a moment staring as if the answers to life were written there on his plain white ceiling; her moan became lower and as her twisting subsided, her eyes were closed again and she collapsed her weight languidly into the sofa and, whatever it was, it was over.

They lay there for some time, his head on her shoulder, her eyes closed, her face expressionless but for a tinge of wonder.

'My God,' he said.

'Phew,' she said in reply.

Ryan called Chean and they all went together to take Malee to her apartment. He felt Malee's hand over his all the way this time, in the dark. He felt her fingers lace into his and he remembered the girl in Kratie. She had done the same thing out on the water, on the day of the dolphins. She had placed her hand over his, then after a minute had laced her fingers like this.

When they arrived at her block Malee jumped out and thought for a second, then spoke as if she had just had a thought.

'Come up,' she said to Ryan. 'Say hi to Cris.'

Chean turned the engine off and said, 'I wait.'

'No, you come too, Chean,' she said. 'You're part of the family as well now.'

Ryan looked up at that 'part of the family' thing, then he and Chean exchanged glances.

'I've seen your apartment, now you can see mine,' she said. 'You know, when I was a child, sometimes I took the family cow away for grass by the river; it was my job once a week for a year. I would take a book to read and study, but sometimes I just sit under a tree and let my thoughts drift away for, like, a whole hour. I think it was the only time in my life ever I was alone. Even riding my bike to school there was usually three of us.'

Malee led them up three flights of stairs and along to the end door in a row of eight. She walked confidently, happy to show how at ease she was in this derelict environment, then she looked around and grimaced before turning the key and pushing through. The two girls inside stopped what they were doing and looked up, their eyes wide at the sight of the two men. Then Cris was there too, jumping up from his couch. The girls were working: Reap was washing clothes in a baby's bath, squeezing a shirt dry of suds before plunging it into a plastic bucket of clearer water. The other girl sat with a wooden board on her knees, next to a saucepan of water that was coming to the boil on a single-jet portable gas cooker; she had chopped a carrot and was just starting on what looked like a turnip or huge radish.

'Hey,' said Cris, and he ran over from the couch to slap Ryan a high-five that Ryan turned into a soul brother hand clasp, just for fun. The kid got the irony in the turnaround and giggled and turned and said something to the girls that must have been, Look who's here. The girls smiled through their embarrassment at being caught out with their washing and their meagre dinner. The room was the size of a small bedroom, but was the living room for four of them, and was now Cris's bedroom too.

'I'll show you around,' said Malee. 'Shouldn't take long.' She went through to the bedroom and pushed open the door. There was a double bunk bed that looked like a child's size, and a foam mattress on the floor with a pillow and a sheet that had been laid out square but in which you could still see the creases from the shape of its nocturnal occupant. There was about a metre of space between the beds.

'The girl from the top bunk went back to the village,' she said, seeing him look at the empty space and the neatly made bed. 'But not the right place for Cris.'

'A cat?' he suggested.

She tilted her head thoughtfully, 'Nah, no space for a cat.'

She stepped out of that room and opened the next door and switched on a light.

'Here is my place,' she emphasised the last word, to show that you could hardly call it a room.

It was an odd little crevice, next to the bedroom, about six feet long and three feet wide. There were medical books ranged up along the end wall, and a single foam mattress had been forced in there. Forced because it was too wide to fit in naturally and was riding up one of the walls.

'We would cut the foam down to fit but, who knows, we might move to a bigger place sometime.' She raised her eyebrows to accentuate the irony.

'Cosy spot,' he said.

'Yeah,' she countered. 'Good security. A robber couldn't even fit in here.'

'He'd have to have an interest in medicine.'

'Hmmm, some intern down on his luck. It could happen.'

He nodded in agreement with that; it was unlikely, but possible.

Back in the living room dried noodles had been thrown into the pot of water, with a little fresh spinach and bamboo shoots from a tin. They were looking forward to this as a feast.

'Is good,' said Reap in English. 'Some night only have noodle.' And she pointed to a cellophane packet in the corner with about a dozen individual serves of noodles, each with its flavour sachet – preservative high, nutrition low. 'We must get strong for demonstration.'

'Of course. Sunday.'

'I'm going too,' said Cris happily.

'We don't know that,' said Reap. 'You still too young.'

'I'm fifteen, nearly. In France you can join the army at fifteen.'

'No, you can't,' said Malee, wagging her finger at him.

'In the days of the Foreign Legion you could. So why not now?'

'This is serious, Cris,' said Reap, switching to Khmer. 'At the last demonstration the police shot bullets. It was not funny.'

'Only rubber ones and only into the air.'

'And you heard what Ma said on the phone today. That raven came back this morning and sat on the house until she threw a stone at it.'

'The raven?' said Malee, the paradox and mockery leaving her face for a second. 'The raven is back?' She returned to English so Ryan would understand.

'But you don't believe that, and neither do I, huh!' said Cris, putting his arm around Malee's shoulder.

'No, no. Of course not,' said Malee.

'And neither does Ryan,' said the little Frenchman, in English.

'Time to go, boss,' said Chean.

Malee went with them to the door and half closed it behind her. Chean went ahead to the stairs. She looked Ryan in the eyes; he kissed her on the cheek, then quickly on the lips.

'Tonight at your place,' she said. 'It was … I never felt like that before.'

She took a deep breath and exhaled. Had something changed in her? It seemed to Ryan that she acted with conviction now, as if she was driving forward with a different strength. As if by assured action and by this alone the world would come to her, not her to it. In this single moment Ryan felt that power, and was at once drawn to it, but was also fearful of it.

'I will see you Sunday,' was her final declaration to him. 'Reap won't be able to stop Cris from coming. We can't leave him here on his own while we all go.'

'One in, all in,' he said.

'Leave them to their meal,' Chean mumbled when they were on the stairs. 'We stay they ask us to share. No good.' His look said, They need everything they have. 'I see much hungry before.'

They walked over to the tuk-tuk and Chean looked back at the building.

'They no choose live here,' he said, and he motioned his hand over the block that sat before them, those beyond, and to the whole world of the garment workers that was this quarter of the city. 'Me lucky, have tuk-tuk.'

His comment was not a celebration but was put neutrally and almost sorrowfully, tinged with an understanding that the injustice of the world was inherent in it, as if he had his tuk-tuk but because of that fact he was only promoting further injustice to a banal commonplace.

For his part Ryan was not speaking. He was sunk in himself, but not with thoughts of the certainties that seemed to have come over Malee. His introspection was something dark and full of doubt, as dank and claustrophobic as Malee's closet bedroom, as murky as the muddy waters of the river that lapped around the stilts of Pa's house in the province of Kampong Thom.

It turned out Janey wasn't able to get away from Sydney with the dramatic flourish she'd hoped for. There were certain clients who had told her so much of their life stories that they were on a hand-holding basis (which she knew she shouldn't do but she did because it felt right). Anyway, no other doctor wanted to see this bunch of loonies, and the patients would see no-one else either, so the mad enthusiasm of the moment had to be tempered by jamming all her regular crowd into the last three days of the week. Janey was leaving on Saturday night and arriving on Sunday, a few hours after the demonstration.

Even though the idea of his sister being there had given Ryan strength, the delay in her arrival gave him time to breathe. Things had changed too quickly in just three hours. When he saw her on Skype he had been ready to declare that he was out of his depth in Cambodia, a protected tourist playing games of pretend in unfamiliar structures. But Malee had come to his apartment to care for him and to give something of herself. But what he'd thought when he was riding home with Chean after visiting the garment workers' building was yet another thing again. Malee had wanted him to see the way she lived. For what purpose? Why had she made such a point of taking them in? Was it tactical, for sympathy alone? To show what he should be taking her away from – graining him into the mix of her family.

But with Malee it couldn't ever be that simple. There was some steel rod of irony that ran through her. It was as if she had an understanding of the world that said, 'Yep, this is the lowest of the low, all right. I don't deserve it but who deserves anything.' She *got* more of the world than any other person he had known. Malee could make acid jokes about her poverty, in a foreign language, and stay a step ahead of a native speaker. But she had such grit that she would never accept her low position. She could sleep on two inches of foam and then get up at seven for school, university and a job waiting tables. She would drive a truck right through the Buddhist acceptance of fate and come through to clear light on the other side. It was the same for the garment workers; unions had been unheard of in Cambodia even five years before – unthinkable. Paradigms were shifting and people were frightened and alive, startled even. If Reap had been born ten years earlier she would never have ventured further than the Kampong Thom marketplace.

So in this world they were all jockeying for position and the powerful people were intent on keeping their own place. If he didn't go to the demonstration to be with them then his positioning within this world became phoney. The visceral connection he felt for Malee would become a predatory thing; he would not be showing commitment to the family. He would become base – physical, not spiritual.

The Kratie girl would be so much easier, but he wasn't born for easy.

The demonstration was called for the same place at the same time: midday on Sunday – the only day off for garment workers. This time they all drove together in Chean's tuk-tuk – Malee and Reap on one side, Ryan opposite them with Cris who, as Malee predicted, had refused to be left behind.

'You go to stay with bong Chamroeun today,' Reap had said, but Cris had said that if they tried to drive off he would grab on to the back of the tuk-tuk and be dragged along in the dirt. And if they hit his fingers to shake him off he would run behind and embarrass them. He had seen demonstrations on TV in France, orderly groups of university types in city streets bearing placards for climate change action or occupying city squares to support some rebel computer hacker guru. That was what he knew of demonstrations and he wanted to see one for himself. Anyway, he was a member of the family now: he just had to go. If Chamroeun would not come that was his problem and fault.

The logic had been difficult to deny. Sure, the last time there had been trouble – rubber bullets. But that was as far as the Government would take it.

'It won't be like that again. We will be ok,' said Reap, her resolute chin stuck out. 'I know it.'

'This time the newspapers are supporting us,' said Malee, as if she was trying to talk herself into believing that it could help.

'The Opposition Leader has taken up the cause,' said Ryan, not sure whether this was good or bad either. One thing clear was that the stakes were raised this time; but still no-one dared mention the prospect of achieving the raise in pay. It was almost as if this was a game played without hope of actual victory, that to speak out and survive would be enough.

'You careful, boss,' said Chean as they jumped out, his face worried, then he withdrew to the shade tree and the other tuk-tuk drivers.

There was a huge crowd – many hundreds, more than a thousand. As they jumped out the same old woman at her little food stand grinned and gestured to her rice and her sauces. He sympathised with her, but he had no stomach for food so he just nodded and returned her sampeah. He was nervous. Police waited in a gang of about thirty blocking the other end of the street. There was a black 4WD vehicle with a megaphone speaker fixed to its roof; a guy with an important hat paced up and down in front of it. No fire trucks, no water cannon. Motorbikes and trucks were still arriving from all directions – chaos looming. He could see that it was not just garment workers now. A few unemployed graduates from the universities had joined them. Maybe this was developing into a broader community protest against the Government, against Hun Sen.

Again the crowd massed against the gabled gates and waited for the first truck to emerge, but nothing came. There was a change of tactics from the apparel company and the police. For twenty minutes the crowd surged against the gates and back again. The only thing he understood from the chanting was: one sixty, one sixty, one sixty – the poverty line dollar number that was the target. Then the vanguard at the front began to shake the gates and someone from the crowd appeared with bolt cutters and made to attack the chains that kept it all together.

Suddenly there was another sound above the already incredible din: the police megaphone on top of the huge 4WD number one police vehicle. There was an agitated man in khaki uniform and police hat with red trim and gold braid in it, shouting into a microphone – Ryan thought of the generals on the stage when Hun Sen was making his speech. He could almost be one of them. His voice was strained, high pitched. Beside him was a row of men in riot helmets holding rifles, behind them a bank of uniforms and Perspex shields.

The man yelled into his megaphone and the crowd shouted back. The sun was above and the heat was rising. The attention of the crowd was now turned away from the gates and onto the police. At the gates a welding set was produced and sparks began to fly. The man with the megaphone now began to scream at the crowd to disperse; the lines of police bristled. Then he drew a pistol from his pocket and fired it into the air. The crack of gunfire panicked some people in the crowd and they began surging into each other, but a young union guy with a megaphone started shouting and the crowd turned to the police and arms were pointed at them and the chanting began again. Then he wasn't sure, did someone throw a rock? He knew by instinct that was going too far and a shiver of fear went through him. More rocks came. People scrabbled among debris at the side of the road and everything that could be removed and thrown was heaved in the direction of the police.

And then it happened. The policeman in the braided hat stepped back, waving his troopers forward as he did so. The men took three steps forward in a line, raised their weapons and immediately began firing into the crowd. It was so sudden that people were in shock for a few seconds. Then people began falling, blood spurted from a woman's stomach. All around him people began screaming and running. He felt the slipstream of a bullet as it made a sound like *whing* as it passed his face. Next to him someone caught a bullet in the knee and went over on to the ground. Malee's eyes were wide in disbelief; Ryan grabbed her and started running. Reap screamed and grabbed for Cris. Ryan lifted his eyes and saw the tuk-tuk drivers starting up their engines, turning towards the city. Would Chean wait for them?

As he ran Ryan saw the old woman rice-seller, lying on the ground, her mouth wide open, her eyes still. A stray shot had come through the crowd and taken her in the throat.

Then as they neared the tuk-tuks Reap and Cris suddenly disappeared from their side. He turned and there was Reap dragging Cris. His legs were moving, trying to run, but not gripping the road. Ryan went back to help and Malee too. Cris had caught a bullet in the back as he was running and now he coughed and choked in his struggle. The three of them carried him in a ragged, panicked, crooked way to the tuk-tuks and there was Chean, fighting off a couple of people who would board his vehicle.

'Boss, quick.'

They bundled Cris into the tuk-tuk and jumped in after him. Then Chean said to the two strangers, 'Now you come,' and they jumped in too. Chean revved his engine hard and they drove away in the direction of the Russian hospital, hurtling past people running, falling by the side of the road in exhaustion, cowering behind trees and buildings.

'Hold his head,' Malee said to Ryan, 'one hand on his face, one here.' She motioned him to support Cris's chest. Reap shoved a hand under his chest and together they supported him while Malee tore the back off his shirt and then stripped off a section to staunch the wound. Cris looked up at Ryan for a second and cracked a half a smile then fainted. The couple they had picked up held themselves together and watched Malee in a kind of awe.

The noise of bullets behind them had stopped. The soldiers had achieved their purpose; the demonstration was dispersed and a lesson of some proportion had been given. Looking back Ryan could see people on the ground, perhaps six or seven of them, motionless. Others were staggering to their feet, then falling, friends and relatives next to them, crying. He turned his face in the direction of the hospital. They passed more people, still running, some crying as they went. Then they were in the clear, ahead of the pack.

He thought of Janey, coming that night. He watched Malee, not calm, but functioning. The couple watched Malee closely and whispered to each other. He saw their admiration, and felt it too, but somehow, in that moment, he did not know her. In the surreality of the action – a tuk-tuk making urgent time along a dusty road in a foreign country, the sound of gunfire echoing in his ears, still blinded by the glint of sunlight off the Perspex shields of riot police – he wondered just how he had got to where he was that day.

Malee felt for Cris's pulse and then she convulsed with her head on his shoulder in a great sigh of relief. Ryan saw it, but he was not there. He was somehow separate from the action, viewing it from the aspect of a cloud, as if he was a raven on a roof.

That bullet had missed him by an inch.

Part Three

He was in a state of shock.

He had read about a demonstration by the opposition in 1997, when pairs of guys on motorbikes had ridden past and lobbed grenades into the crowd – twenty people killed. The bikes had then driven straight into a hundred-strong rank of Hun Sen's own praetorian guard, which had mysteriously turned up to watch this opposition demo and had then parted to let the bikes through in much the same way as the Red Sea had opened up for Moses. Since then newspaper proprietors had been shot dead in the street, sure. But he'd always thought of that as the old days, ten years back at least.

The scene was different now: not so much the battle for political supremacy between factions, this was about profits and kickbacks for an established elite. But as much as profit, he could see that it was about social order. It was unthinkable, even ten years before, for a thousand Cambodians to parade themselves in the street in disobedience of their superiors: social, economic, political – call them any kind of superior you liked and they were it. The Prime Minister was probably genuinely shocked. Sure, everyone adjusted their position in life according to what their karma allowed – he had certainly done so. But in Hun Sen's eyes this would have been a disgraceful display, and also one that threatened Cambodia's forward economic march.

Ryan's mouth was arid and his temples ached. Cris had seemed some kind of glue that kept him, Malee and Reap together – that brought him, Ryan, deeper into the family.

'Jesus,' he said to himself and wiped sweat from his brow with the sleeve of his shirt. He went to the bar fridge in his apartment and took a bottle of water and drank a mouthful. He'd not had a drink of any type for five hours. He had been prickled in the hospital; when the doctor emerged to talk about Cris, the women had taken over and he had been waved away. Malee had almost forgotten he was there. She turned around to him at the last moment.

'Oh,' she'd said distractedly. 'I'll see you later.' And then she'd turned away with Reap and the woman in the white coat and stethoscope – as if he had been family when Cris was there, but now his usefulness had evaporated into an invisible mist. He and Chean had no course to take but to walk away into the car park. Chean started up his engine and said seriously, 'Home boss.'

He sat and stared at the blank dark TV screen.

He remembered Malee's text: *Do you speak French?*

He heard a motorbike engine and the tuk-tuk tyres swinging around in the street and he stood to look out the window. Chean was completing a U-turn outside and drew his vehicle up as if for an appointment. It took a moment for the message to knock on Ryan's head.

'Janey. Oh Jesus.' He said his sister's favourite exclamation out loud. Janey was due at the airport in thirty minutes. He rushed around the apartment thinking panicked thoughts.

Just at the moment that he was patting his pockets to check that all was in place, his phone rang. He thought, could it be her already? Was the plane early, or had he and Chean got the time wrong? He looked at the phone. It was Mr Dith – the kind of phone call that he should have just let go by. But he had a broad streak of duty and responsibility in him – curiosity too.

'Hullo.'

'Mr Davey. It is Mr Dith speaking.'

'Yes. Yes. I know. I mean, I saw.'

'Mr Davey, have you seen the television news this evening?'

'No, no. What? The news?'

'Yes, the news. There was a lengthy item about the demonstration today.'

'There was? Oh, but of course, there would be.' Ryan still couldn't see the point of the call.

'Mr Davey, there was much visual coverage. You were there. There was a film of you arriving with the student Malee of whom we have spoken previously. As a Westerner you are a curiosity and would be a source of interest to news cameramen.'

'Ah, I see. Yes, I did notice that I was being noticed.' He began to see it now.

'You were not to come closer to this student. And I have already received two phone calls from people who have recognised you. The story will spread very quickly and the owners of the college are certain to find out about this. When I hear from them I will be able to announce to them that I have already terminated your services. I will go to your desk tomorrow morning and remove your personal items and place them in my office. I will make an arrangement with you to collect them from me at a later date.'

'You're giving me the sack.'

'I am terminating your services immediately. I am very sorry. Goodbye, Mr Davey.' And the phone went dead without another word.

'Jesus, you look like what the cat dragged in but decided was too unwholesome to chew on.'

'Ta.'

The look on his face didn't go away so she slung her carry-on bag down and looked at him closely, 'My God, I think I'm glad I'm here.'

'I think I agree with you.' They gave each other a little squeeze and shoulder pat.

'It occurred to me that whatever was the matter might have blown over by now and I would be hanging around getting in the way.'

'Hmmm, I'd always be able to find a problem for you to solve, if I thought about it.'

Then words came tumbling out of his mouth as if he had to tell the stories all at once. What Janey heard was that Malee was a big mistake, that they were only after him for his money and that Pa was some malevolent *éminence grise* of the family who manipulated them all for his own benefit. That Reap was working like something out of Dickens, that Malee was the great hope and that he was a part of Pa's plan to advance the family. He even made it sound like they had forced him to get attached to the boy Cris and then they'd shot him just to make life awkward.

Janey felt for his pulse and told him to shut up and he did. She looked into his eyes and felt his forehead.

'Just checking for shock but I think you'll live. Did they look at you in the hospital?'

'They don't do things like that here. Everyone's in shock in this place, every day of their lives.'

'I'll wait to be my own judge of that.'

They walked out past the alleyway of phone and merchandise stalls and through the waiting crowd and into the carpark. Ryan was wheeling Janey's bag and she had her arm in his and it wasn't clear who was guiding whom. Chean straightened up as soon as he saw them coming.

'You ok, boss?' he said to Ryan, then, 'I take, I take,' and grabbed the big bag and swung it up into the seat behind the driver.

'What is this, you have your own driver?'

Chean turned to Janey and placed his hands together in sampeah and raised them as high as his forehead.

'Chean is my friend. And we drive around together too.'

'I met Mr Ryan on this spot – on this very place. Two month ago. He told me that the sky was very low that day. No-one ever talk to me about the sky before. Hotels, Angkor Wat, garment strike, yes – never sky.'

'Oh, I see. I am very pleased to meet you, Chean.' And she made a sampeah too, as the moment seemed to require.

'You never sampeahed me that high, Chean,' said Ryan.

'I see straight away, your sister great lady.' Chean spoke from his deep sense of agreeableness, wishing as Cambodians did to overlay every situation with the congeniality that would get them through each day. But also this time he spoke from an appreciation of something he could see in Ryan's sister – the kind of first impression that counts.

'This is the most charming man,' said Janey, as she took her seat and Chean gunned the motor. 'Why aren't you more like that?'

'The insights into your character that Chean expressed are so obvious to me that they barely merit the expenditure of breath,' said Ryan as they pulled out into the highway.

'Hmmm,' said Janey, 'you're more like yourself every minute.'

Immediately they were in the shoving jostling traffic – petrol fumes, honking horns, proprietorial 4WDs gliding through, scattering before them the rattling clapped-out motorbike engines that were the true pulse of Phnom Penh, moving across each other at speed, blaring, warning, all with an incomprehensible sense of purpose that was so urgent it seemed more like an abiding role-play than something that could ever be real. Janey gripped the side rail of the tuk-tuk hard with one hand, held Ryan's arm with the other, and jammed both feet up against her luggage to steady herself.

'Jesus, I can see why everyone is in a permanent state of shock here.'

Ryan almost felt for his own pulse then to see if he was running fast, and at that moment it occurred to him that he needed to get away from the city; that, in wanting to become close to this place, he had come too close too quickly and it was time for distance. Janey's visit was not quite that of a guiding angel, but something he could use to steer himself in another direction. He realised in a switched-on second that he had always needed someone else to help him make his moves. Tom took him to Kratie and the river girl. And Cambodia itself? It was Amanda; it was all about Amanda and Dermott. But whether he was using Janey, or just making a decision for himself, he needed some space to think in.

'Tomorrow we're going to Kep,' he said. 'To the beach. The French built summer houses there.'

'I don't blame them,' she said, fanning herself. 'I place myself in your capable hands.'

Capable? he thought. He could hardly be certain of that.

The next morning Ryan woke drowsy from the temazepam Janey gave him that she had brought for sleeping on the plane.

They had gone to his apartment and Chean helped them with Janey's bags and made the sampeah once more and left. They talked. The apartment was better than Janey had expected. She complained about Ryan sleeping on the couch while she got the only bed. He said he'd washed the sheets specially and if she didn't use them what was the point of all his good work, so they put her things in the bedroom.

Janey couldn't slow herself down so they walked to the Quay and absorbed the buzz of the night time city. She bought a trinket from small girls peddling wristbands and a photocopied guide book from a dwarf in a wheelchair.

'Now this is what I call a souvenir. They really photocopy these things?'

'Cost you five dollars, but they still make a profit out of that.'

Tourists of all ages and stations jostled along the narrow footpath, felt their way over loose bricks, dodged around racks of sport shirts and every now and then a trio of scampering urchins swarmed past. There were travel agents, massage parlours, cafés and bars with tables and chairs obtruding passers-by; it was like some snakes and ladders game – paradise to pitfall in any second.

They chose a place and ordered beef lok lak. While they waited

Janey could not keep her eyes from the street and its constant teeming parade.

'Is all of it so … charmingly chaotic?'

'Pretty much.' Cambodia and chaos: sure, but the craziness was like a clown's suit on a wise old man; there was a less apparent order beneath – everyone hustling but still knowing their place, their limits in karma. 'We'll have time for the FCC after.'

'FCC? Sounds like a blood disorder.'

'It will be if you keep drinking like you are. It's the Foreign Correspondents' Club.'

Janey raised her eyebrows. 'Sounds important.'

'The journos moved on a couple of decades ago, but it's a big spot for expats and tourists – a view of the river, the confluence of the Tonle Sap and the Mekong.'

'We're going.'

'You ever get lost in Phnom Penh, just wave down a tuk-tuk and all you have to say is 'FCC' and you'll be safe. Every single driver will know it.'

'I get the impression safe is a commodity worth having here.'

'The place looks frayed, but it's really rare that a tourist gets bopped without doing something to really seriously deserve it.'

'Nice to know. But how safe are you, little brother? In here.' And she pointed at her chest to where a heart would be.

'Oh, that.'

'Yes, oh that. The most important thing there is in the world. That.'

'Emotional safety, it doesn't exist, you know that.' He leaned forward in his seat. 'You know, the first day I met this Pa guy he told her to get me to take her shopping. And I did it! You know, up goes the curtain, out comes the actor, reads from the script!'

'But Ryan, as I see it, you will never be the proverbial penny in the slot machine. Isn't that why you clashed with Amanda? Maybe there was a part of you that actually wanted to take her shopping. Huh?'

'She did look pretty nice.'

'Ok, so tell me something that's more important than a girl looking nice, I mean in the history of the whole wide wonderful world.' He stroked his chin in mock thoughtfulness so she went on. 'Anyway, how much did you spend on her?'

'Twenty bucks, well, fifteen. I know that doesn't sound like much but it is over here. And it's the principle.' Janey gave him a raised-eyebrow look. 'Then the same night her brother comes at me with a mate and a couple of fence palings. Jesus.'

'Your sudden and unexpected appearance may have provoked some family disagreement. What is this Pa fellow like?'

'Not that unexpected is my guess. You should have seen the look on his face when I pulled out a wad of bills at the Pizza Company – Christmas, New Year and Happy Birthday all at once. People that know this place say that once you start with the money train you never stop and it just gets bigger and bigger until you are paying for fancy weddings for all of them and a Land Rover for Pa.' He was exaggerating but he knew that Janey knew he was so he was able to run away with himself.

'All right, all right, I get the picture. Just how many siblings does this girl have?'

'Nine.'

'Fucking hell!' To say that Janey took a long tug on her South African sauvignon blanc would be correct, except it was also true that she had done little but that since she sat down. She signaled for another.

'Three of them are pretty much settled, so that leaves only six to go. Seven counting her …'

'Whose wife-ness is at issue because she will not return to the village. Interesting.'

After dinner they walked out into the street. They stopped outside a travel place, still selling bus tickets at eleven o'clock.

'Well, let's get this ticket to Kep. I want to see these French villas. But I want to see this girl of yours too. I want to see her with my own eyes. Only then will I know. For God's sake, I can't trust every word of what you're saying tonight. Tomorrow she may seem a different prospect completely.'

He looked at her queerly. 'I don't know,' he mumbled.

'Exactly. Now where is this Foreign Correspondents' Club? I've only had three drinks and I have a terrible feeling that that will not prove to be enough to get me off to sleep after this exciting day.'

'There,' he said, pointing up to a first-floor balcony, where complacent florid faces chatted and drank, framed by stately arches that gave out to the river view.

'Jesus,' she said, 'this city is full of surprises.'

'You don't know the half of it,' he said, and led the way upstairs.

On the bus they saw a Korean action movie, with two super-hero girls fighting giant spiders and anacondas, escaping falling nets, rushing down waterfalls on perilous rubber rafts and occasionally slicing through a dozen or so soldiers in samurai sword fights. Then, if that wasn't comic relief enough, on came the perpetually warring couple he had seen on the Kratie bus. Their comedy routine was like an old friend and he cheered, then eased happily back in his seat. Some Khmers turned around and smiled, pleased as they were with his familiarity and appreciation of their culture.

'Check these guys. They're good,' he said to his sister, all wise and knowing, pressing his insider credentials.

'How much do they remind you of Mum and Dad in the old days,' Janey said after a minute, 'before she gave up?'

'A bit,' he said. 'But with these guys you know no harm is going to come to anyone.'

'Do you think he harmed her?'

'He ran her life. She was an ornament. On display.' He looked at her. 'She gave up acting to be the wife of the President of the local Rotary and the Anglican Layman of the Year.' The layman of the year bit was made up but Janey knew what he meant.

'Are you sure we weren't part of that decision.'

He crossed his arms and looked again at the comedians on the screen.

'You mean the whole baby thing?' He kept forgetting that you had the power to change someone's life like that, without even being born. The thought of babies suddenly was oddly redeeming; it suggested an application to duty and a freedom from choice. It associated in his mind with the perverse freedom of arranged marriages. It was also the kind of liberation from the burdens of individualism that the Khmer family had – no need to decide what to do with your pay packet each week.

The bus dropped them in a seaside town square at the foot of a hill which was the backbone of the little peninsula that Kep yawned around. A row of cafés and hotels stretched around the open space and Janey was already making eyes at the dress shops with their goods spilling out on hangers. To see the sea and sand from the bus, after months in Phnom Penh, was so alien that he could not take his eyes from it, like returning to childhood and simplicity. Rich magenta bougainvillea leant out of huge cement planters. The human machine ran at one quarter the pace.

He had made an error with the booking. Instead of two single rooms he had somehow made it one twin room.

'Lucky it wasn't a double is all I can say,' said Janey.

'We can change to separate rooms, no problem,' said the man at the desk.

'Nah,' she said, looking at Ryan, 'It'll be like old times.' She leaned forward in a conspiratorial whisper to the man, 'He's my baby brother.'

They went away with their parents from time to time when they were children, to resorts on the northern coast of New South Wales. They had liked to have twin rooms. They could listen to the sea outside their windows, moaning and restless. It was like no other sound. At home they were close to the ocean and could go to the beach any day they wanted and crash right into the waves, but this was different. At night and with you tucked up in bed the sea became something mysterious and endless. On their holidays they would talk and compete to see who could stay awake the longest. Janey usually won, partly because she was older, but also because she was highly strung, could never settle. Ryan was the one who allowed himself to be swallowed in the quiet tidal roar.

'I give you key to room opposite as well,' said the man on the desk, delighted. 'If too much like old time you can change and pay me in the morning.' They all laughed at his little joke and the man was pleased. They were all pleased.

They dropped their bags and decided to stretch out for a walk on the beach before it rained. Clouds were beginning to build; it was four o'clock in the afternoon.

'One never knows what people really want,' said Janey. 'What does Chean want? It might serve you well to stop and ask yourself that for a minute. What does he really want beside the obvious entity of the next fare?'

'Chean has a wife and two little kids – girls. He works so they can go to school and don't have to sell bracelets in the street. He is fifty-three years old and his kids are twelve and ten. He has big reasons to keep on going. He was thirteen in the Pol Pot time.'

'That's what they call it?'

'Sometimes they just say "in the Pol Pot"; it's become like some abstract idea now. Pol Pot is a person but also a thing. Most people talk about those times in a matter-of-fact way like it's something that just happened to everyone, but Chean never says a word – gives some vague answer or just clams up completely. I think school stopped for him at age eleven. Now he's a tuk-tuk driver and he can't read a map and has trouble with street signs. You know, in just a few years away from education you forget so much and he hasn't been anywhere near a school in forty years. But he knows about guns, broken bones, how to dress a wound, how to fix a motor bike engine, even a bit about being a farmer – how to plant rice anyway, about the seasons, the rains, markets for different produce. He can tell you the best way to wring a chicken's neck.'

'Great.'

'He was in the army after the Vietnamese came, fighting the Khmer Rouge until he was thirty. He must have been good at it, because all he will say is that they wouldn't let him leave. So, now he probably just wants to get home safe and see his girls and put some food on the table. In the West he'd probably be borrowing money to get a second and third tuk-tuk and building up a fleet. Here he considers himself lucky to be putting along on one.'

'He has an extra space for you, in his heart.'

Ryan thought for a few seconds before he answered. 'I guess I'm about the age a son of his would be if he'd had one at the regular time of life a man might have a son here.'

'Connections,' Janey said wistfully. 'The family we wished we had.' Perhaps she was thinking about Joel and the family of her own that she didn't have. It is easy enough for us to conceive of idealised versions of things we don't have, and Janey would probably do that and keep it held within her silent grief place.

'Either you're thinking about how much I could be better at everything, or more likely about babies. It's not too late for you, Jane.' When he called her by her real name, not 'sis' or 'Janey' and certainly not 'Bubbalinks', the point was being made that this was a truly serious topic of conversation. She was not just his sister here either, she was being addressed as a public person whose decisions would have a ripple effect on everyone around her, including him.

'I think I'm fated to be the eternal auntie. It's a safer journey than the other. And as for babies I see enough of the little mites five days a week.'

'You don't think your own would be any different from the rest?'

'You have to have a partner and what are the chances of me keeping one? I'm too nutty for most of them, which leaves you as the designated breeder.'

'Joel understood you.'

'But this brings me in a roundabout way to another important matter. The coming wedding that was the closest thing to incest without being that …' By changing the subject away from herself, Ryan could see it was something Janey had already thought about too much, so profoundly that she could not talk about it. He stared at the sand in front of them. The word 'wedding' was so loaded and serious … he was thirty and Janey was thirty six; their mum would like grandkids. Just how much of your life should you have to live for others? He had stayed silent, so Janey went on.

'It's all off.'

'Off!' He awoke as from a dream. 'What's off?'

'This wedding.' The news electrified him out of melancholy. The world lurched forward, tilting on its axis; somewhere a black hole closed over and with it an odd sense of balance was restored. 'Yes. Off.'

'You mean she saw through him? At last? Or did she catch him? Catch him at it?'

'As her attraction began to wane, she also caught him, what you would say red-handed.'

'Ha ha ha,' Ryan made a parody of knee-slapping hilarity.

'Almost literally red-handed except that wouldn't be the part of the body in question.'

'My God, that conjures images I only want to steer around. But, Janey, she's known him for seven years. What possessed her, in the first place …?'

She looked at him sideways. 'What possessed her? Probably you, in the first place.' He was silent again, so she went on. 'You don't think you could ever be a little, um, what shall we say, frustrating for a girl? Disappearing into a bean bag with books of poetry for days on end!' Is this what she had come all the way to Cambodia to tell him?

'You mean I should be the hundred pounds of clay, to be moulded into shape by a woman with sound social ideas.'

'More like two hundred. I mean because you're always thinking like that and, what's worse, saying things like that. Amanda is not a bad girl. Yes, there may be some small cultural differences between the two of you, she would clutch at things too hard then not know how to sit them up straight when they fell, but she would find excuses to visit you, wouldn't she ...'

'Yep, like coming to tell me she was going to marry my brother ...'

'Yes, *you see*, like that. She could have sent you a text ...'

'That's what I asked for ...'

'Oh, Jeeesus.' Janey pretended a scream and held her hands up beseechingly before her, but no God or Buddha appeared from the clouds to show her brother the way to be with girls. 'Remember that the girl has a soft spot for you, at least, and probably a very warm one as well. Did you ever consider that the marriage thing with Dermott may have been an attempt to attract your attention?'

'It worked on that level.'

'She may have been consciously telling herself that Dermott was better for her, but adding up sums and coming up with a relationship doesn't work for most people. Some yes, her no. She's not practical at heart; she loves you, which is the living proof of that fact.'

Ryan was thinking but not speaking.

'Do you think her move to Real Estate was concocted purely from her love of standing around in draughty houses for days, telling half-truths to all that would enter and then following that up with endless hours of tedious paperwork.' Still Ryan said nothing. 'Do you think she may have wanted someone to chase her? Unfortunately the other brother did so.'

They walked back up to the Hotel de la Plage. He had a large beer and as she was on holiday she had a little red margarita, and then another.

'Lastly, I must tell you that your father has been on the verge of plunging over the cliff for three weeks. You picked an interesting time to make your exit. We have two minor crises and you're in both of them.'

'Have you come to bring me back?'

'I came to get away, just like I said. And to tell you things, in person – that much is true. To be honest your quandary here made a very nice excuse for me. Ma said, Go. If he dies, he dies. You know, you want it to end, but you don't want it to end. But I think she is also praying that it will be soon.'

'Ma said that? If he dies, he dies?'

'Your departure has had a greater impact than you might think. It never occurred to anyone that they could actually do what they want in life. Or say what they really think. You may have promoted that "life's too short to …" mentality. You know what I mean?'

'Yeah, but …' How could he explain it? The Western idea that life is too short to not engage all your wants and fantasies just had no currency in this country. He thought of Cris slumped in his arms in the tuk-tuk, Malee taking his pulse, looking up every five seconds, willing the Russian Hospital to appear; all that family had their obligations, but he could go anywhere in the world that he wanted. If he stayed would he be just a provider, or a real part of it? He remembered the crazy Western goon on his pushbike outside the Pizza Company. 'You'll never be one of them.' From the mouths of fools comes truth. Cris was in the hospital and Malee was with Cris. He felt a surge of anger, and of foolishness. To bring his sister to Kep was a fine thing, but there was a sudden emptiness that he would never share this kind of thing with Malee. It would be her family, always.

'But there's more to it than that,' he said at last.

'Indeed, baby brother. Just when do you jump off the cliff? When do you take the wheel and when do you sit in the passenger's seat?'

'If you jump in the hot seat too often you're going to get burnt.'

'Then again, a hot seat may be better than a fucking cold one.'

They raised glasses and drank to that, then signalled for two more.

They drank some more and ate fish amok. The rain came in a sharp burst, then the clouds lifted away; late sunrays dwindled and at last the sea grew dark. Ryan was glad the day was done and he saw the tired look in his sister too. They planned a trip to the pepper farms the next day to give their time in Kep some shape and reason.

Ryan laid down on his bed and listened to the sound of the sea that was maybe a hundred metres away, but whose arriving waves were so insistent that they could have been breaking against the wall beneath his window. It was ten o'clock. Boys kicking bags of sand to each other in the square had gone home and the place was quietening. A group of diners shuffled softly in the street, returning early to their hotel places – occasionally a voice; the idea of a late night bar was a distant and disturbing thing, and the tight black outfits of Phnom Penh bargirls like a nightmare down here.

Ryan heard the street die, listened to his sister brushing her teeth in the bathroom. It was the sound of childhood and he brought the blanket up under his chin as he had on cold nights when he was a boy. Then he closed his eyes and turned to the wall while Janey settled herself down. He wondered what Malee was doing now. Was she with Cris, as he recovered in the hospital? Ryan had told himself he should be with his sister, but if that was true and his loyalties really lay with his family, why had he come to Cambodia in the first place?

But Janey *was* his family. She was all he had; and Colin, if you counted reprobates who cared. And he was not in such a position that he could afford to say no to anyone who cared.

He felt a swift downward spiral of loneliness. He turned over in bed and tried to settle facing the other way. In a minute he turned back to the wall. He listened to the waves but they did not take him away with them now. It was not northern New South Wales and he was no longer a child.

Then from somewhere came a distant whining sound that at first he thought was a mosquito in the room, until he placed it outside the hotel, in the distance, on the street – a sound that grew and heightened in pitch as it came closer. It was a small motorbike, of the kind that Reap rode to the garment factory every morning. The sound spluttered and then abruptly stopped as the bike pulled up outside the hotel. A rush of thoughts and feelings about Malee came over him: Khmer girls on motorbikes, fragility and toughness juxtaposed. It couldn't really be. Then there was silence for what seemed a long time – too long to be anything. He sat up in bed, ears straining for sound. Was it a conversation in the lobby downstairs? Were there voices raised? A disagreement? Pleading?

Then, distinctly, there was a foot on the stair: a quiet foot, so light as to be barely audible, taking steps one at a time, but at a pace – running almost. His mind returned to Kratie, another time he had heard a girl's foot upon the stair from his hotel room; then it had filled him with confusion and fear. But now it was different. He swung out of bed and pulled his trousers on. He heard Janey sit up. Then there was a knock on a door. It was not their door, but very nearby. He quietly turned the handle of his own door and stepped half out into the passageway. As he did a girl looked up from outside the next room. She was knocking on its door. It was dimly lit but there was no doubt.

'Malee,' said Ryan.

'Och!' she cried out, and he rushed up to her.

'I couldn't see the numbers. They are so small and it is so dark. The man didn't want to let me up, but I made him.' He held her in his arms. He felt her shoulder blades through the thin wet shirt. She was trembling. She crushed her head into his chest and squeezed her eyes shut.

'Here,' said Ryan. He dried some tears from her face with the bottom of his T-shirt.

'I only ever cried once before,' she said, in amazement at herself, 'and that was yesterday. It seems like two weeks ago. I had to come. I couldn't stop ...'

The door of their room was swung open again. Janey emerged. 'Oh, my dear,' she said softly. 'Let me look at you.'

Janey advanced down the passageway, shown the way by the spectral light from her phone.

'My God,' she said, when she had come close enough. 'You are the most beautiful girl I have ever seen.' Looking at the helmet in her hand, 'You came all this way on your motorbike?'

'Uh huh,' Malee managed, wiping her nose on her shirt.

'In the rain? With all those trucks and buses?'

'You just have to make sure you miss them.'

'Now that is what you would certainly call logical. I am taking the key to the other room,' she said to Ryan, and went inside, returning in less than twenty seconds with her bag and toiletries.

As she crossed the corridor and tried the key and opened up, the last words she had to say were, 'Push the beds together.'

When they were alone Ryan said to Malee, 'How did you find us?'

She raised her eyebrows, 'You said Kep Beach and there are only five hotels along this part; the bottom two were scungy and the top two were expensive.' There was a small shrug of the shoulders that said, Simple really.

He stood back to look at her. Not five feet tall, maybe forty five kilos, maybe not.

'If you hadn't found us what would you have done?'

'Probably sleep on the beach.' Why hadn't he thought of that? 'I brought some plastic for shelter just in case.'

'You don't have any money?'

She pulled out some notes and made a show of counting them, 'After petrol, two thousand five hundred riel.' About sixty five cents.

'Enough to rent a nice pile of sand for the night.' They fell into nervous banter, standing there in the corridor, on the edge of something else as they were, both too edgy to pass through the door of the hotel room to everything that lay beyond.

'Couple of geckos for company.'

'You have to watch those geckos; they'll mop up the last of your beer if you turn your back.'

'Yeah,' she said, 'I knew a couple of those girls pretty well once upon a time.'

'You the party animal.'

She leant in to him, whispering, 'I'm not sure what that is, but let's not worry about it now.'

'Time to go inside?'

'You could help me get out of these wet things.'

They closed the door behind them and she put her arms around his waist and they held each other for a minute. He kissed her but it was a long way to bend down there so he picked her up and held her in his arms. She was light to hold and she clung to him close, her knees clapped around his waist. They kissed for two minutes: mouth, cheeks, ears, neck and then mouths again.

She spoke first. 'You will have to let me down sometime or else hold me up all night.'

He laid her on the single bed he had left seven minutes before as a lonely vexed and worried single man. He drew the sheet across them as he got in. He had no shoes and she had slipped her thongs off as soon as he picked her up. They held each other close.

'You had your phone off, naughty boy.'

'I … I was trying to work out what I really felt.'

'I missed you. I love you, I think. But isn't love supposed to be like in Korean pop songs? Where they stand beside a waterfall and they are dressed in pink and yellow silk and look into each other's eyes and sing.'

He knew she didn't think that. 'I won't sing for you,' he said.

'Why don't you just do what you did before?'

She did not need to explain what she meant by 'before.' It had been on his mind for a week.

'But you're in these wet things.'

He picked up a towel that was on a chair next to the bed. He opened her shirt. She was still wet from the highway. His drying sweeps with the towel lingered on her breasts and then remained there, stroking her until the towel dropped and then she was undressing him while his lips went over her breasts. The world was silent except for the waves that rolled beneath the window; perhaps they were the waterfall backdrop of this Korean pop song. She closed her eyes and began to moan softly. He ran his warm hands along her back as he licked and kissed her. Her eyes were closed but when he kissed her mouth again he could see small tears in the corner of them. He unbuckled the top button of her jeans and she helped him slide them off. He ran his hand across her buttocks and then between her legs. She gasped, her voice high, her breath quick.

'Malee, darling.' He kissed her again. 'You are a virgin?'

'Yes,' she gasped again, 'Now!'

'What about babies?' He was gasping for breath himself.

'I don't care about anything.'

And at that moment he too cared about nothing in the world except her and him and being together; not one thought for anything else or for any other person. She held him in her little fingers and guided him to her and he entered her and broke her. He stroked her soft and slow. Her mouth was open and her moaning rose in pitch until it became quite breathless and she gave a little scream that was suppressed as she bit her own hand to hold down the noise and tears came from her eyes. He could hold himself no longer and with two hard strokes he came with her, and within one minute of beginning they had both finished. They lay each in the other's arms for some time, not sleeping, dreaming their thoughts, not different but to-gether.

Malee and Reap had been in with the doctor a long time.

'They have to save this boy, don't they,' said Colin, shaking his head. 'This will be cataclysmic news in the village – a boy shot in a garment worker demo. Out there they won't know what a strike is.' He turned to Ryan. 'A lot of people in the city don't.'

'Do you reckon they would have told them about the demo? I mean, their Ma and Pa.'

'Not likely. It would scare the shit out of them if they thought their kids were throwing rocks at the coppers. Ha,' Colin threw his head back and snort-laughed at the improbability of it, 'these people had a thousand years of being told that if they did the right thing by the rich man they'd have a better life next time, then the Khmer Rouge smacking people on the head with a shovel if they spoke out of turn. Nah, it would freak them out if they knew. Your Malee's a pretty adroit operator from what I can gather. No point in telling the old ones.'

Ryan had never thought of it that way. Malee would never tell a lie, he was sure of that, but perhaps a small omission here and there to make things move smoothly.

When Colin had sent Ryan a message to see what he was up to and Ryan had replied that he was in the Russian Hospital, Colin had gone straight down there. 'I want to meet this girl of yours too,' he had finished. At least he's honest about it, thought Ryan. Colin sent him a text each week, asking if he was ok, but he had not seen him since the Heart of Darkness night.

'With Meach and Kim gone, everyone was jostling to be the ones that brought him up.' Ryan brought the conversation back to Cris. With only one leg in the family, Ryan could still speak of them with the kind of critical eye that can be born from a state of partial exclusion; he still didn't quite get them.

'There's merit to be earnt there for future lives, as long as you don't want it too much. Let's have a look at you.' Colin examined his head for bruises. 'You're a quick healer.'

'You heard about that.'

'I have sources.' Tom, thought Ryan. But Colin went on.

'Big brother probably didn't really want to bring the boy up, but he wanted it to look like he did. Now that he's had a piece of you, he doesn't have to worry. He's evened up the score and he can let the girls have the kid, no probs. He's shown that he cared.'

'By beating me up.'

'Yep.'

'His face is good now.'

'Yep. Good as yours, ie a bit battered but not that ugly.'

'Jesus.' The idea of the family now seemed to him like a claw around the throat – just for a moment. But then his own brother had done nothing but trip him up as long as he'd been alive. 'But a family is just an idea; you *can* be free of it,' he said, looking down at the worn-out linoleum tiles.

'It's more than an idea around here. Your family *is* your safety. No social security safety net around this place. No family …' Colin seemed a little exasperated, 'they don't even have a word in the language for being alone. Even if your family are all dead you end up in someone's family.' Ryan though of Tommy, at the Pizza Company lunch. He seemed not to have all his wits, but now he thought he got it. Pa was taking care of him. Tommy had been adopted and everyone just accepted that.

'They've been in there a long time,' said Colin.

'Something's up,' said Ryan.

'Or down.'

That morning in Kep they had filled Malee's petrol tank and she zoomed away like a girl who had made a right decision and had grown during the night. She had never acted so impulsively before and now she had slept with a man for the first time in her life. It had worked out, or so it seemed. He offered her more money and she refused.

'I'll make it there,' she said. 'If there's a problem I'll call.'

In the morning she had curled into him like a wanderer returned home. Her eagerness had startled him. Where had it come from? Her reserve had been swept away, perhaps by the spray of trucks and cars along the road from PP to Kep. And her alacrity had become his. What else could you do with a girl who had ridden three hours in the rain? All the resolutions he had been promising himself about staying away and taking his time seemed like sterile chatter in the face of the profundity of the earth itself, the stumbling of a self-defensive fool. He watched her ride along the seafront road, in the direction of Kep City, out to the dangerous highway. To Ryan it was as if the most vulnerable part of him had gone out there, a girl on a bike against trucks and speeding buses, creeping hay-carts, other motorbikes and cars buzzing between it all. He wanted to keep her in Kep, but he could not: she had missed her first ever lecture and to stay would mean doing the same again in the afternoon.

He and Janey had walked around the town and decided they'd seen it all. 'Besides, that girl of yours is the most interesting thing I've seen in Cambodia so far.' Ryan had not had to say a word at breakfast; it was a two-way chatter between Janey and Malee. They went straight in to a bus ticket shop.

He stared at the rubbery plastic tiles of the hospital waiting room floor. They must have been laid in the early sixties, during a brief boom period: pop music, night clubs, Modernist architecture, and the latest thing in rubber tiles. It had been a time when the innocence of the people was wrapped around inevitable official corruption, which had grown and festered into Lon Nol and then the savage reaction of Pol Pot.

Innocence. It remained there still in many places. Malee had given him her virginity. In this country, with a girl of Malee's type, it was the gift of a life: I have decided – it is you. To abscond from that would be reprehensible, yet it would still be so easy to walk away.

He could be on a plane tomorrow, to any part of the world – this afternoon, really. He could walk out of that waiting room, catch a tuk-tuk to his apartment and pack up his scant belongings in ten minutes.

Half of him wished that she was pregnant; that would mean the time for decision was past and he would go with her. If she was not, he could decide to spend his life in East Sydney, or Cambodia without her, or somewhere else. Or he could marry her and take her with him.

There had been a night of love, but that had happened to him before and the feelings had dissolved into a residue of sadness and delusion. And what had it really meant for her, for Malee? How natural was a family anyway? Before the role of seed in reproduction was known about, children were raised by the village and named after the earth mothers who bore them …

But before he could gather his thoughts any further, there was a shuffling of feet on the corridor tiles and Malee and Reap were there, with the doctor. They were solemn.

The doctor held her hand out to Janey in a Western shake. 'We did everything we could. Any hospital in the world …'

'He is not with us,' said Malee, with a lift at the end of her line that had a question in it.

Colin withdrew from the group and sat down on the hard plastic seats. 'Shit,' Ryan heard him say softly, to himself. No-one cried. Reap sniffed. They had all known how strong the chance was that Cris would leave to join the spirit world.

'The government,' Malee's eyes were narrowed and the words were steely. In Cambodia the custom was to channel grief into ritual – chanting and incense, monks and achars. The expression of anger was allowed only to the wealthy. If you were poor, anger had to remain bottled and capped, and it stayed that way until it sometimes exploded.

The doctor raised her hands in respectful sampeah to the group. She nodded to each of them, then turned and returned to her endless work, her sandals flapping softly away.

The next day there didn't seem much left for him to do but to walk over to the school to collect his things from Mr Dith. Chean was due in ten minutes to take Janey to the Wat Phnom, so she could sit in the shady glade on the hill for a while. She might do lunch in the French colonial elegance of Van's and from there she would be the lady of leisure at last and walk back through the Riverside area, as far as she felt, and see the city on her own.

They were putting the finishing touches to their packing for the day when they heard steps on the outside stair – slow and deliberate. They both listened.

'That's not Chean,' said Janey.

'Mr Thiounn wouldn't let him up without a fight anyway.'

A quiet knock came at the door, so Ryan passed a look to his sister and went through the kitchen and opened up.

'Mr Dith!' he said. Dith had not figured on any mental list Ryan might have had of possible visitors.

'Mr Davey. Good morning,' said Dith, bowing slightly, pressing his hands together and raising them to his face. 'I am sorry to disturb you. If this is an inconvenient time I can return later, but there is one thing I wanted to say to you, which I found I had to say in person.'

'Of course, Mr Dith. Please come in. My sister and I were going out in a few minutes so you have caught us at a good moment.'

'Your sister,' said Mr Dith, stopping for a moment and turning to Ryan, as if he was afraid that his visit could be construed as an intrusive or impolite act.

'My sister I'm sure is very happy to meet you.'

'Very well, Mr Davey,' said Dith with some hesitation. 'We shall proceed.'

They entered the living room and Janey rose to greet them, making an impeccable sampeah to Mr Dith, who smiled and bowed his head in appreciation at her politeness and returned the gesture.

'Good morning, Miss Davey. I am very pleased to meet you.'

'You wouldn't believe how pleased I am to meet you, Mr Dith. Ryan has said so many things about you I have been dying to meet you in person.' The polite exaggeration hit its mark.

'Oh, oh, is that so …' Mr Dith seemed struck by Janey's comments and he bowed once again. He looked at her once more and blinked slowly as he nodded almost imperceptibly in a way that Ryan had never seen him do before. He motioned to Mr Dith and they arranged themselves around the coffee table.

'Mr Davey. It is clear that I was intending to speak to you in private.' Dith's grounding in protocol made him broach the matter so he could get at least an implied permission to speak in front of the unexpected third person.

'Mr Dith, whatever you want to say to me can be said in front of my sister.'

'That is excellent, Mr Davey. I wanted to say to you that my understanding of your situation has changed since I last spoke to you. It came to my attention last night that you have suffered a great loss.'

'Ah … yes?'

'I was deeply, how shall I say … shaken by the news of the shootings at the demonstration last Sunday. The television news coverage which I saw did not include any mention that there had been killings, or shootings of any kind. There was much footage of demonstrators with angry faces, shouting, pushing at the factory gate.'

'I suppose there would be.'

'The television completely omitted mention of the level of violence used by the authorities in response to that situation. But on Monday morning the newspaper ran the story. Seven people killed, dozens wounded. People were being treated while they were waiting on the hard floors in the corridors of the Russian Hospital. It was very distressing. One of the dead was an old woman selling rice – an innocent bystander.'

'I saw her.'

'You saw her?' Dith asked. His face was filled with true compassion.

'You never told me this,' said Janey.

'I thought it was, I don't know, I guess I've never seen anyone lying dead before, and with a bullet through the throat. Still dealing with it perhaps. Anyway, I thought it might frighten you unnecessarily.'

'I think you were right about that.'

They paused then, and looked to Mr Dith to continue.

'I was very moved by these things, Mr Davey.' And Dith nodded towards Janey as well, as if to include her in this form of address. 'We have not had this kind of violence in the city for many years. The nature of this government response has changed my view of the incident. I think all of Phnom Penh is shocked. And now, yesterday, I hear that the cousin of your friend, our own student Malee, has been lost also. This now affects all of our community at the school. Mr

Davey, I understand that you were with the boy, Cris, when he died.'

Dith was silent for a moment. His hands were together, in front of his mouth, fingertips touching the end of his nose. He was tapping his fingers together, as if he had made a decision which was a watershed moment for him, and this was the moment to take the leap into enacting his new resolve.

'On Monday I placed your personal things in a packet which I have kept in my office, as I told you I would on Sunday evening. But I would rather that you do not take them away. I would like you to keep them there and then return them to your desk. I would like you to remain with the school. With your permission I will report to the senior management that I have re-employed you.'

'Mr Dith I …' He was going to say that he had not really been with Cris when he died and that the rumours had exaggerated his role. But he hesitated a second and Mr Dith went on.

'This is not only because I want to re-employ you for my own reasons, but because the students want you too.' And at this Dith, for the first time that morning, smiled. He had crossed some Rubicon; he had said something important that he had been working up to and his face was relieved. It may have been the first time ever that Mr Dith had taken a chance.

'Mr Dith, I am honoured by your offer. I must say, honoured. I … I have much to think about at this time. There will be a funeral.'

'Of course. I will wait for one week for you to return to Phnom Penh. I will take some of your classes; Mr Andersen will also help.'

At this moment there was the rumble of tuk-tuk wheels in the street outside and two sharp toots of the motorbike horn. Chean had arrived, one minute ahead of time as always.

Mr Dith rose, his speech over.

'Phew,' said Ryan, exhaling audibly. Having Mr Dith in his house had been a difficult and unexpected experience for him.

'It has been a great pleasure to meet you, Miss Davey.'

'It has been an extreme pleasure to meet you too, Mr Dith. I hope I have the pleasure of speaking to you again while I am in Cambodia.' Indeed, she seemed to have been quite charmed by this polite and self-effacing gentleman. At this, Mr Dith stopped in the middle of the room for a moment, as if flustered. He felt in his pockets and after a few moments he produced a simple white business card, which he then placed, without ascribing any specific purpose to this act, on the coffee table, facing Janey.

'Ninety dollar offer,' said Reap. 'Ninety dollars!'

The Government had offered to increase the minimum wage by five dollars a month. The girl from the apartment next door had come in to tell them the news she had heard on the radio. Reap and Malee did not know how to feel. The fact there had been an offer at all was overwhelming to them. Up until now the girls had felt they were invisible, that their time did not belong to them but to Amalgamated Apparel; and that the action they took in the streets was just an outlet for their frustration – not real but a psychodrama they played out to create a delusion that progress could ever be possible.

But now there was an offer. An unseemly low offer perhaps, but it was evidence that they had been noticed, talked about in high places and even taken seriously. The delirious joy of recognition was tempered by the amount offered: five dollars per month increase from eighty five to ninety. The unions had asked for the poverty line: one hundred and sixty.

The four girls put in twenty cents each and the girl from next door went down to the convenience store for the *Phnom Penh Post*. To read the newspaper was an unusual event and they crowded around the little coffee table in Reap and Malee's flat. It was Sunday and the girls were not working, except Malee who had studied steadily through the morning. There was a preview of the demonstration the next week and speculation whether the offer would change anything. There were pictures of the last demonstration, and a statement from a representative of a British department store that sold the clothes they made. He said his store deplored the violence used to disperse the garment worker strikes last month. An American jeans manufacturer said the same thing; the paper said there were a number of comments supporting the garment workers from companies around the world.

'We are winning,' said the girl from next door. Her eyes were wide.

'If they like us so much,' said Reap, 'why not give us more. Five dollars is nothing.'

They looked at Malee for answers to the difficult questions, but she took a moment to decide what to tell them.

'I think it's because the ones who sell the clothes are not the ones who pay you to make them.' The other girls were silent a moment, not understanding. 'You say that sometimes Korean people come to look at the factory.'

They all nodded. They had heard the strange voices and seen East Asian men in Western suits and ties. No-one had ever told any of them who owned the factory; this was their only clue.

'Then it is Koreans who own the factory. They sell the shirts to American companies to put in their stores. In other places it is Taiwanese or Chinese people owning. So the people who sell the clothes don't really have anything to do with the factory.'

'So they can say nice things,' Reap got the point at once, 'and no-one cares.' They saw that the store owners in the West could say bad things about the Koreans or Chinese who own the factory, but that didn't stop them going on and buying the jeans and shirts. Only the Government could raise the minimum wage.

'But I think it does mean something,' Malee went on. 'They never said anything like this before. Last time Hun Sen went too far and everybody knows it. We will all go to the demonstration.'

Yes, yes, they all nodded. They could feel a lift in their spirits — articles in the newspaper, an offer, even of only five dollars; this was new ground.

'Poor Cris,' said Reap.

'Poor Cris,' they all agreed. 'We must march for Cris too.'

Ryan walked down the stairs with Mr Dith and Janey after their meeting in his apartment. Chean was waiting in the street to take Janey away to Wat Phnom.

Ryan kissed his sister on the cheek and shook Mr Dith's extended hand.

'Mr Dith,' said Janey, 'how did you get out here?'

'I took a tuk-tuk also.'

'Perhaps I can drop you near your school. I think it is not far out of the way.'

'Why I …' To accept a lift from a Khmer woman would have been a difficult thing. From a Western woman was different. 'Perhaps if you drop me on Norodom Boulevard I will walk the next block. That will be easy.'

Sensing a change in instructions Chean jumped down from the driver's seat and walked the three or four steps over to their group. Then a very peculiar thing happened indeed. The eyes of Chean and Mr Dith met for a moment; their looks were locked for perhaps only three seconds, but it was long enough for each of them to drop his guard and for both to assess and confirm the identity of the other. Mr Dith stiffened and drew himself up to his full height. By contrast, Chean's head dropped a fraction and he drew within himself.

'Mr Ung,' said Dith, using the formal title, perhaps the only name for Chean that he had ever known. There was silence for a few seconds. Ryan and Janey exchanged looks.

'Well, let's get goin' then,' said Janey with a forced brightness, trying to cover over whatever it was that existed between the two men. 'We will drop Mr Dith off on Norodom Boulevard, Chean.'

'Yes, miss,' said Chean, jumping on his motorbike, keen to go.

During the five-minute trip up Norodom, Mr Dith was quiet. When Chean stopped the tuk-tuk he climbed out and thanked Miss Davey and bid her good morning. Chean pulled the tuk-tuk into the traffic and headed north to the Wat Phnom, without looking around.

'How ya bin? I seem to have lost my drinking partner just about permanent.' It was Colin on the phone. 'I hear you've struck a snag or two.'

'Is there anything you don't hear?'

'I ran into Tom.'

'Ok. Don't tell me where. I don't want to know.' It was a joke, really, referring back to the Heart of Darkness night and Tom's avid interest in the wildlife around him. But since Kratie Tom had been quiet, brighter-eyed at work, few stories to tell. To Ryan's relief he had even dropped some of the Tex-Mex lingo.

'Look, I rang him up and we went out for a drink. I have to know how things *really* are with you and at least he'll tell me. Good lad – got his own problems though.'

'I know.' Tom's anxiety had not been that hard to see. He may have run away from something but was still pursued by himself, and he dealt with problems in different ways to Ryan.

'You got sacked.'

'Yes, well done. You found out.'

'It's your altruistic streak fucking up your life again. Those bloody demos.' Colin just had to give his tough side a run before he could get to himself.

'I guess that's it.'

'But listen, I must say that since I've been in this country I have not heard another thing that equals all this in shitness – and in this place that's a big statement. Young kids, and that old woman rice-seller with a bullet through her neck.' Colin went quiet for a moment; Ryan could feel him shaking his head at the other end of the phone. The rice-seller seemed to have got to everyone.

'We have to march again next week.'

'Fucking hell, so you *are* going? I have to admit that half the reason for calling you is to find out what you were doing about that. Now I can worry about you. Still, the same thing can't happen again, I wouldn't think—' Colin stopped in mid-sentence for a minute – unusual for him. 'I have to tell you that I kind of, kind of love you for it. You're weird but, you know … respect.'

Ryan's shoulders felt as if some mystical masseur had eased a weight from them. Colin had stepped across a communication line that had separated them before. They had talked about personal things, but there was a place where familiarity stopped and intimacy began and Colin didn't cross that line; Ryan had never heard him use the word 'love' before, ever – not for anyone.

'What was the other half a reason?' Neither of them knew where to take an open statement of affection between men. What do you say? 'Love you too, man.' Not likely, so the subject was changed by mutual unspoken agreement. Their relationship would change from here, in subtle barely perceptible ways, but not by candid declaration.

'You need a job; I've got one for you.'

'One thing your gossip circle didn't do for you. I got my own job back.' Another silence: he had said 'my own' and taken ownership of the school, his job, Dith – everything.

'You're right. That's one thing I did not know, but if you asked me tomorrow I probably would have. But I'm a bit surprised. The blokes who run those schools are seriously Big End.'

'He came here.'

'To your flat? Dith?'

'I was amazed. Shocked. There is still a heap of stuff I don't get about Dith. He surprises me all the time.'

'That's probably normal for this place. Not still worried if he was Khmer Rouge?'

'I stopped trying to guess. But then, today, when he was leaving, we bumped into Chean downstairs. They knew each other but no-one said how. Dith knew his surname.'

'Only his surname. That's interesting.' Ryan could hear Colin thinking on the other end of the line. 'That means Chean was in a position of respect somewhere sometime, or authority at least. Anyway, Dith deserves to be honoured for reinstating you. He'd be acting contrary to the expectations of his superiors; they'd be conservative and powerful. But when you're thinking about this don't forget that my job pays five times the amount.'

He could live on the teacher's pay if he was very frugal and he was moved by Mr Dith's visit, but in this country NGO pay was wealth. He had another ethical decision to make.

The waiter at *La Tour Eiffel* came to the table and Janey watched Mr Dith bow and nod at the Khmer girl as she stacked plates and skilfully cradled them up her arm. They had been through the opening small talk and politeness and then the subject of the city of Phnom Penh, then Angkor Wat and a little on medieval Khmer kings. It was all new to Janey and she listened avidly. Mr Dith was a charming and knowledgeable man, amiable dinner company, but his points of expertise were just little keys to unlocking the man that she wanted to know about.

'It was very good of you to call me, Miss Davey,' said Mr Dith. 'When you asked me to choose a place to come, I could not think of any other place but *La Tour*. The atmosphere here is so,' here he paused to gather his thoughts, '... just as I imagine a Paris bistro to be.'

Janey had to admit that it was a pretty decent facsimile.

'You've never been to France?'

'No, no.' Dith shook his head and chuckled, and Janey suddenly felt such a fool to imagine that Mr Dith could ever fly off on a trip to Paris when he had family to look after.

'I'm sorry, of course ...'

'It was always my wife's dream to come to a French restaurant.' Mr Dith had interrupted her, if only to save her the embarrassment of explaining her faux pas, which he perfectly understood. 'And mine also. I think that, at my time of life, I have done enough that I can now begin to allow myself an occasional small luxury.' And looking around him at the restaurant, he added, 'It would be very nice to come here, say, once a month ...'

Janey wondered at the reason Mr Dith would have for taking this direction in the conversation, but after this suggestion of a personal message he returned to the factual.

'In the 1960s, French dining was very fashionable, but my wife and I were poor students. We could not afford to come to a place like this, and there were enough of them in Phnom Penh in 1969. The king was a great lover of French things. He owned Peugeot cars, he made movies in the French style.'

'Movies?'

'Yes, he made films and was the star actor also, and then he set up awards nights and he won for best director and so on. He was, in his own eyes, the father of his people and we were all his children. He even sent students from mandarin families to Paris to study, thinking that they would come to love French things as he did. He anticipated that they would return and support his programs even more strongly.'

'It didn't work is my guess?' Janey knew that Mr Dith was talking about Prince Sihanouk and that his reign had ended decades before. She was murky on details but she knew something about him hanging on powerless and bitter.

'For some of the students, yes it did. But at that time Maoism was very popular among French students and so some of our expatriates returned as Communists ...' Dith smiled ironically and held his hands together in sampeah, as if to honour the best intentions of his former monarch. 'It seemed that some of the children were of a mind to repudiate their father and his claims to genius.'

'I think I get it. Some of these students became quite well known?'

'Yes. Saloth Sar was among those students of this kind.'

'That one is vaguely familiar.'

'Yes, he came to be known by the name of Pol Pot.'

'Oh my god.' Janey didn't know what to say. She remembered that Ryan and Tom had been talking about Mr Dith as if he had been a member of the Khmer Rouge. Could he really have brought her out to this French restaurant to lionise the man who created the killing fields? She had been to the monument there only the day before and stared at the hundred-foot glass tower crowded full of skulls dug from the fields surrounding. Looking at Dith now she could not believe it. But then, what does life do to us, she thought, but make us into things and then unmake us again. What were most of the Khmer Rouge cadres but country lads, changed by six months of indoctrination from obedient rural Buddhists into violent revolutionaries? Who are we really? What chance had made her a doctor? She'd made a random decision to join the dramatic club at university, then fell in love with Joel and felt the disdain of his parents that she would never be anything but a school teacher. That was enough to make her grind through years of medicine, to prove them wrong, but which only steered her more damagingly to the rejection which was all she had ultimately achieved from them. And now here she was, sitting in Phnom Penh listening to a middle-aged Cambodian man who was as great a mystery as anything she had known, even in all the years she had spent talking to her patients with all their maladies real and imagined, their anxieties and secrets.

'Did you have … much contact with the Khmer Rouge?' She had meant to pursue the subject as diplomatically as she could, but she knew that as soon as she had spoken that she had again said something stupid. How could anyone avoid contact with the totalitarian Khmer Rouge in the 1970s, without leaving the country?

'Miss Davey, my wife and I had a little boy in the Pol Pot time. We were taken from the city to a labour camp near Battambang. My boy died of starvation after two years and my wife died of dysentery six months later. I had to bury them both. I wanted to put my wife in the same place as the boy, but when we went out to the jungle it was all overgrown with saplings and vines and we could not find it.'

At that moment the girl brought their desserts: camembert au lait cru for her and mousse au chocolat for him.

'Merci, 'demoiselle,' said Dith.

'Cheers,' said Janey.

'Ah,' said Mr Dith, his face brightening. 'This is the part I have been looking forward to most of all.' Then, after a momentary pause that would have done credit to the timing of a professional actor, he whispered to Janey with half a wink, 'I have a sweet tooth.'

The weather was hot and it was past mid-afternoon so Ryan went to the fridge for a beer. As he sat down with it the phone rang once more. It was Malee. They talked for a moment about Janey, and he told her how she had walked all over the town and that Chean had finally had his wish to take someone to the Killing Fields. Then he told her that Dith had offered his job back. For some reason he didn't tell her about Colin. He felt that the teaching offer was something she should know about, but the job with Colin would make him almost too grand, too juicy as wedding material. He would bide his time with that.

'That is so good,' said Malee. 'But not this week, right? You come with me to the homeland tomorrow? I want Janey to come too. She will be an honoured guest.'

'Janey will come.'

'We need a car. That will cost money.' He could feel it coming. 'Pa is paying for the achar and everything else in Kampong Thom, but we need the coffin here and to pay for the driver. We have to put him next to his mom and pop in the stupa when he is burnt.'

'Of course, it couldn't be any other way.'

He allowed a silence to develop between them, as if to emphasise what had to come next.

'How is your cookie jar with spare cash looking?'

'Not too good after my trip to Kep,' she laughed, reminding him of the risk and sacrifice she had made to reach him.

'I'll pay for the coffin and the driver then.'

'Would you?'

'I would. Will a hundred dollars cover it?'

'With some left over for the party. I'll ring the coffin man now to say go ahead. See ya.'

What they would have done for a coffin and a driver without him, he decided not to ask.

He went out to the back door and looked across into the grounds of the wat that fronted the next street. A group of novices were just heading inside the pagoda. An adult monk closed the door after them. Dust settled in the compound they had left and all was quiet under the two huge banyan trees. From two blocks away a jackhammer rattled into the day and there was the endless distant honking from Norodom Boulevard.

He kept thinking of the look that had passed between Chean and Dith. It was a surprise to him that they would know each other. Mr Dith was educated and steeped in the etiquette of a man of some position; Chean was rough and knockabout, but keen to please and to be accepted. Their social positions would seem to provide very little opportunity for them to meet. And the title, 'Mr Ung,' was the only name Dith had known, spoken without irony.

It was time for him to go to the market and buy some things for the evening meal. For once he hoped that Chean was working and not waiting at the corner. He wanted to walk and to be alone for a while. He picked up his back pack for shopping. But when he locked the ground floor gate and turned into the street, Chean had parked at the entrance to the lane, waiting for him.

'Boss,' he said, straightening up and grinding his cigarette into the greasy footpath.

'Chean, not in your usual spot.'

'Boss, I have to tell you. You talk to me about your Mr Dith, but I never think anything because there many Dith in Phnom Penh.'

Here he stopped, as if that was enough to imply that he knew Mr Dith, almost as if it should somehow imply the rest of his story, which Ryan should guess or understand by osmosis.

'Yes, he knew your name. He called you Mister.' Ryan started off the conversation in a friendly, chipper tone although he could see something ominous in Chean's face.

'Boss,' again Chean stalled in his attempt to speak. 'Boss, I told you I was in Pol Pot labour camp.'

'You did.'

Here Chean hesitated for several seconds, staring un-focused at the footpath, as if collecting in his mind exactly what he was going to say.

'I *was* in the camp. But before that I come into the city. I walk down that street.' Chean pointed up to where cars and motorbikes streamed past, about a hundred metres away.

'Norodom?'

'Yes. I wear the black clothes and have the rifle. You see pictures of Khmer Rouge boys walking into Phnom Penh, April seventeen?'

He had.

'We look very mean. But I tell you now, we just very hungry. Three weeks in the jungle, no food. We scared. I scared. We have to go through the apartment blocks and tell people to move. I think they going to kill me. But they move. They do what we say. Me and my family very poor. My father have very little rice field. Now these people, rich people, they do what I say. I tell people to go with me and my friends. We go west, to Battambang. Walk all the way.'

Chean's speech was five times longer than anything he had ever said before. Telling his story, in a foreign language, had caused him extreme effort, and pain.

'That's where you knew Mr Dith.'

'Yes, I know Mr Dith. His family dead.' Chean said this as if it was the end of the story, the last thing he would say on the matter. Whatever he had done in Battambang and whatever Dith knew him for would not be spoken of. It was as if he had said, Think the worst and you've got it.

The two men sat in silence. It was Ryan who spoke.

'I talked to Tom once, about this.'

Chean looked up with surprise, as if someone had jabbed him in the side.

'We talked about what we might have done if we had been in a position like yours; in the country, teenagers. We thought we probably would have joined up too. We would have turned red for sure.'

Chean immediately understood the meaning of these words: he

was not being judged. Ryan would not moralise against him.

'One thing. You told me you fought *against* Pol Pot.'

'That true too.' Chean jumped at this. 'When Vietnam come they many guns. They kill us. We run into jungle, crazy crazy. I run away from the Pol Pot people; in my heart I hate them. Vietnam people find me. I say I talk to villager for them, fight for them. I stay six year – pay good.'

'You defected.' Ryan shook his head in wonder. 'Good move. If you'd stayed you might be dead.'

'Fifty fifty – maybe I hide in jungle with Pol Pot for ten years.'

'Phew.' Ryan exhaled, considering this possible fate, then put his hand on the shoulder of his friend. 'Look, Chean, I'm going down to the market. I'm going to walk. I need a bit of time to myself. But if you happen to be on the corner at seven o'clock, Malee and I will go to the Riverside I think.'

'*Yes*, boss.'

Ryan walked away in the direction of Kandal market. He had been surprised by Chean's story, but not for long. At the corner of Norodom he waited for the traffic. For a moment he tried to imagine the thirteen-year-old Chean, marching in single file with twenty other youths, a mean look hiding his fear, and a rifle around his neck.

'This is the third day after he died so the ceremony must take place today,' Malee said to Ryan. 'If not, tomorrow is ok.' She spoke seriously and deliberately, but an eyebrow was raised.

'I see. That's clear enough.'

'When I was little, funerals took place *seven* days after death. I can still remember one.' She looked meaningfully at Ryan. 'Not nice. This is the new way.'

A marquee had been put in place, in front of the house, abutting the road to such a degree that the occasional vehicle that passed had to slow, in respect; motorbike riders brought it down a couple of gears and putted slowly past.

There was white bunting draped around all four sides – simple and elegant. Malee was all in white. Ryan had brought a white shirt from work. No-one had any pants that were big enough for him so he was loaned a white robe that was draped over his shoulder and pinned at his hip to cover part of his camel-coloured jeans, the lightest thing he could find. That showed sufficient respect. Janey had gone to the market in Kampong Thom and was wrapped in white from head to toe.

A monk was busy lighting fistfuls of incense sticks and placing them in holders around the marquee. The smoke and scent collected in the sultry atmosphere and then drifted out the open sides to announce the service to villagers for two hundred metres in every direction. Under the tarpaulin the effect was balmy and pleasant – dreamy. Not like the choking eye-watering incense swinging of priests he had been brought up with in oppressive closed church spaces. He remembered Wednesday afternoons and eucharist: tall hats of white and gold, slivers of what they told him was bread.

'Now I finally get what incense is all about.' She gave him a questioning look. 'It's a bit like curry spices in Southern India.'

She gave him a questioning look.

'Well, they cover up the …' and he sniffed the air.

'Like that, yeah.' She gave him another look and shook her head sorrowfully.

The body of Cris had been washed and dressed in Phnom Penh and placed in a coffin there. The achar travelled from the village and supervised the proceedings. He and Reap and Chamroeun had then driven back with the coffin in the car. Three freezer packs had been placed inside the coffin but by the time they got to Kampong Thom they were all warm, said the achar later, and so was Cris.

'Cris had the back seat all to himself,' said Malee to him. 'Reap sat in the front seat between the legs of Chamroeun.'

The thought of Reap and Chamroeun that close, huddled together in the front seat all that way. The family was so entwined it was almost like a single organism. He had not gone to see them off because of Chamroeun. He didn't know what to expect. Would the guy still be angry? It was said that Ryan had been with the boy when he died, Chamroeun had not. He had also not attended the garment workers demonstration. But today could be a time for him to regain face.

Cris was in his coffin to be viewed. The wooden seal had been removed and revealed a face with a beatific smile, a boy at rest. There was no embalming and although he was pale there was a kind of sheen on his face, which had not lost all of its glorious golden colouring.

The monks had come the night before and recited a sermon over the body, which then lay inside the house. Malee had insisted that Janey come with them to be there for that and they had travelled on the bus together. He and Malee had sat together with Janey behind them, but there was so much chatter between Malee and Janey that he swapped seats with Janey so he could get some peace on his own.

'Did you know,' said Janey when they got off the bus and waited for Malee to arrange a tuk-tuk to take them home, 'that your girl has never been to Angkor Wat.'

'Not many of them have.'

'But it's only another hundred and fifty kilometres up the track.'

'Something like that. It costs too much. Just the transport up there and then the fare from Siem Reap to the temples is over the top, without taking account for a hotel and other stuff. The only holidays they get are New Year and Pchum Benh and even then they have to be here, to go to the temple.'

'But this is their national treasure.'

'They've seen the pictures; they think that's ok.'

'But the grandeur of the place is what it's all about, or so they say. You can't get that from pictures.'

'Every one of them wants to go. Believe me. But it's for the elite, and funnily enough the elite don't seem to value it so much.'

Later they had slept upstairs, Janey in the women's quarters and he in the men's, separated by a screen through which they could share some whispered talk. The matter of the temples had stayed on Janey's mind through all the services for Cris and the meetings with family and the introductions and bowing and sampeahing.

'You must take that girl to Angkor Wat. You haven't even been yourself.'

'Ok, sis. I'll do that,' said Ryan, tired. He wasn't a very good tourist; he'd go to a place to be with the people, not to see temples, unless they happened to be where he was at the time. 'Time for some sleep, eh.'

'How can I sleep in this place; my head is spinning.'

'Night, sis.'

Ryan was not prepared for the entrance that Pa and Ma made to the marquee. They came down from the steps of the house, Pa first, Ma second, and Chamroeun behind them as a kind of groomsman or assistant. But it was their look that fixed him on the spot.

Pa's head of thick black hair, which had so impressed him at the Pizza Company, was gone. His head was shaven, and so was Ma's. Pa was naked to the waist with a white and gold krama tied around his middle, then tucked under him and hitched at the back. Ma wore a kind of sari of white with trimming in gold. On their feet they both wore their everyday sandals. They were both dignified, monk-like, ghostly. Pa was serious, as though he was on the verge of tears; with his mop of hair, it seemed, had gone his vitality. Ma was likewise, although upon her persona the aspect of mourning sat more naturally. Behind them Chamroeun was grave and noble – the dutiful son assisting his parents in their time of travail. His hair had been trimmed very short, as if run over by an amateur barber with a number one cutting comb. It suited him; his face was there to be seen, purposefully erect, where before it had been cowed and hidden. He too was bare-chested but wore a light jacket with pockets that were so large they almost seemed to flop open, although Chamroeun never placed his hands in them, but folded his fingers together in front of him.

Throughout the prayers and rituals, the chasing away of bad

spirits with incense and monks, Chamroeun stayed close to Pa and Ma. And then, when the achar and the monks had finished their incantations, a strange thing happened: the villagers began to come forward to Ma and Pa in their twos and threes to pay their respects, but not only for that purpose. From each one of these little groups a member pressed a fold of notes of money into the hands of Chamroeun who received them with a respectful nod and then slipped them into the capacious pockets of his funeral jacket. The whole procedure was completed in a respectful hush, so quiet that the rustling of the notes could be heard, along with the occasional cry from the birds in the trees along the noiseless village road. The procession was immense, with thirty or forty groups of neighbours filing past and bowing, passing over bundles of riel.

Janey made for her purse and began to extract some notes. Malee held out her hand to stop her. 'You don't have to,' Malee said. 'But I'm going to,' Janey replied. She grabbed at Ryan's arm as if to say, you're coming too. It was a moot point whether Ryan should go up with money, for that was a point of respect paid by villagers to their neighbours, not by family. But was he family, yet? The appearance of Westerners at a funeral was probably unprecedented in the village, in the province perhaps.

But up they went. This time Pa showed no outward delight at the money; he bowed respectfully and they passed through to Chamroeun. As they handed over the cash first brother Chamroeun bowed to them and made a sampeah to them both and as he held out his hand he took the money with his left hand, not his right as he had with all the other guests. As he was sliding the money in his pocket with his left hand Chamroeun held out his right to Ryan in the manner of a Western hand shake.

Ryan was shocked for a moment and he froze, but the hand stood out there for that second and it didn't go away. Ryan reached out and took the hand.

'Thank you, bong,' Chamroeun said warmly, in English, as he shook. 'Thank you.'

After forty minutes or so a donkey was brought into the marquee and the palanquin upon which the coffin had been laid was then hitched up. The seal was placed on the coffin and a couple of boys jumped up onto the tray to ride with their dead friend who they may have met only two or three times.

The procession was then led away from the house and through the long strung-out village to the temple. People stopped along the way to watch them pass through. Boys quit their games of football and cleared the road for them.

'Chamroeun shook my hand,' said Ryan to Malee, his mind unable to leave what had happened back at the marquee. 'He didn't have to do that, did he?'

'He didn't have to do that.'

'If I had been any other Western guy, would he have shook hands?'

'I don't think so. It was because he was with Pa.'

'You mean Pa made him do it?'

'Oh, no no. He was with Pa and he was being dutiful first brother. He had his place back; he had his face back. Then he can be a fine person. Then he can be good to you.'

'So that meant he could be magnanimous.'

'Hey, that's a good one – magnanimous,' she repeated, rolling the word around in her mouth. 'I never heard that one. Yes. If he saw you at my place, like if you were there as my friend and he was there as my brother, then I don't know.'

'We would have been equal and he wouldn't have been able to be generous.'

'That's right. But today he is like the next Pa. He is able to welcome you to family; he can call you bong, in front of everyone, and that gives him face. You were there when Cris was shot so you have earned respect. You won face then and he did not. He must respect you. He has to do everything right from now, and I think he will. This is a serious time.'

'So now,' said Janey, who had been listening all the while, 'this could be a turning point for your Chamroeun.'

'I think so, could be,' said Malee. Janey squeezed Ryan's arm as if to say, You did good.

At the back of the temple a pit of dried twigs and charcoal had been prepared. The body of Cris was laid in it and the dry wood was lit. Janey and Ryan stopped to stare for a moment, unable to wrench their eyes from this scene.

'I am a medical person, but I can tell you that is something I have never seen. A body laid out like that for burning.'

'They don't hide much, do they,' said Ryan. 'In Australia the coffin is rollered off through a curtain and never seen again.'

The procession moved away into the temple and they left two monks to watch the fire. It was in the latter phase of this burning procedure, he had heard, that a stricken loved one might retrieve a chunk of charred bone to take home, to show the deceased that they would continue to be loved, or as a kind of talisman, that the spirit of the deceased would protect them in the life remaining on this earth.

Later, when the session inside the temple was complete, when the protection from bad spirits was ensured and all others save Pa and Ma and Chamroeun had dispersed to their homes, the ashes of Cris were collected by the monk and placed in an urn that looked like some Moroccan cooking pot. The monk placed that in a concrete stupa, shaped like a three-metre high bishop's mitre, next to the urns of his mother and father. No-one collected the charred bones of Cris; there was sorrow, but not ownership. There was collective sadness at the snapping of such a promising life; but there was also a feeling among the villagers of a tragic inevitability surrounding his passing — as if in their sad shaking of heads there was an acknowledgement of the inexorable forces of destiny that had taken him, just weeks after the passing of his repatriated parents.

The Sunday of the third demonstration came. The three of them, Ryan, Malee and Reap, climbed into Chean's tuk-tuk and made for the industrial zone again.

Janey stayed out of it. Mr Dith would call for her and they would go to a place he knew for a lunch of Khmer food. 'I have my own friends now,' she pretended to admonish them with her hands on her hips. But, seriously, she said it was 'awfully sweet' of him. While they were gone she would also ring their mother in Australia.

Where there had been excitement on previous trips to the demonstration area, there was now silence in the group. It was not just the sobering absence of Cris – everyone arriving at the site had a more businesslike manner about them. The crowd was the biggest ever, if anything; the murderous events which had occurred on the previous demonstration had brought even more supporters from the apartment blocks, from their Sunday rest and chores of washing clothes and preparing for the week ahead. And once the action began there was no screeching megaphone, no bolt cutters at the padlocked gates. They were there to occupy the space and to show that they were not going away – no backing down. There was a feeling now that all they had to do was push on, to keep coming back. Everyone knew of the initial offer that had been made, of the comments made by international companies in the press.

Police lined up in the same position as before. There were just as many as there had been but now they wore soft hats: there were no riot shields. An organiser stepped up onto a milk crate and began the chant of 'one sixty, one sixty'.

He was new. He had to be. In the week after the last demonstration Hun Sen's men had picked up fifteen organisers from the unions and placed them in jail. It was his way of saying that if there had been deaths, they were the fault of the mad unions. And now new men, barely twenty years old, were leading the singing. The police stood in a double line with their hands clasped in front of them. After forty minutes of chanting there had been no dispersal charge from the police and someone in the crowd produced confetti from her bag and threw it joyfully in the air. Others followed her as if by prior arrangement. People's shoulders relaxed and they began to smile; they could see that the police had been told to lay off. Within ten minutes the new organiser spoke to the crowd. A representative from the factory had come down from his office to tell him there would be a negotiation with the factory owners the next morning at nine o'clock. If a satisfactory resolution was not reached they would return in two weeks' time for another demonstration.

When the crowd dispersed they found Chean.

'All good, boss?'

'No problem.'

As the tuk-tuk gained momentum Ryan turned around and watched the crowd wandering away to motorbikes, some on foot to nearby blocks of apartments, in the tired and resigned way they would if they were leaving another day of work, veterans that they were now of civil disobedience.

They dropped Reap at their block and Malee came with them back to Ryan's place. She could not wait to see Janey again and to see how her date with Mr Dith had gone.

'So what did he actually say?' Malee sat on a chair facing Janey on the couch, with Ryan next to her reading the *Phnom Penh Post*. He had not mentioned his talk with Chean. He was still processing it. He wanted to hear what Dith had said.

'With regard to the speculation that he was a member of the Khmer Rouge I can say as a matter of fact that he was not, unless he is the most brilliant actor and liar that I have ever known.'

'That I don't think,' Ryan mumbled.

'Your Mr Dith was married to the love of his life who died of dysentery in the Khmer Rouge years.'

'Ok,' said Ryan, nodding.

'Ew,' said Malee. 'Most people went that way. Four times more died of disease than were killed as enemies of the state.'

'He told me that he buried his own son at the labour camp they took them all to in Battambang, out in the jungle near a stream. It was the place they buried all the dead ones. There were rows of graves three feet deep. I have read about these things.'

'You have?' said Ryan.

'The library at home was surprisingly well stocked and you can learn a lot in five days if you have no social life.'

'That is so good,' said Malee. 'You don't want to come just to see the temples and the torture prison.'

'We'll get to the temples in a minute. Anyway, after the Khmer Rouge years he returned to Phnom Penh with the daughter who survived the holocaust.'

'Daughter?!' they both exclaimed. No-one had known a thing about this.

'He has a grandson. He said they keep him alive, and the school. When he got back to Phnom Penh – don't get me off the track again …'

'But we didn't—'

'*When* he got back to Phnom Penh he didn't know what to do. He was blank, confused – shell-shocked. Do you know he had to rough his hands to make out he was a workman and hide the fact that he had an education. They would have killed him if they knew he spoke English.'

'Yes, presumed him to be an American spy.'

'That's what he said – taken for an agent of the CIA. When the United Nations came everyone wanted to speak English in a hurry and he started teaching, then someone asked him if he wanted to run a school. Now his boss is ex-Khmer Rouge colonel.'

'I heard that.'

'No surprise,' said Malee. 'Everyone has to live together – *As long as the killing stop*,' she recited a line she'd been brought up with.

'Yeah. *As long as the killing stop, no worry.*' Ryan finished off; everyone had to live together no matter what the memories. 'Did you hold his hand while he poured this out?'

'As a matter of fact I did, yes.'

'Whaaat?!' They were both incredulous. 'He let you touch him?'

The allowed physical intimacy of a middle-aged Khmer man might extend to the occasional encouraging pat on the back to a male colleague, but not to touching a woman. And Dith was the model of discreet propriety.

'I shouldn't have done it. I wish I hadn't now. I think I said a couple of stupid things that I should have thought through better and I was overcompensating. It might have been the first time any-one has touched him in thirty years besides his five-year-old grand-son who lives out in a province and he sees twice a year.'

Janey stopped for a moment and she rubbed her hands anx-iously, as if they were guilty things. Ryan remembered the gesture from his childhood – Janey vexing about something she had done that may not have been right. 'It's my fault. I'm too touchy-touchy and I know I shouldn't do it. I brought my culture with me and I led him and it wasn't right. It was like some lightning rod went through him.'

'Oh, sis,' Ryan half sighed and consoled at the one time and made to put his arm around her.

'We're nowhere near the end of this, by the way, so un-hug me now.' She took a deep breath. 'He asked me to marry him.'

'Whaaat?!'

'Not in so many words, but he told me he was lonely and would have to retire before too long and there I was holding his hand. He is such a sweet man.'

'Did you lead him up the path?'

'Well, not really. I had to change the subject smartly enough and I told him I was going back to Australia on Wednesday and I wouldn't be able to see him but maybe once more. He was very nice about it, but he took his hand away from me.' Janey took two tissues from her handbag and placed them over her eyes, wiped, then blew into them and held them in her hand. 'There was a little silence be-tween us after that.'

There was a little silence in the room as well. Ryan broke it.

'You're not really going home on Wednesday are you?'

'Yes, I am. I rang mother. She told me that after his lengthy ill-ness our father has passed away.' It was said with the kind of even-toned compassion that a medical professional would use to make such an announcement.

There was another silence in the room. Ryan sank back into the seat as the importance of these words was processed by him and Malee. If Ryan went home for the funeral, would he come back? Instinctively Malee's grip on Ryan's hand loosened and she took in a breath to steady herself. It was as if Janey had taken all the fragility of their relationship out of her handbag and put it on the coffee table and said, There, look! The reality of death which, in the case of Cris, had perhaps brought them together, in this case could drive them apart forever. Ryan thought of home, and Amanda, and of a reality that could make his three months in Cambodia seem like a freak, a fluke, a quirk. Would this be something that in ten years' time he would remember as he shook his head in wonder? Would they talk about his adventure with Malee as Janey might about Mr Dith?

'There is one thing else I must tell you.' This was truly Janey's day.

'Before I leave this place there is no force on earth which is going to stop me from visiting the temples at Angkor Wat. Also, I must say that I do not intend to go alone.' She paused a moment and the two of them wondered what she was going to do next. She wouldn't go with Dith? Surely not. 'And you both are going with me. I bought the bus tickets this afternoon. We leave tomorrow at ten and the next morning, after a restful night in Siem Reap, we will be watching the sun rise over the great temple.'

Again there was a little silence in the room. It was broken by Malee.

'Ok,' she said. 'I'm in.'

An hour later Reap came to take Malee back to their apartment and Janey and Ryan were left alone.

'He's dead,' said Ryan. 'It felt like a bit of a game, thinking about the possibility of him not being around. And that he wasn't ever *really* going to pop off at all. Just to think of him lying still is weird – not joking over a beer, or pushing his finger in someone's face and telling it how he reckons it is, or showing someone what he's not doing well enough – not even coughing or wheezing. Just still. Have you ever seen him just still?'

'Nup,' Janey shook her head, 'I don't think I have. Even at the movies he was animated.'

'Yeah. Nodding agreement, guffawing.'

'No-one like him.'

'Except maybe George W. You know, you're totally with me or you're my enemy.'

'And Dermott was totally with him.'

They had been talking and avoiding the point that was the issue. Janey would be going back on Wednesday to be with her mother in preparation for the funeral. It would be half expected that Ryan would go back too, but only half. It was a long way to go and people would understand, perhaps. But there was Dermott, in place for the family takeover. If Ryan stayed away Dermott would say he was not committed to the family. If he went back Dermott would say he had come for Amanda and was stirring up trouble. Dermott would do whatever he could to bad-talk agendas and assert his primacy. But a feeling had transmitted to him that maybe Amanda had grown up in the last few weeks.

'It won't happen until next week,' said Janey, reading his mind. 'No-one will make you go.'

'What about Mum? She'll want both of us to be there.'

Janey fished in her handbag for a couple of seconds and pulled out her phone. She pressed some buttons and then held it out to him.

'Find out for yourself.'

He pressed the green button and the phone rang three times and the voice came on.

'It's not Janey, is it? I can guess that much because she wasn't speaking already before I got a word in.'

'Yes, it's me. Hey, I heard your news. Well, our news, everyone's news.'

'Yes, everyone's news but mainly my news, I suppose. He has been a long time going down. Don't ever smoke cigarettes is the only thing I will tell you.'

'I don't. I won't.'

'And another thing I want to tell you ...'

'Hey, I thought there was only going to be one.'

'You thought I would stop at one?'

'No, I didn't. I never really thought that.' Mum and Janey were more alike than either of them would admit.

'Well, you were right.' There was a moment of silence as she gathered her wits and as Ryan waited respectfully for his homily. 'I'm going to tell you what I really think. I think you should go and live your life and don't let anyone stop you. Certainly not me.'

'Mum, I—'

'I'm talking, you're listening. You think you are coming home to be with me? Forget it. I won't be here. We are going to do this thing next week and then I am going.' She had emphasised her words, then gathered herself for the next part. 'As soon as there is a respectable distance of time. To Alaska.'

'Alaska!' Ryan could not stop himself interjecting.

'I always wanted to go. All that ice and snow. So clean and pure.'

'But Mum it's as polluted as ...' But he stopped himself. What place was not polluted? You read stories. Were they all true? There must be incredible places up there. He remembered his mother saying something about Alaska years before, that it was the place she had wanted to go. That was ten years before, more. She still had the dream.

'Even your father knew it. The day before yesterday he said to me, in the hospice and juiced to the eyeballs on morphine, he patted my hand and he said two things. One, he said, "It doesn't look too good" – he was right there. Two, he said, "Go to Alaska." And do you know, I hadn't said a word about that place to him in fifteen years. But he remembered. He knew what I had given up for him and he knew I did it willingly. And he remembered Alaska and that is something I will always treasure.' He heard the sound of sniffing on the phone – weeping. He said nothing. He waited. Love was truly a very peculiar thing that sprang up in the most unlikely places and who was he to interrupt his mother's weeping.

'He was hard on you, but he thought it was tough love. It was all he knew and it didn't work out. That's life sometimes; you were never going to follow him. But do you know one thing? He knew he was out of his depth with you.'

'He did?'

'What would he know about poetry or *Oscar and Lucinda*? Anyway, don't let anyone force you to come back for the ceremony. You've made a move; it's up to you.'

'Okay, Ma,' he said, his own voice thickening in his throat. 'Will do.'

'Be happy, that's all I ask. Now you should put me back on to Janey.'

He handed the phone over to Janey and went out to the little balcony at the top of the stairs at the back of his block. There was another block across from him. A woman had her washing out on a line that stretched across the alley to the block across from her. Away on the other corner he could see into the wat. There were stucco walls and high trees, a temple. Boys in saffron robes had gathered in the forecourt, maybe the same lads he had seen a few days before. They dribbled a football around in a desultory manner, as if they were not sure whether they should be boys or monks, whether they should let themselves go in the delirium of the game or act in the decorous manner expected of a novice. But that was the problem for all of us. How natural can we afford to be? When we make a change are we just switching sets of expectations and making ourselves work within those?

After a couple of minutes a monk appeared at the top of the eight or so steps that led into the temple. He said something quietly and the boys filed inside; he seemed to approve of their restraint. The football bobbed away a few paces and laid still in the shade of a banyan tree. Ryan thought of his sister, bound for home; he thought of Reap and Chean – they had no options beyond continuance and survival. They had duty. Mr Dith – same. But for himself and Malee the options were complex. He had heard it said that when it was time to make important decisions, do nothing for a while. A couple of weeks had passed since Kep. They had not had sex since then, but once was enough and he had had no news from her since then.

He had never thought it possible that he had defeated his father.

It was the last minutes of darkness before dawn. There was a distant lustre, as if the first rays had appeared somewhere behind the jungle a hundred miles away and had lightened only the sky above that jungle and had left the rest of the world in darkness. It was no more than a looming sense that there was light, somewhere else, in some other world. For the three of them in practice it was dark, and they felt their way warily along the cobbled path. There were a hundred other pilgrims ahead of them and behind, shuffling, some of them with torches, all of them quiet or speaking in low voices.

'We should have thought of the torch,' Janey whispered theatrically.

'I think so, yes,' Malee giggled. 'But we can kind of see where to go from their light.' She could pretend to guide the stage-panic of Janey.

'At least it won't get any darker,' was Ryan's view.

'Hmmm, of course.'

'Yes, I agree.'

'Not for some hours.'

A stone concourse of two hundred metres led up to the great temple at Angkor Wat. There was an ancient stone gate that they passed through as the sky began to lighten in the east. On the left of the concourse, before the giant moat, were already gathered fifty or so visitors, a few with cameras on tripods – past them a couple of little shops selling peanuts and other snacks. They stepped down the ancient steps from the concourse into the viewing area as the first distant streaks of pink and yellow stabbed the sky.

'Hurry, we'll miss it,' said Janey, as if she would barge to the front of crowd.

Malee giggled. She knew that Janey would exaggerate, but only to introduce some faux craziness into the morning.

'We will see everything.' Malee said in her knowing, even tone, like the straight man in a comic duo.

The moat shone at them. Like an old daguerreotype immersed in photographic liquids, the silhouette of the temple began to appear slowly, slowly. With a shade more clarity each minute the four towers emerged into the sky, with the great central point rising in between — the greatest building in the world in its time. Ryan and Malee stood holding each other, Janey next to them with a camera. The pink effusion behind the temple turned to orange and then began to recede into yellow and blue. The temple towers were clear now, stark and mysterious in the morning glow.

'It almost seems too cheesy to take pictures of such an incredible thing,' said Janey. 'But …'

'You're snapping for the three of us here, sis. Better get to work.'

Janey raised her camera and pressed the button, then again. A hundred people did the same. Janey moved away for a different angle, then took pictures of the people taking pictures, then of the causeway angling up to the temple.

Malee did not move from her place, her arm around Ryan's waist, silently watching the sun come up over the symbol of her nation. The wat was somehow the old way, beyond words. From the age of the Hindu kings, even before the Buddhist conversion, it was so far removed from history and culture that it did not belong to any one era or place. From so far in the past, it had become associated in the national psyche with survival and newness.

By ten o'clock the sun was burning hot. They had looked over the bas-relief friezes, the battle of Lanka where Rama defeats Ravana, and Vishnu's two hundred servants using the serpent Vasuki to churn the Sea of Milk. They stopped before the carvings of a dozen apsaras – bare breasted dancing nymphs. Malee reached out her hand to the sleek wall carving and glided her fingers past the row of figures; she could not lift her eyes from that perfection. She had never expected to hold her fingers just a centimetre from a thousand-year-old dancing girl.

'This … is the real one,' she said, her hands flickering before them, her eyes filled with the magic of it. 'This dancing girl – it is like she can do anything. She can live forever.' In her own youth and beauty, and at the beginning of another life, Malee may have felt for a second that she was like that girl in stone, immutable and indestructible.

'In a way she can. We can get a temple rubbing when we leave. I saw them on the way in. Apsaras in red or blue.'

'Red,' she said, without thinking, then confirmed it, nodding. 'Red.'

Inside the main temple there were rooms, open now to the sky, with deep pools where the king and his concubines had bathed eight hundred years before. The two of them stood silently and imagined the event. Would they have been serious or frolicsome as they took to the waters? Lascivious or demure? He had read an eye-witness account by a Chinese visitor who had suggested they were more frolicsome and lascivious than the other. Even the peasants in the field were uninhibited. The rural life would have been simple, but attractive. So how had the arc of civilisation brought them to the place they were in now? Reap at that very moment sewing hems in a hot box in Phnom Penh and the wage dispute tottering towards an unsatisfactory conclusion. Were the kings of Angkor kinder to their peasants?

They climbed one of the four towers that surrounded the main citadel. There was a view over the jungle, haze in the distance, in the foreground the moat and lake of Angkor, the squared-off compound and the dead straight wagon road that led the eyes out again through the great gate to the steamy horizon. Malee drank it in, her eyes open wide, as if only in that way could she appreciate it all in the heartbeat of time she had to experience it.

The main tower was before them; the steps were heaven-steep as the access way to the touching point of the Gods should be.

'Shall we go up?' Malee eyed the hundred or so steps.

'Phew,' was all Janey could say, and wiped a handkerchief over her sweating forehead. 'I think you have to be under thirty-five to even think about it.'

'Ha,' Malee laughed. 'I'll grab some snaps while you have a rest.'

Janey handed over her camera and Malee moved away to the parapet.

They watched Malee take a shot, then were unable to take their eyes away as she braced herself for a new angle; knee-length shorts they had bought in Siem Reap the night before showed her sinewy calves flexing as she leaned into position. The fisherman, Ryan thought: up at four in the morning helping Pa to pull in nets, picking out the fish, pushing the boat out, rowing, holding her steady in the current.

'She looks puny with her long pants on.' It was Janey who broke their silence. 'But now, Jesus, look at those calves.'

Malee disappeared out of view to the East side of the building.

'Are you still having doubts?' said Janey.

He didn't have to ask what about.

Janey grabbed Ryan's hands and pulled him to her. This might be her last opportunity ever to play big sister.

'This girl is a winner. She has charmed me completely as she will charm many others.'

'She has charmed me completely too. But that's the point, isn't it. Charm.' He took up for a moment the serious clichéd documentary voice. 'What lies behind the Khmer smile?'

'This is no time for that crap. If you don't take her now, someone else will.'

'But where is she going to get a better deal than me?'

'Stop it. She will get offers. If you don't marry her you are insane and I will kill you.'

'You would?'

'I will.'

'Well, that would be the sure way out of my problems.'

But, for once, glibness would not be allowed as the way to slip a net. This was more important than that.

'Just look at me,' she said. He looked at her. 'What I mean is, look at my life. What do I have?'

He didn't dare say that she had a great job that she had worked hard to get, that she had patients who loved her and a family who did too and girlfriends who would do absolutely anything for her. That wasn't the kind of thing she meant.

'Here I am fifteen years after my one life romance and still stuck on a Jewish boy I loved and whose family wouldn't take me. After so many years they wouldn't accept me.' Janey had missed her one chance. 'She loves you. I could see that from glance number one in the corridor of that hotel in Kep. She is an extremely practical girl, and that frightens you. But the way I see it she doesn't have any choice, and with you in the equation someone has to be. But you love her too; I could tell that before we even went to Kep. And her family, well …'

'They want me.'

'I think they want you for every reason. Not just because you're Mr Moneybags but because you are one gorgeous hunk of kid. Even first brother can see that now and he's probably killing himself for what he did to you. Go back and help to save him. He needs it. If you validate him he will sing with joy, believe me. You have more power than you know. Don't come back to Australia with me and don't follow on next week. It's time to do what's important, and attendance at this forthcoming ceremony of dispatch is not important.'

Ryan did not answer back even to point out that she had contradicted herself about going back to see Dermott. Indeed, there was no time to be glib. Malee was approaching from the other side of the tower, shaping to take their photo from a distance. Janey and Ryan posed; the shot would be them together with ancient tower and end-less blue sky.

'She'll take you places you never dreamed of going,' Janey whispered to him as Malee lowered the camera and came towards them.

The bus back to Phnom Penh two days later settled into its rhythm. The morning sun came from behind them over a patch of jungle trees that were the backdrop to ripening rice fields. It was November now and the floods had ebbed into their river and the fields were drying out. Water buffaloes and cows stood on firmer ground, chewing hay. Tourists in the bus chatted happily or slumped in their seats, recovering from a night in Pub Street, Siem Reap.

Janey was in front of them, talking to a girl with dark blonde hair and an international look that could have been from anywhere: Germany, Sweden, Britain, Canada, even Australia. The girl was talking softly and every now and then Janey's voice would pipe up, 'Really, I don't believe that', extracting confessions from the girl about her life, loves, her pets and even what they did as a family at Christmas – his guileless chaotic sister. Too much sympathy almost; her questions would lead the other person by instinct in a direction they wanted to go, as if by their answers they had found their own solution to the problems they'd flagged. Janey went with people more than she went with herself.

Malee gazed dreamily out the window at the patchwork of fields, the peasant farmers methodically working their way across then back. She would think of herself as spoiled, he knew that – being brought to Angkor Wat. She would need to return to work and study even harder now, to prove to herself and to others that she was not changed by her new fortune, by the great temple, by Ryan, by Janey.

But she was changed. With her fortune there was an edge lost from her irony. Her studies were nearly over and she would be qualified and then there would be more decisions to make. She was the top student in her class and they had all done practical placements in hospitals and job offers would be certain to come. She was nearly there and could almost cry with relief.

'There is one thing I should tell you,' she said. 'Something which concerns you.' He froze and waited; this was an announcement. 'I can tell you pretty much for certain as of this morning that I am not pregnant.'

'Oh, I see.' He exhaled in his own theatrical way. 'That's good.'

'What do you mean, that's good?' she sat up, not sure whether to be outraged or mock outraged. 'You don't want my baby?'

'Darling, yes, but not now. You have a few things to do first, don't you?'

'Just a few. I made sure anyway.'

'How do you mean?'

'Well, sure as you can be. I gave myself a vinegar douche.'

'You what?' He could not believe what he had just heard.

'I brought some vinegar from home for when we did it at Kep. I may be a scientist but you're foolish if you ignore the traditional methods. But there is science behind it; even Hippocrates knew the vinegar trick.'

'But, but … It was all so spontaneous and loving, and, I don't know, epoch-making.'

Malee raised an eyebrow. 'Epoch-making, that's a good one.'

'Fucking hell.' Ryan pulled his hand away from Malee and crossed his arms and looked past her at the Malaysian bulls in the field that passed by the window. Janey had already pointed out that Malee was frighteningly practical.

'Japanese rice wine vinegar,' she went on. 'The best. We don't have many luxuries but for something like that …' Her voice trailed off so he could think for himself how appropriate her idea had been.

'I guess it was the right thing to do.'

'Mmmm …' Malee nodded her head in assent, quietly sending up his Western romanticism. 'I couldn't afford to get pregnant for about five different reasons.'

'It's right because that now leaves the field open for me to ask you to marry me without it looking like you had the shotgun at my back or any such thing.'

She closed the medical magazine she had been idling through. She stared up at him. 'You really want to marry me?'

He made to glance around the bus. 'Well, there's no-one else around here worth taking.'

She made to slap him playfully, then held on to his arm. In half a minute he prised her from him. Her eyes were dry, but closed in a dreamy meditational way. She opened them and looked at him.

'About time,' she said.

Ryan shook his head.

'You're a hard case,' he replied.

'But you know I have to be.' And he knew it to be true.

They travelled a couple of kilometres without speaking, their fingers touching and their eyes closed. Ryan was thinking of what he had just asked Malee. After talking to Janey the day before it seemed so right; yes, he would be foolish to let her go. But then he recalled what Tom had said to him on the bus back from Kratie, 'It seemed so right at the time' or some such thing. But here Tom was in Cambodia trying to sort himself out after one year of marriage. But he was not a rambling man like Tom. Was he?

Malee's phone gave a double buzz indicating a message.

'It's from Reap. She got to work this morning and they say there has been a new pay offer. It's in today's paper. She ends her message with three exclamation marks.'

'Exclamation marks – not like her to be so emphatic,' he said, with a trace of his own irony.

Malee's grimace in reply attested to the truth revealed.

'But wait, didn't you buy the *Post* before we got on the bus?'

'Well, yes, I did.'

'And you read it?'

'Ah, yep, part of it.'

He looked through his carry-on bag for the copy of the *Phnom Penh Post*. It was folded to the inside back page.

'What have you been reading?'

'Er, cricket scores. There's a Test Match, Australia vs England; you have to learn how important these things are.'

'Oh my god,' she rolled her eyes. 'You didn't look at the front page then?' Ryan grimaced maybe not. As soon as he turned it over the words 'Hundred Dollar' smacked them in the eye.

He folded out the paper and they read the headline 'PM Hundred Dollar Minimum Wage Offer.' Hun Sen had raised the offer from ninety dollars; that meant every garment factory would have to pay it. Ten dollars didn't seem like much at first glance, and it fell a long way short of one hundred and sixty; but with the other five dollars up from eighty five it meant someone could buy good vegetables to go with their noodles every night, and maybe even a chicken once in a while, and still send a little more home to parents. The five-dollar offer was nothing; this was something.

'Oh my god,' Malee said quickly, in a different way than she had said it a minute before. She held the paper in her hands to read the first few sentences of the article. 'Oh my god,' she repeated, shaking her head. 'At last …'

'An offer.'

'It's hard to believe.' She looked at the headline again.

'Do you think they'll take it?' Ryan thought there was a good chance the answer would be yes.

She stared at the back of the headrest in front of her for a few seconds.

'They'll take it,' she said, then looked at him sideways, 'for now. If the others are anything like Reap and her friends, they'll take it. Everyone is so tired. Every second week you spend your only day off on the outside of the factory not on the inside, and this is nearly seventeen per cent on what they are getting now.'

'I hadn't thought of it that way – seventeen per cent. Fifteen dollars seemed so little. That means no more demonstrations.'

She closed her eyes and shook her head.

'Thank *god* for that,' she exhaled. It was the first time she had even implied a word that diverged from the family line. She had expressed her feelings to him, assured of his confidence, and they were closer because of it.

'Thank God for that,' he repeated. They shared a laugh that was in relief, but which was tinged with nerves as well, as they both knew the story would never end so simply.

As they settled back into their seats Malee repeated her two words in mitigation. 'For now,' she said thoughtfully as she pulled back the curtain and watched the fields go by once more. 'In six months it will start again, that is for sure. It will take years of grind. But six months is far enough away for me now.'

'In six months you could be in a hospital in Battambang or some place like that.'

'Or Siem Reap. How would that be.' Just two hours down the road from Kampong Thom, he thought. A vague feeling of disquiet at being closer to Malee's family crept over him, but he wasn't able to balance on that for long.

'Or in Kratie,' she said. 'They have a hospital there. You've been there.' There was something mysterious and suggestive about the way she said her last sentence.

'Kratie, yes,' he murmured.

She sent him a raised eyebrow. 'I know about Kratie.'

'You know? About wha—'

'The walls have ears. The river has ears. And the school has teachers who talk too much. Things get around in five minutes.'

So she knew. She knew she had competition, or at least she thought she might. The ride to Kep, the vinegar trick. She is so practical, but she has to be. Is that what Janey had said to him, or was it what he had said to her? He rubbed his forehead and tried to bring back conversations and to bring them to order in his mind, but it was too much for him.

'Don't worry. You were meant for me, darling. Even the Australians are said to take on doctors from outside. You know, let the

Third World country spend half their GDP training medical professionals and then just take them away for nothing so they don't have to train their own.'

He was shocked numb. She was three steps ahead of him again.

'Indians and Sri Lankans, maybe,' she said, digging him in the ribs 'but I don't think so much Cambodians. Not yet, anyway.'

'So we're staying in Cambodia then?'

'Looks that way, at least for a few years.'

'Ok, thanks,' he said. 'That's nice to know.' And Malee took his hand and the bus sped on to Phnom Penh.

Ryan creaked down the steps of the bus, his long legs cramped up from the six-hour trip. When they'd set out on the return trip from Angkor Wat all three of them were buoyant and optimistic. It was as if they were setting out on a new adventure, not returning home from one. But with the passing hours their weariness with uniform countryside had congealed into visible unease. Janey had lurched unsteadily out of her seat and now swayed down to the ground and heaved a huge sigh and stretched her back. Malee skipped down the steps after them. She had tugged her legs under her thighs through the trip and, after accepting her marriage proposal, read a book of medical study and in this way was content all the way back from Siem Reap.

How could she do it? Ryan had watched her in wonder through the trip back, concentrating, marking passages in pencil. Her respect for books came from her school days when they were objects to be treasured and venerated, shared and preserved. Pencil could be erased for another student to start afresh one day. The lead points never broke; her touch was light but firm. This book would probably be passed on or sold at the end of the semester. Every twenty minutes or so she would place a scrap of paper in to mark the page, look out the window for a few seconds, then turn to him and smile. She was as happy as a Khmer girl could be. She had a chance and she was taking it; she had a role in her family. She had a future.

Janey groaned and stretched her ample frame. Some of the local passengers tittered at her open display and meant no harm. 'These buses are tailor made for Khmer people, I'll say that much for them. And maybe Chinese tourists, some of them.'

What is seen as a bus station in Cambodia does not resemble its counterparts in the West. No open-sided aircraft hangar with neat painted-in concrete resting points for buses and an under-cover kiosk selling coffees and chocolate bars and tickets, with a TV monitor displaying departure and arrival times. The bus station here was a shop that sold tickets and had a regular city street outside. The bus driver had to find a place to park his rig that wasn't blocking the road *too* much. Today that was a hundred metres up the street, so they had to tramp back with their luggage. When Chean saw them he jumped into his tuk-tuk and idled up to save them half the walk.

'Chean, you saved my life,' said Janey.

'Always, Miss. Never problem.' He swung her bag up so she could sit with it between her legs.

They went straight home and Malee went on to see Reap. She and her sister had much to talk about.

Ryan flopped himself down on his couch then got up to look in the fridge. There were two beers there that he had forgotten about – perfect. They would be a consolation to the constant presence of Janey within three metres of him. She had come to Cambodia to help him and in her way she had done that. Much had happened since her arrival – so much that he could hardly make sense of it. She was a single woman in her mid-thirties who had resigned herself to the idea that there could be only one true love in her life. And that true love was gone. She was determined that she would find no other, or so it seemed to him. But perhaps she knew something about herself that she wasn't telling anyone out loud – that her overwhelming manner had to be taken in small doses. The man who would take her would have to be a mouse. And she could never love a mouse.

Such was the irony of relationships, he thought. What we want we usually can't have. Now Janey had channelled all her romantic force to live through him and he was all but married to Malee. But when they had talked on the beach at Kep she had also done more than just hint that Amanda was now free. She is not a bad girl, Janey had said pointedly and hinted that he, Ryan, may have been a difficult person for Amanda to cope with too. He wondered just how much Janey thought things through before she spoke. She went into all things on instinct, but her grounds could shift around so much, and he had taken her advice back there at the Wat. But what if he had taken her hint at Kep?

In the next room he heard Janey muttering to herself. 'Jesus Christ,' she said out loud. 'I'll have to wash and dry these things to-night.' Of course, they had been away three days.

'Buy a new set at the market,' he called out.

She came to the door. 'You think the markets here are going to have underclothes of a size for me?' She had a point.

He drank the two beers in no time. The first one had been for thirst and the second one for effect. He could go down to get some more from Mr Thiounn, but it was almost knock-off time for the office workers and Colin was usually thirsty.

Janey came to the door holding black lacy knickers in her hand; Ryan turned his face away. 'Why don't you go and visit Colin,' she said. 'You could do with some male company.'

'That way you can have the place to yourself to wash your knick-ers.'

'Exactly.' His sister might bowl people over sometimes but she could also show a faultless insight.

They arranged to meet in a bar just off Sothearos Boulevard, just up from Colin's office. It gave Ryan a twenty-minute walk to finish loos-ening his limbs from the bus and to see if any epiphany might strike him. It had felt so right on the bus, spontaneous and loving, and with Janey in the seat in front of them they had seemed an unshakable team of three. But Janey would be gone tomorrow and it would be back to him and her, and her family. Chamroeun had made a gesture at the funeral, but that was with a hundred people watching. His handshake had been appreciated by them and was, in part at least, the expression of his own grandness; he could just feel all those people smiling and nodding to themselves at Chamroeun's coming of age. And Pa would be quietly content now, another daughter successfully settled. This one he had probably seen as his biggest challenge, but brilliantly resolved.

The Back Street Bar had that combination of a down and out name with trimmings that aimed straight at the new middle class Cambodia, with a few knowing Western customers thrown in for balance. This was one notch up from the Blue Pumpkin. Bar tables and chairs had been artist-made from salvaged tyres, wooden pallets and metal scraps from building sites. The wall art pieces had been crafted from coconut bark, fish scales, leaves and eggshells, depicting rural Cambodian scenes. Bottles of French and Australian wines were displayed in shadow boxes along one wall. The arty rustica achieved a marriage of the old rural Cambodia with the new city middle-class who had not only the trained skill to make Westernised artefacts, but had the leisure and finances to sit and look at them too. Some people were doing well in Hun Sen's Cambodia.

'Good place to bring the missus when you're hitched,' Colin said after about one minute.

'What the fuck? What do you mean … married?'

'Well, you've popped it, haven't you?'

'What you mean, Colin, her or the question?'

'The question. I already knew about the other stuff.'

'What the …? I never told you about that.'

'Didn't have to.' Then, after a pause, he narrowed his eyes and made his pronouncement. 'On the subject of marriage, I could tell by the look on your face. There is a mixture of contentment and anxiety. Usually you show anxiety and bewilderment in equal measures – you've changed.' Ryan said nothing, just folded his arms and gave a look that said, Go on, I'm interested.

'You've just come back from a trip to the Wat. Not bad going, I must say. Must have been nice. There's a beautiful, optimistic, eternal kind of atmosphere up there, isn't there.'

Ryan began to unwind. 'You've got to say that's true.' Colin had got his back up a little and any fears he had been having about Malee's family and their motives were now washed away by his countering need to assert himself with Colin. 'But you're not saying it was all planned by the devil-woman, are you?'

'Which one? You've got two of them on your case, maybe three.' Colin watched him closely and then chuckled and gave him a playful punch on the shoulder. 'Just pulling your chain, pal.'

'I actually came here to tell you two things. Firstly, that I'm going to be with Malee no matter what effort or difficulty it takes and as a consequence I won't field any more comments from you or Tom about Khmer women. Well, not about Malee anyway.' There, it was out of him. The more convinced half of him had sprung forth, if only in self-righteous repudiation of Colin.

'Did you decide all that on the way down or just in the last ten seconds? Look, you can be impulsive. That's why you're here isn't it, in Cambodia. I just want you to be sure of yourself. Ok, what's the second thing?'

'You said something about a job. I'll take it if it's still going.'

'Little woman got in your ear then?'

'I said I wasn't having any more of that. I haven't even told her about it.'

'Sorry, sweetheart, I was only teasing. I think it's about time you and Malee came over to meet Sokha.'

'Sokha?'

'My, well … partner. We've been together for fifteen years.'

Ryan thought this through for a second and Colin sat back in his chair, a little smugly, Ryan thought, and watched him.

'Fifteen years,' Ryan said flatly, buying time before he had to say anything else.

'Married for seven.'

'You fuckhead.'

'I had to give you the bad word first, mate. There are pitfalls in this game, plenty of them, as I think you are aware. I didn't know anything about this girl you were stuck on. Had to paint the worst case scenario. But I did eventually make a few enquiries, as I'm sure her family did about you – as much as they could from their distance and with the limited resources available to them. But there are always ways. They don't want their little flower petal crushed any more than I wanted mine.'

'Thanks, Colin.'

'But she's close enough to on the level …'

'Close enough?'

'As you'll get.' He leant forward in his seat. 'Any woman and her family are going to expect you to have your hand in your pocket to a degree. It's part of the culture, mate, but still a sight cheaper than getting married in the West if you want to look at it that way.'

'Yes, Colin.'

'Right. On the other matter, we have just completed the job interview and you are employed as of this moment. Your first task after one half day of training will be to sit in my office while I go to Sydney for your Dad's funeral.' He fished in a pocket and tossed a swipe card and a couple of keys on a plain ring in front of him. 'Here's my spare set. You answer the phone and sweet talk anyone on the other end of it. I'll leave some things for you to read and a list of jobs to do. I fly tomorrow afternoon. Anyone wants to have a piece of you for not coming back, I'll shut them up.'

Ryan lounged back in his seat, jingled the keys on his finger. It was a long way back to Australia – a hop to Singapore and then a punishing all night run straight after. And at the end of it, Dermott and Amanda – separate now, but they'd both be there. No question. How would Dermott be? Chastened perhaps, literally and figuratively. And Amanda. She had been foolish, so be it.

Ryan placed the keys back on the table.

'I think I'm coming with you.' Colin stared at him, waiting for something more. 'Face the music, you know. He *was* my Dad after all. The other two? Well, I'll talk to them. The way things are it feels like they're the children now and I'm the adult. I'm going back, for one week.'

After a few more seconds of silence Colin reached over his desk, picked up the keys and put them back into his pocket. Then he spoke.

'I've got only two words to say to you.'

'What are they?'

'Good boy. What sort of pissweak stick of shit would have piked out of it?'

'That's a lot more than two words, Colin.'

'You're right, out of the three of you, you just might indeed be the most grown up now. Nothing like a few months in Cambodia to knock the edge off the ego, is there.'

And so that night Ryan met Sokha, a jolly Khmer widow about forty years old. While the boys were away, the girls made friends. She loved Malee on sight, and probably had done so for long before they had even met.

Epilogue

It was the same marquee they'd hired for Cris's funeral but now it was dressed up like a tableau from Disney's Fantasyland: the white canvas was draped with festive candy colours, yellow and pink; inside, white cloths covered the circular tables and chairs were wrapped up with pink bows at the back. There was a little hardwood floor for dancing. With all this in the main street of Kampong Thom, no-one could miss how Pa's face was growing in the community.

The villagers were honouring the occasion in their shiniest and brightest – print dresses of orange with gold or aqua sashes pinned at the hip, men in black slacks with their newest shirts of blue and red. As well as villagers there were people from the town, probably shopkeepers that Pa had dealt with over the years – business associates, men that he still wanted to impress and their wives who would spread the news of the day deeper into the community.

Reap and Sister Number Four were bridesmaids, in golden dresses with clip-on fingernails that they displayed like apsara dancers. Their hair had been permed and with Malee in between them they had the aura of Cambodian pop stars of the 1960s – the Khmer Supremes; Diana Ross had nothing on this.

The marquee was closed all but half of one side and the guests crammed there spilled out on to the road in the kind of Khmer chaos that unwound him with its inexact relationship to rules. Inside, Ma had set up a little table with a writing pad and a couple of biros, for what reason he had no idea. Tom had come early and was standing with him.

'So what are you doing this year? Back to school with Dith, or what?'

'Yeah. That's a good one. I dunno.' Tom stood with his hands clasped in front of him, looking as official as he could make it, a kind of unofficial groomsman figure. 'I talked to Marie a couple of times.'

Tom had been quiet since Kratie. He had been brighter in the mornings at school, not taking two hours and three coffees to get him mobile. He had twice asked Ryan for books, novels, to read. Ryan wondered if he was saving money.

'Oh yeah? So … how'd it go?'

'Apparently it's still fucking cold in St Paul.'

'You're kidding. No global warming issues up there?'

Tom shrugged his shoulders. 'I don't care what happens, I'm not going back there. It reminds me of too much negative stuff,' he looked sideways at Ryan, 'and not just about Marie. And to be honest, all this …' – he glanced around the marquee at the costumes, the bunting, the fancy foods laid out waiting – 'all this stuff would freak me out, man. Mr Darcy and his little Lizzie Bennet. Sorry, but that's the way I am.'

'Nothing to apologise for. It's doing the same for me, but this is the way it has to be over here.'

'Yeah, well, this is the way it has to be to get someone like Malee.' Ryan remembered something Janey had said about ripple effects of the decisions we take, and looked closely at Tom.

'You been making plans?'

'I might as well tell you. I've been looking at jobs in Arizona. Marie is thinking of moving down there.'

Ryan turned to look at him, closer. 'Serious? The two of them? To be with you?'

'Phoenix. They got thousands of kids down there need to learn proper English. There'll be big problems with some of them for sure but, still, it is a job. If the kids want to learn like the school says they do, it won't be all bad. We – well, we talked about stuff. She said she had been kind of rethinking things. Can you imagine that?'

Ryan shrugged his shoulders as if to say, beats me.

'She says she thought everything she did was all for us. Like everything she wanted was going to be everything I wanted automatically. She thought if she just ploughed on ahead it would all fall into place. But, you know, we *are* all different.'

'I guess so,' said Ryan, looking about him at the Khmer wedding that was taking shape around him.

'Relationships are, well, hard work if you really want them to stay around,' Tom expanded the theme, 'but I think you worked that out already.' Ryan looked closer at his new relatives now filing into the marquee, smiled and nodded.

'I guess so,' he said. 'You'll be with your little girl.'

'Yeah,' Tom nodded his head and thought before choosing his words. 'I didn't really want to miss that.' That was as strong an admission as Tom would ever make out loud.

Pa's hair had grown back black and strong with just the few white hairs that Ryan had noticed at the Pizza Company on the day they had met – Pa eager to see the new beau, come to the city on an odyssey and eating the strange new meal, the first time he had ever seen melted cheese. Ryan thought about that day now. Something of the avid expression was back in Pa's face and eyes. Ma's hair had grown back too but it was like steel wool – it frizzed in all directions, was grey and yellowed with age, but somehow looked hip and punk. Ryan bowed and made his sampeah. By their side again was Chamroeun; he would take the part of Pa today – the giving of the bride.

Guests began moving through steadily now and Ryan got down to the business of making sampeah and beaming. The whole of the village must be empty today, he thought, and half the town as well. Invitations had been handed out with a white envelope attached. Guests stepped through the canvas flap of the atrium and handed envelopes to Ma who was sitting at the small table; then she began to take money out and was writing down the names of the people and the amounts they had given.

'What in heck is she doing?' Ryan said to Tom.

'Charge of the ledger.'

'Isn't that a bit …' He hesitated to use the words that came to mind.

'It's protocol. She's not checking up on people or anything. But if they make a note now they'll know how much to give back when they're invited to these people's weddings down the line. It's a delicate situation but this lady looks like she's right on top of it.'

'But right here, right now?'

'Best to get it out of the way. The marquee man is probably hanging around waiting for his money, then there's the achar, the priests, the flower people, the food …'

'Yeah, yeah. I get it.'

Tom glanced across at Ma again.

'I think your mother-in-law might be the velvet hammer of the family.'

'And I'm finding this out now?' Ryan held his hands out in appeal.

'You know what they say about mothers and their daughters, muchacho.'

Then there was a discordant Australian voice in the street.

'Colin is here.' Something settled and unwound in Ryan's fluttery stomach. Colin had known him since he was a baby. He was a kind of uncle, but in the last three months had become something more than that. He was Ryan's whole family in this nation and with Tom there too he felt a more substantial person, one on each side of him – strength.

Mr Dith came, with his sister. They bowed and made sampeah to Pa and Ma and then to Ryan and Tom and Malee and Reap. When Ryan mentioned the wedding to Chean all he said was, 'Mr Dith go; I stay.' In the last two months, Ryan had rung Chean from time to time for a job and he was there on time every time and cheerful, but something had changed between them. Chean never waited for him on the corner anymore. He went back to a place among the crowds on the Sisowath Quay, where he could be alone with those things that troubled him.

And Janey would not come. She had seen everything she wanted to see and done whatever she had needed to do. Ryan set up his iPad on a table in the main room and Janey and his Mum would watch what they could from the living room of the old family home.

'We have our French bubbly and our Kleenex. We need no more than this.'

The monk gathered everyone in the main part of the marquee and began with prayers and a short sermon. Then there was laughter during the ritual hair-cutting of the bride and groom. The duty was performed by Sister Number Five and she was nervous and Ma had to help her and everyone smiled and laughed in an indulgent way so she was not embarrassed. Number Six came forward with cotton threads which had been soaked in holy water and tied them around the wrists of the couple. Then Ryan placed a scarf around the shoulders of the bride. It was midnight blue and edged with gold and the tradition was that the groom was from afar and had brought the scarf from his homeland as a gift-symbol of marriage into the bride's family. He was certainly from afar, said most people, so the scarf was greeted with smiles and nods.

Then the couple had to be blessed with good luck and fertility, so the married people formed a circle and danced around Ryan and Malee to keep bad spirits away and so happy ones would know to help them. Single people were not allowed and divorced people were bad luck. Colin joined in with his Khmer wife. Some of the group watched and grinned, waiting for the Westerner to fumble the dance steps. But Colin had done it all before and he put his feet in most of the right places and his dance ended with applause and smiling faces.

Then the sound system got going and deafening Korean pop music began.

'Hell,' said Tom, 'if it was ZZ Top I'd manage.'

'I'd be happy to kick back with a bit of *Tupelo Honey*,' said Ryan.

There was a sit-down dinner and lots of drinking. The Khmer people clinked glasses at nearly every sip of beer and toasted 'Chuol moy'; it seemed that no-one intended to stop for a very long time. They had kept at it right through the main courses and into the bowl of mango with ice cream and chocolate sauce. Then came the sugary dumplings filled with sesame paste that auntie had made.

Ryan was feeling queasy.

But as he looked around the room he could not see one person who had treated him with anything but open-hearted joy. He felt embraced into the family and valued for himself. As far as the ceremony was concerned no-one had asked him for a single cent; he decided to make a point of this to Colin when he next saw him. He had been expecting requests for fifty or a hundred dollars here and there, but there had been nothing. Malee had been almost coy when the question of finances had popped up; she just twitched her eyebrows and gave a tiny shrug of her shoulders. He had let the issue ride so far, but he could see that his options were to either ask about it now or let it rest forever.

'It's a great party,' he said to Malee.

'Yes,' she said, taking hold of his arm, 'it couldn't be better.'

'Must have set Pa back a bit.'

'Oh,' Malee hesitated for a moment, surprised. For once he had caught her a degree or two off her composed equilibrium. She saw him see her thinking, and she was thinking that he had been thinking about this matter. It seemed best, at that quite early stage of their marriage, to speak the truth, especially as she could think of nothing else that would sound convincing.

'Not so much a problem,' she said, cautiously but clearly, as if explaining something to an intelligent child. 'Janey sent me seven hundred dollars six weeks ago, and I gave it all to Pa.'

Something swayed in Ryan's stomach. It was not the mango ice cream and sesame paste sitting on creamy fish amok. The warnings of Colin and Tom were in his ears.

Ryan sat back in his chair with his arms folded. It was as if he had been cornered in a game of chess, and the only way out of check took him into more trouble. No wonder Pa was jubilant. He had made great face in the village, and even in the town. It was the best wedding of the year and would be remembered. He would walk around with his head held high for the rest of his life now, and hadn't had to find a hundred riel. For a moment Ryan wanted to walk across the room to the iPad that was still propped up on a table and punch some buttons and make it spring back to life so he could have a strong word with his sister. It was all very well to hold the hands of your patients while you told them what they wanted to hear, to chatter away to people on buses and to extract a life story from Mr Dith. It was all done by being sympathetic – the road too easily travelled. But sometimes things just weren't your business.

For a moment he watched the flap of the tent flicking up in the evening breeze; it was an object that was, strictly speaking, inanimate, but it was given life by the incessant force of nature gusting it in one direction then the next. He stared at the gaudy hot pink bows that were wrapped around the back of every chair, and at the diners and drinkers and their faces flushed in worldly success, all of them a force of nature with which he may even now be at odds; or, at least, the power and purpose of which he did not yet comprehend.

Malee stood up to pay her respects to an auntie who had travelled from Siem Reap for the wedding. There must have been five aunties on the day, each wanting their equal portion of attention. It was his moment to slip out, to leave the wedding feast to do what it would do in its own way. He needed to feel the freshness of the breeze for a minute, to quell the anger of powerlessness he felt building within him.

He stepped into the street, with the raw feeling of having his delusions stripped away. His sister had decided what was best for him – still, even now, up here. He had got away, but not far enough, or so it seemed. He thought of Colin in there, with his wife. The first day he had gone to see Colin and they had drunk beer in his office

he had asked Colin whether he would ever settle down, and Colin
had not answered him. He had been wary of Colin, afraid even, the
man who had given nothing away until the last moment. But now,
Colin was some kind of rock in his life. Colin and Sokha, Ryan and
Malee: there was symmetry to it, but now he was not convinced that
was enough for a life. Had he ever really decided? For a moment he
could think no further into the future, but was swamped with ideas
of change and growth and problems.

The town of Kampong Thom was settling from its day, but still
there was movement in the street. The last market stalls were packing
up, the first lights were flicking on. Then a man on a motorbike
crossed an intersection and tooted his horn at nothing – no car or
moto blocked his way – simply to happily announce his presence to
the world. Whatever that man had in life, he accepted it. He saw Ryan
loitering and he slowed and turned around in the street to come up
to him.

'Motorbike, sir? Where are you going?'

'Going?' He grimaced at the question – just where was he going?
'I dunno,' he said, as much to himself as to the man. Then he spoke
up, 'I really don't know.'

The man's face turned quizzical in acknowledgement of this am-
biguity, the way Chean had done on Ryan's first day in Cambodia,
when he'd asked about the sky over Phnom Penh.

'You want motorbike?'

'No, thanks,' Ryan laughed and held up the palms of his hands
to show denial, 'not this time.'

'Maybe tomorrow,' the man grinned in his own kind of irony.

'Yeah,' Ryan repeated, 'maybe tomorrow.'

The motorbike man turned again in the street and went on his
way; he nodded and grinned at Ryan as if he understood everything
that had been said to him, but surely he did not. He remembered the
idiot on the pushbike outside the Pizza Company the day Pa had
widened his eyes at Ryan's fold of bills. 'You'll never be one of them'
the man had cried out as he turned in the street. That was the first

day he had been with them, as a family. And Tommy had come too, the adopted one; there was kindness in them. His thoughts swirled and could not settle.

And then Malee was there, by his side. Her hand slipped inside his arm and she leaned her head against his shoulder. They stood like that for a few moments, listening to the dying sounds of the town. Ryan was the first to speak.

'I just …' he began, then hesitated, collecting his thoughts.

'Ssshhh,' said Malee, and she looked up into his eyes. 'Darling, everything is going to be all right. It is normal to worry.' She paused for a moment, thoughtful. 'For *you* it is normal.' She tapped him gently on the chest with her finger then stood up on her toes and kissed him on the lips. He took her in his arms and held her for a full minute; there was nothing else he could do.

Malee stood back for a moment and looked at him again.

'This is the happiest day of my life. Now I think we should go inside and talk to my relatives, don't you think?'

'Yes, I expect we should. Some of them have come a long way.'

He allowed her to guide him back into the banquet arm in arm. When they pushed through the tent together there was a scattering of applause from some of those inside, as if this was some scripted and prearranged nuance of the festivity that should be acknowledged. Ryan was sure he heard a few of the ladies exhale, 'Aaaahhhh,' at the sight of them.

Malee went about her duties, speaking to older ladies, bowing, making sampeah, hugging. But he slumped in his seat, suddenly very tired. He picked up his beer glass and took a long swig. Pa leaned across the table. 'Chuol moy,' Pa said enthusiastically, using the only two words of language they understood in common. Ryan wearily raised his glass to clink with Pa, who then turned back to the friends and family gathered around. Pa was going to enjoy the rest of his night.

Malee sat down again beside Ryan, looked across at her Pa with a curious smile, and took the arm of her husband.

Acknowledgements

With thanks to Pip Lewin, Mark Badger, Ben Smith and Denise Keenan for their reading of early drafts of this novel and for their insights and suggestions.

An early version of this novel was completed during a Doctor of Creative Arts candidature at the University of Technology, Sydney, under an Australian Postgraduate Awards scholarship.

About the Author

Robert Horne has been an avid reader of fiction since childhood when he started on the classic novels his mother put in their bookshelves. With a BA under his arm, he worked at many different jobs before spending sixteen years as a senior secondary teacher in English and Classical Studies. His first visit to S-E Asia in 2008 developed within him a burning interest to write about that area.

His articles have appeared in the Sydney Review of Books, Mekong Review and journals of the Universities of Barcelona and New Delhi. He is the prize-winning author of two books of short stories and completed a Master of Arts in 2012, and in 2017 a Doctor of Creative Arts in Creative Writing. He is now a freelance editor of academic writing, as well as an interested gardener and grower of organic vegies. But it is the flame of fiction writing that still burns most strongly in him.